WHISKEY FLIRT

A Foster House Novel

WALKER ROSE

LE Publishing

Copyright © 2025 by Walker Rose

Editing by Razor Sharp Editing

Proofreading by Fairy Proofmother Proofreading, Deaton Author Services, and Judy's Proofreading

Cover design by Ever After Cover Design

All rights reserved.

No part of this book may be reproduced in any form or by any electronic or mechanical means, including information storage and retrieval systems, without written permission from the author, except for the use of brief quotations in a book review.

The characters, places, and events in this story are fictional. Any similarities to real people, places, or events are coincidental and unintentional.

No AI Training

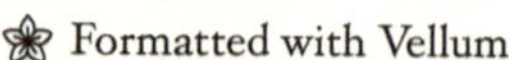 Formatted with Vellum

My name may be front and center on my bakery, but my past is sealed up tighter than a mason jar. I returned to tiny Huckleberry Springs, Montana, to start over, keep my history to myself, and ignore handsome flirts like local distillery owner and rancher, Cruz Foster.

Cruz might make me forget how to frost a cookie, but I've been taken in by guys like him before. When he turns up the charm, I punch his efforts down like a first proof of my dinner rolls.

He backs off but continues being sweet. My car dies, and he's there. I need a ride, and he's there. I tell him that I miss the whiskey flirt with the lopsided smile, and he's there with a sizzling kiss.

The real Cruz is even better than the one he shows everyone else. I can't help but fall for the guy who loves his family, works hard, and leaves his troubled childhood far behind. With my past, is it any wonder a man who can fix himself is my weakness?

But secrets like mine don't stay out of city limits. If I don't want Cruz sinking to the bottom with me faster than blueberries in cake batter, I need to break my heart and go back to minding my own business—without him.

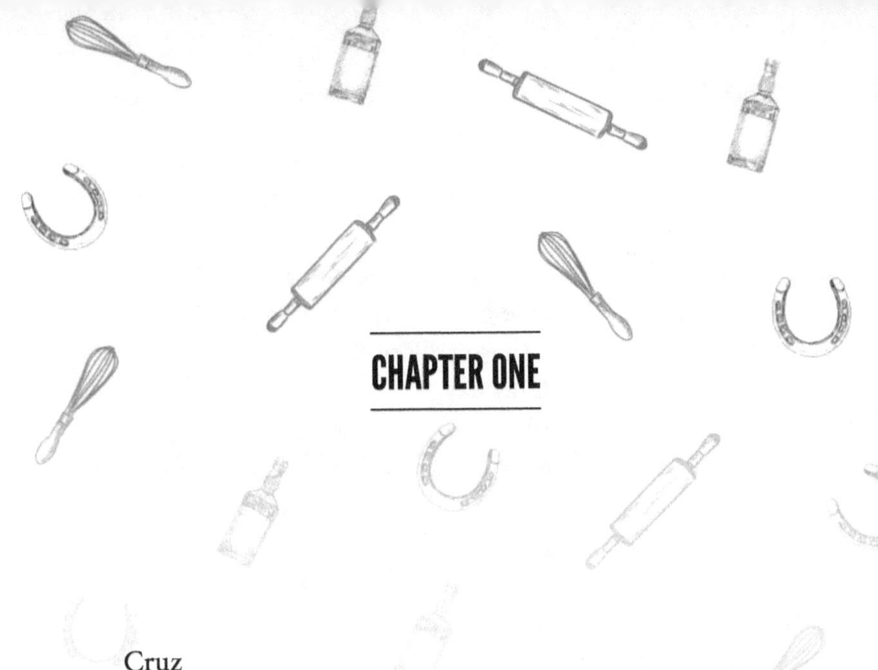

CHAPTER ONE

Cruz

The early morning Montana sky spans above me like a dark blanket, and the highway into Huckleberry Springs from my house disappears beyond my headlights. I yawn, letting out a whoop to wake myself up more. Back in the day, I used to be up until the ripe hour of four in the morning, doing nothing productive and everything destructive. Nowadays, I'm snuggled in bed with a kitten or two by ten p.m. Who in their right mind would start work at this hour?

Elodie Palmer.

The pretty little baker who hides behind her glasses is already at the bakery. Word around town is that she gets up at three in the morning.

The pretty little baker also turns into the quietest woman in town when I'm around, no matter how hard I try.

The pretty little baker has burned my pride enough, so I've got to behave around her. I'm done making an ass out of myself.

Today, I'll be nothing but professional. I'll drop off the stash of spirits Lane gave me for the bakery to use in a collaboration with the distillery we're part owners in and continue on with my day.

I reach the buildings on the edge of town and roll through until I approach a brick building with timber accents and a white sign reading *Dee's Sweets* hanging above the door.

She told Lane to enter through the back, so I drive around to the alley. I'm supposed to be the contact for this collaboration between her bakery and our distillery for some local craft fairs, but she still goes through Lane. I'd be jealous, but she doesn't look at Lane any differently than anyone else. Elodie Palmer is a reserved person with everyone, and as much as I want to be, I'm not an exception.

I park to the side of the door in case she's got more deliveries coming. The clock blinks four o'clock. I'm a half hour early. I was too afraid to be late, so I got up before I needed to.

Getting out, I straighten my shirt and jeans. A piece of lint glows under the streetlamp on my shoulder and I flick it off. There. Professional.

No hitting on my little baker. Not anymore.

I lift the box that has a bottle of each type of spirit we make and a bonus bottle that I couldn't resist including. As soon as I open the pickup door, a thumping beat vibrates through my body. From what I've figured out, Elodie lives on the second level, which can't be that big with its peaked roof and the bakery below it. On the main level, the front with the counter and seating area is roughly half of the floor plan. The buildings next to her are closed and their second levels have businesses, not residential tenants.

Is *Elodie* playing music that loud?

Light floods onto the sidewalk from the open back door of the bakery. I ease through the screen door and step inside. I'm enveloped in a sweet, yeasty cloud. Trays line a long stainless-steel table pushed against an island. Heavy bass music fills the air.

I should announce myself, but I haven't seen the elusive woman yet, and I'm drawn inside like a moth to a vanilla-scented flame. When I round the corner, I stop short and barely keep from dropping the box.

Elodie's back is to me. She's by a wall of cabinets, dressed in her normal baggy pants and oversized shirt. She's also dancing. Gyrating, hip-thrusting movements that are raw and raunchy. A full-bodied expression of the real person inside the quiet baker.

Fuck me. I'm frozen. I knew she had curves that would make me salivate, but her punctuated movements pull her loose clothing tight. She's a moving, pumping tease.

A tease who thinks she's alone. I should turn around.

My feet don't move. It's like my boots are pasted to the floor.

"Ugh, yeah." She pumps a hand in the air and grinds low to the floor, holding her apron out of the way. *"Make me wanna come with you, grind with you, sixty-nine with you."*

My throat grows thick and swallowing is difficult. Hearing her say "sixty-nine" when she's not counting out my change has upended my world. I grip the box of spirits with both hands.

Turn around. Me or her, it doesn't matter. One of us has to put an end to this scintillating purgatory.

"Put it right here, baby, down there, baby." She winds her way back up and drops low again, shocking me with the speed. The dark hair wrapped into a floppy bun on top of her head bounces as much as her ass cheeks.

The beat of music winds its way low in my body. *Goddamn it, turn around.*

The brain-body connection comes online. My boots finally move. I put my back to her.

"Elodie?" My voice is rough, thick.

The music drowns out my voice.

"I'll make it good." The sound of her shoes scraping on the floor. *"Put it right here, baby, down there—"*

"Elodie!"

"Aaack!"

I spin around just as a container of sea salt flies from her hands and hits the floor. I take a step to get it for her, but my hands are full and her eyes fly wide behind her thick-framed glasses.

Her expression grows more horrified. "Oh my god!"

"Sorry! I'm sorry."

My heart is racing, both from her dancing and the shouting, but I got a glimpse of an Elodie I sure as hell would've never seen otherwise. Does anyone witness this side of her?

"I knocked," I explain lamely. How do I fix this? Be professional. *Do your job.* I force a smile past the swirling emotions of the last few minutes. "I have a special delivery."

She blinks and steps back like she's going to close herself into the pantry. "Lane was supposed to be coming."

"He got called to the main distillery in Denver. You got me instead." I smile to defuse the situation.

"You're early," she says with a panicked whisper, her hazel eyes owlish behind her frames. She's closing down on me, and I can't let that happen.

"Good thing I was, or I would've missed your deepest secret."

She gives an astounded shake of her head.

"That you can dance." I say it lightly, but my heart is pounding. I've mucked all this up. Can I save the morning? I balance my load on one arm, stoop to pick up the salt, and hand it back to her. I flash her my winningest grin. As seedy as it sounds, it usually works with women.

She doesn't accept it right away. The grin or the salt. A deeper flush creeps up her neck. "That was private."

My stomach sinks all the way to the ground. My chest does one twist and holds, thinking of a question that's none of my business, but I need the answer more than I need to be professional. "Was it for Lane?"

"*No*," she says, scandalized, and snatches the salt. "It wasn't for anybody, but why isn't Lane doing the drop-off?"

I've never seen her this riled up, but then I barely see her, period. Something I'm trying to remedy, but not today. "He asked if I could make the drop, and I didn't think it'd be an issue."

Her stern stare makes me want to squirm like I'm back in elementary school. My instinct is to claim I didn't do it, whatever *it* is. Do I look like hell? My clothes are clean and I brushed my hair, but I discreetly glance down to check myself regardless.

She drops her gaze from my face down to my boots. I gave them a quick polish before I left. They're work boots, but clean. When she wrinkles her nose, I want to sniff an armpit. I showered last night, but something about me is not up to her standards. My stomach sinks further.

She squares her shoulders and marches to the island. "You can set the bottles here."

I follow her and set the box down. I can't leave like this. She's upset with me, and possibly with Lane. I've gotta save this. Not just for the distillery. For me.

It's been years of trying to get to know the elusive baker better, but unless I eat cupcakes, muffins, and cannoli three meals a day, I don't usually see her around. The one time I finally get a glimpse of the real her, and I've scared her?

The back of my throat burns. That won't do. "I really am sorry that I scared you."

She lifts her chin. "You *startled* me. Next time, I need to be notified of any delivery changes."

There's still something in her tone. Something that feels personal, but not in the way I've wanted from her. Has it all been for nothing, trying to get to know the only woman who's caught my attention in years? "Do I bother you?"

She draws back at the abruptness of my question. "Your flirting does."

"I wasn't trying to hide my interest." I've been called shameless before, but I don't go where I'm not wanted. I had enough of that growing up.

"Oh." If possible, her face turns redder, and she blinks several times. "But you aren't, you see."

"I'm not what?"

Her eyes narrow. "Interested."

"Why wouldn't I be?" I shouldn't do this here, but she's actually talking to me. Confusing me, but I appreciate the dialogue nonetheless.

She huffs out a frustrated breath. "I don't know what you want, Cruz. I'm not the type of girl you date."

The pleasure that ripples over me when she says my name is dulled by her disbelief. The first time I stepped into Dee's Sweets, I got caught in an aloof, hazel tractor beam. I was brushed off by the woman with a mop of mahogany hair that's as haphazard as the clothes she wears. I developed a sweet tooth that only craves shy bakers.

I need to drop this whole entire topic, yet I can't quit. Her attention is on me, but again, not in the way I've wanted. "And just what type do I date?"

I don't date much. I've done my share of fucking around, but since moving to Huckleberry Springs, I've kept my personal life tame.

Vulnerability flickers in her eyes before she shakes her head, ignoring the question, and pulls the box toward her.

Quiet and stubborn. That's apparently my type.

I plant my hands on the counter and lean forward. Is she . . . jealous? Is she really interested? Should I have taken my chance and asked her out? Should I do it now?

I left playing games in my childhood. I open my mouth to shoot my shot.

"Have you washed your hands?" Her gaze drops to where I'm touching the countertop.

Here's a bar of soap, Cruz. Use it.

Old shame wells inside me, and *Want to go out sometime?* dies on my tongue. "I'm not dirty."

She hits me with a plaintive look, but there's a thread of understanding. "I didn't say you were," she says softly, "but I serve food to the public."

Right. I was too defensive. This is her place of work, and I'm not an unwashed kid anymore. I peel my palms off the table and hold them out in surrender. "Yes. I've washed them."

"You don't have a hairnet." She shoos me back, but there's a brusqueness behind that keeps it from feeling personal. "Thank you for the delivery. Sorry for hollering at you." She says the last part with equal efficiency, but there's a hint of real remorse there.

Elodie keeps a lot of herself from showing. That elusive part of her calls to me. She doesn't foist her overwhelmed emotions on anyone else. Usually. Except for this morning.

If I'm the exception, I'll take it. It's something to show for this one-sided obsession. "No problem."

Her attention swings to the bottles, and she frowns. "Wait. I only ordered one bottle each of whiskey, gin, and vodka."

She did, and she told us to surprise her with any flavor. We gifted her three bottles. We're not going to charge her, but I have the feeling that news will be as appreciated right now as asking her out. "I tossed in a Butter Barrel. It's made like a bourbon, but we didn't follow the aging or proofing guidelines. What we were after is a buttery flavor with a bourbon richness. Thought it would make a good flavoring for something."

"Like what?" she asks, slightly interested.

I have no idea beyond wanting to surprise her with something. "An icing?"

She nods and works her teeth against her lower lip. Then she gives her head a shake. "I have plenty of ideas for the other bottles, so this isn't necessary."

Maybe it's the early morning or that I got caught ogling her or the flashbacks to being a loser kid, but my attitude roars to the forefront, tired of being repressed for so many years. I don't like to be dismissed. "How about a thank-you?"

She winces and nods once. "Thank you. You can leave it on the invoice."

Great. I'm treading too close to being a jackass. "It's a gift. We appreciate local businesses and want to help out. Keep it and enjoy a glass."

She slides the box closer to her and studies the bottle. "I don't have time to enjoy a drink. It would get old and go to waste."

"It might get a little rusty tasting after a couple of decades from oxidation, but it'll still taste good. You keep it in case you come up with something. Bourbon's meant for sharing."

"You said it was whiskey."

Ah, I'm starting to track this woman now. She either doesn't like to be messed with or she's very literal. "Sure is. Want a sip?"

"I'm working."

"It's part of my job, so it's normal." I give her a reassuring smile. A private tasting is the least I can do for disrupting her.

"It's five a.m. somewhere?"

"Ha! Yes." Damn, she's got a hidden sense of humor. I can see her mind working behind those cunning eyes.

The baker's got me thoroughly fascinated now. She's shy but bold, like a young whiskey, clear and strong like a quality vodka, and prickly like a potent gin. "How 'bout we have a taste and I'll go?"

That came out flirtier than I meant, but I do like showing off our products.

She chews the inside of her cheek, assessing me. Her creamy skin has returned to its normal color, but her lips are a ruby red.

Her guards are firmly in place. Dammit, she's going to kick me out, but I give it another attempt. "It'll only take a minute. Two sips for a tasting is all I'm asking. Promise."

As soon as *promise* leaves my mouth, the shine in her eyes dulls. "I have to get back to work."

Dang, that went south. I would've kept my promise, but someone in her life must not have, for her to shut down that fast. If I keep pressing, she'll trust me even less. I've waited this long, and today I got to know her just a little better. I've got time.

I back toward the door. "If you want a taste tester for any of the new recipes, hit me up."

Her lips form a troubled line. "Do you need to approve my food before the fair?"

I'm caught on what to say. I want to tease her and say absolutely I do, but she's wound tight and I don't know which way she'll spin. "Not at all. Everything you make is perfection. You could've named your store that. Confection Perfection."

"That's actually not bad." She purses her lips. "But Dee's has meaning."

"I'd like to hear about it sometime."

Her expression shutters. "It's, um . . . it's private."

Mercurial. That's not a word that would normally pop into my head, but it does now. "An inside story?"

She moves the bottles from the box to another counter and pushes them close to the wall. "I'll bring some samples by during the next crochet group so you all can approve them before the Billings craft fair."

Okay, the reason for the name behind the bakery is off-limits.

Her privacy is intriguing. My business was splashed all over the neighborhood as a kid. But Elodie's is locked. She's got her shit together, and damn, that's a turn-on.

She's also locked me out, and until she opens that door, I'll have to stay outside.

"I'll let the guys know." She could make vodka-flavored mud and we'd hope our spirit lifted out the best flavors of the dirt. Besides, it's Elodie. She's got the whole town nursing a sweet tooth. But she offered, and while I have to back off of the pretty baker, I'm not missing an opportunity to see her again. "Have a nice day, Elodie."

Elodie

Saturdays and Sundays are my busiest days. I'm closed Mondays when I do a lot of admin and baking for the upcoming week, along with any special orders. I often spend the whole day working, but today, I have somewhere else to be. The crochet club is a small reprieve from constantly toiling away on my dream business. A little bit of hope that I might see a flirty cowboy I should stay far away from.

A flirty cowboy who saw me pop nearly every joint out of socket during my morning wake-up jam session.

A flirty cowboy who acted like a gentleman instead of his usual incorrigible self when I was dying of embarrassment.

Before I leave for the Foster House Distillery, my uncle Karl is here to pick up his order for the church.

I step outside and soak up the warm July sun. He's got the door open to his car, and he grins when he sees me. He has on a short-sleeved blue shirt and his white pastor's collar with black slacks. The sun gleams off the dark skin of his head. He's been bald as long as I've known him, only now he no longer has to shave his scalp each day.

"There she is." He rushes to take my load of flat boxes filled with cinnamon rolls from me. I have another tote bag full of samples, but those aren't for him, and a second one filled with my crochet supplies.

"And there's my favorite customer." It's not polite to lie to a pastor, and as soon as the words are out of my mouth, I have to bat away the image of Cruz Foster aiming that lazy grin at me across the bakery counter. He's perplexing and frustrating, and after he saw me shaking my ass like I was in front of a crowd willing to pay all my bills, he's all that times a thousand.

My uncle balances the goodies in his hold. "If these weren't for a funeral, I would sneak a few myself."

I wipe my hands off. "You know I've got you covered. There's an extra half dozen for you and whoever else is around."

"I knew there was a reason you and Clem are my favorites."

My sister, Clementine, and I are his only nieces. He has no nephews and no kids of his own. It's why my dad's sister left him, but Uncle Karl couldn't leave his congregation. "You're my favorite uncle." I have more uncles, but he really is my favorite.

He gives me a quick once-over. "No apron. You headin' somewhere or do you want to stop by and enjoy a roll with me?"

"I'm leaving right after you. Thank you, though."

"Something's actually getting you out of that bakery?"

"I work almost as much as you," I joke. The church would have to hire two pastors for all the work Uncle Karl does, but he can't sit still and he loves his job. Retirement is a curse word for him.

I get a quick hug before he climbs into his car. I smile and wave at him as he drives away.

My stomach sinks. I would love to have lunch with him or just stop in at his house for coffee. I'd be overjoyed if I could meet my sister for dinner. As it is, I only see her when she comes to help me.

My sigh comes out on a long exhale. There's work to do and I have bills to pay. Some more unexpected—and larger—than others.

The lick of icing I had earlier curdles in my stomach. The next payment is due at the end of the month. The local food fair Campbell Hawthorne thought up to boost tourism, Taste of Springs, isn't until the second weekend in August. I'll need that influx of money for whatever bullshit amount I have to pay at the end of that month too.

I lock up the bakery and trudge to my beater of a car. The damn thing needs new tires; there's a grinding noise when I turn, and the engine knocks. The shape it's in is karma biting me in the ass.

It was my money too.

Repeating the mantra doesn't help.

I get behind the wheel and gaze at the bakery. Dirty money. *My* money. I clench my teeth together. If it was purely my money, I wouldn't be trying to do right by it, to even the balance before my precious business pays for my misdeeds.

Driving off, I roll the windows down until I hit the highway. *Knock, knock, knock.*

Damn. I have to get this thing looked at. I roll the windows up and turn the music louder. Thumping bass fills the cab, barely blocking out the noise. I'm heading toward the distillery for Hookers and Booze. It's my favorite day of the month and the only hours I'll give myself off for the months ahead. I need to bake and cook and do cartwheels with my finances to make enough money to cover my ass.

As I turn into the parking lot, the distillery looms large, all timber, glass, and rock. Large, inviting windows allow a peek at the tall stills inside. The shiny copper columns are my favorite over the steel stills. I should design a cupcake tower for the fair to resemble them.

Is vodka made in the copper ones? The frosting I made with their huckleberry vodka turned a nice blush. It's not exact, but it might be close enough.

I park and suck in a deep breath to prevent my heart from racing. *He's* not here. He's never here for crochet club.

This is only the third crochet club ever.

I look in my rearview mirror and my pulse jumps. His silver-and-blue pickup is parked right behind me, and it looks like it's vibrating thanks to the music rattling my windows. I let my eyelids drift shut. His mischievous smile should be repellent. *It is.* I just have nowhere to go when he's in the bakery.

Then he caught me dancing last week. I was sure I had plenty of time before Lane showed up. But I spun around and there was a tall man with sexily rumpled dark hair that brushed his ears, wearing an obscenely tight T-shirt, blue jeans, and cowboy boots.

His eyes are the same blue as the denim he wears.

It'd be easier to ignore him if he weren't unfairly handsome. Panties burn off when he walks down the street. Women throw themselves at him. He's always smiling at them and joking around. Then he comes in and asks me questions, like about what baking soda does for muffins. Or how to get the perfect moist cookie. His questions are never innuendos and he listens to my answers. It makes him endearing, dammit.

There's a light knock on my driver's window. I bark out a cry and turn the music off. A large shadow with biceps I could lick looms on the other side. I didn't notice him while I was staring in the rearview mirror at Cruz's truck.

The man hinges at the waist and it's *him*.

His mouth moves and I cock an ear toward him while turning down a song much like the one I was grinding to when he caught me. My cheeks warm as he grins. Is he remembering the scene too?

"Can I help you carry anything?" he calls, that easy smile in place.

He can help by not being so nice. It'd assist me a

lot if he weren't the hottest guy I've ever met. I'd find it so useful if I didn't get so acutely *aware* when he's around.

"No," I mutter. He cocks an ear. He can't hear me. I push the door open and he backs up, but all I get is a window full of rugged man. Powerful thighs and a long-legged stance. The slight scruff on his face sets my heart beating faster. I have to look away before the tingles all over my body announce how epically long it's been since I've gotten laid.

The man is arresting, and I don't need more men and arrests in my life.

"What can I grab?" He peers through the back window.

Why is he so relentless? "I've got it."

"I'm here. Use me." He holds his arms out to the sides, snugging his shirt to his torso. Ranching and distilling do a body good.

I'd use him so hard.

Nope! I have ninety-nine problems and a guy is very much one. I don't need to round it out to an even hundred. "You can get the tote with the samples of my fair items."

I back all the way up to let him into the back seat. He bends over and my attention goes right to his ass. So damn firm I could bounce a quarter off it.

"You need this other bag?" he asks, his voice muffled.

My crochet supplies that never left the car after the last monthly crochet club. "Yes, but I can get that."

He backs out and hip checks the door shut. "It's no problem."

It's a huge problem. The way he's holding his arms, a little out to the side with his biceps bulging, and his stance? With that tight shirt and cowboy boots? It's obscene.

I want to climb his tall body like I'm a kitten and he's both the tree and the fireman who'll save me. I have to look away before the image in my head becomes two naked humans. "Thanks."

He beams like he's pleased that he finally gets to help me. That's worse. He tips his head toward the building. "Ladies first."

I start walking and he falls in step beside me. I have nothing to do with my hands since he's carrying everything. I have on loose gray linen pants and an oversized Montana shirt I got at the gas station.

"Everyone's here already." Does the silence bother him, or is he always this chatty? "You're not late though. Durban's running drinks. Campbell's here, of course."

I never tire of seeing Durban Hennessy and Campbell Hawthorne together, or Durban's brother, Iverson, and Campbell's sister Jamison. Those couples are real. The love in the guys' eyes is real. They've been nothing but trustworthy and upstanding citizens in the community. I knew of the three Hennessy brothers before they bought into the distillery, and before the two oldest fell for the oldest and youngest Hawthorne sisters from the guest ranch outside of town. None of the gossip about them was scandalous. It was barely salacious, and that's because all the Hennessys have the same effect on women as Cruz. Lane's the same.

I just notice Cruz more than anyone else.

"You excited to crochet?" he asks.

He's always trying to make small talk, and the less I speak to him, the harder he tries. I can't succumb. "I'm sure crochet is boring for you."

"Nah, it's cool to see everything you guys make. Edna was showing me the blanket she's making for a silent auction at the fair next month."

"I'm putting together a package for that." I bite the inside of my cheek. No good will come from making conversation with Cruz. I'll just want more, and I know his type. Charming flirt. Skin deep. Even if I could trust a guy again, it's a bad time to date.

"I can't wait to see it. You do that white chocolate cake, and it'll bring in a hundred bucks. At least."

My insides get all warm and gooey. That flavor is my favorite for a cake. "I'm actually putting together a baking basket. It'll have all the utensils, ingredients, and instructions."

"That's a great idea. It's going to get a big bid."

"You think so?" I've been a little insecure about it.

He smiles at me. "One hundred percent sure."

I refrain from rolling my eyes. More boastful promises.

When we're inside the tasting room, all the women shout greetings. My smile pokes through, but I still want to hide behind Cruz's big body. I don't like having attention on me.

Edna waves. "Now it's a party."

My sister is sitting at a table next to Edna and four of her friends, who are all past retirement age, along with one of their grandsons who's home from college. Clem's hair is dark like mine, but she's got hers down today. The tasting room is cool. Must be why she has the green gradient shawl she crocheted over her shoulders. Campbell is poring over an instruction pamphlet for some project, her long chestnut braid hanging over her shoulder. I wistfully admire her athletic shorts. Why didn't I throw a pair of shorts on? I've gotten too used to dressing like this. My linen pants today are very sweats adjacent.

Durban is behind the bar. Does the distillery buy tight T-shirts and blue jeans in bulk? Except for Cruz's older brother Lane, who wears suits once in a while, that's all I've seen the five owners in.

Technically, there are six. Lane and Cruz have an older brother who stops into the bakery to pick up various desserts when he's in town. Myles Foster is the founder and owner of Foster House, but he brought in his brothers and the Hennessys to invest and run the Huckleberry Springs site they call Foster House Gold.

I hear and see a lot in the bakery, and I like to be in the know. Because then *I'll* know if my personal business ever starts making the rounds.

I weave around the tables toward Clem. She grins at me.

"If she gets out of line," Cruz says to me, "we'll put her to work."

Clem gives him a playful glare. I ignore him.

"Don't listen to him," Edna calls, not missing a beat in her crocheting. "We'll move this shindig if the guys try to ruin our fun."

Cruz chuckles, and gah! It's such a deep, pleasing sound. "As long as no stools go through the window. And Durban will need you all to sign a disclaimer before there's any dancing on the tables."

Durban nods, but the smoldering glance he shoots Campbell suggests that there's been some private table dancing already.

"Where can I put these?" Cruz holds up the bags.

"I've got them." I set the containers with the samples

on the bar counter. He doesn't leave my side as I unload them. "Thanks," I say in a way that sounds more like goodbye. He doesn't move until I shoot him a deliberate stare.

He ducks his head, but his smile is all *charm your pants off*. I immediately look away. A thousand pairs of panties can burn off, but I'm not going to do anything about it. After I arrange the containers of baked goods, I bring them to the bar counter.

"I have enough here for all of you to taste test," I explain to Durban even though Cruz is leaning on the counter and hanging on my every word. "I put the huckleberry vodka in the batter and the frosting of the cupcakes. Your spiced gin was used for the oatmeal raisin cookie. Then"—I move the samples around to stimulate my memory—"another cupcake because I wanted to play with the gin. This time I put it in the filling. Oh, I also made a single-serving spiced cake with a buttery whiskey glaze. If there's something you don't like, don't hesitate to tell me."

"Samples?" Durban peers at the goodies. "You didn't have to."

"I told you I would." I shoot Cruz a questioning look. Didn't he pass the message along?

"That's right, you did. I must've forgot." Cruz's lopsided grin probably makes all the girls forget when he doesn't keep his word.

I don't play relationship games like that anymore. It's easier not to do relationships at all. No one's made me want to—until Cruz turned my head. But I swiveled it right back to my goals—to run an honest, successful business and pay it forward as much as I can.

"Thanks, Elodie," Durban says to me before turning

to Cruz. "I've gotta pop into the storeroom. Be right back."

Cruz nods, his attention on me.

I'm going to smolder and start smoking if he leaves it there, and it'll burn away my resistance. I grasp for something, anything, to deflect the heat and keep my wits about me. It shouldn't be so easy, and maybe it's not fair to Cruz. He could've legitimately forgotten, or he could be like someone else I once knew and playing games.

"Don't say you're going to do something when you don't mean it." I keep my voice low so only we can hear.

He blinks. "I'm sor—"

"Don't apologize when you don't mean it." Anger that Cruz isn't responsible for rises from the depths I try to keep it in and aims right at him. "Don't keep trying to help me. I don't want it. I don't know what you're looking for, but it's not me. No more flirting. No more fake promises. You need to leave me alone."

His jaw goes slack. Oh my god, did I go too far? The bewilderment and, dammit, hurt in his eyes turn my well-aged fury to panic. I should've kept my mouth shut and ignored him like usual. Only Cruz doesn't make it easy.

The urge to apologize is strong. To tell him I don't mean any of it. But I do. I have to.

I take refuge with my sister at her table, my heart racing. Eventually, Campbell sits with us. I struggle to draw a full breath and the middle of my shoulders aches from the tension I'm holding. The handsome distiller reminds me of too many bad boys I've known in my life. It's not his fault, but I need space. Lots of it.

Cruz chats with Durban before he steps away from

the bar. I slip a stitch on my project. I lashed out way harder than I meant to and much harsher than he deserved. I glance up and my gaze collides with his. He only gives me a tip of his head and disappears into the main distillery.

I slump in my seat and keep working on the bodice of an apron for the silent auction basket. Guilt and longing mix in my chest and breathing is hard again.

Well, there's the space I wanted.

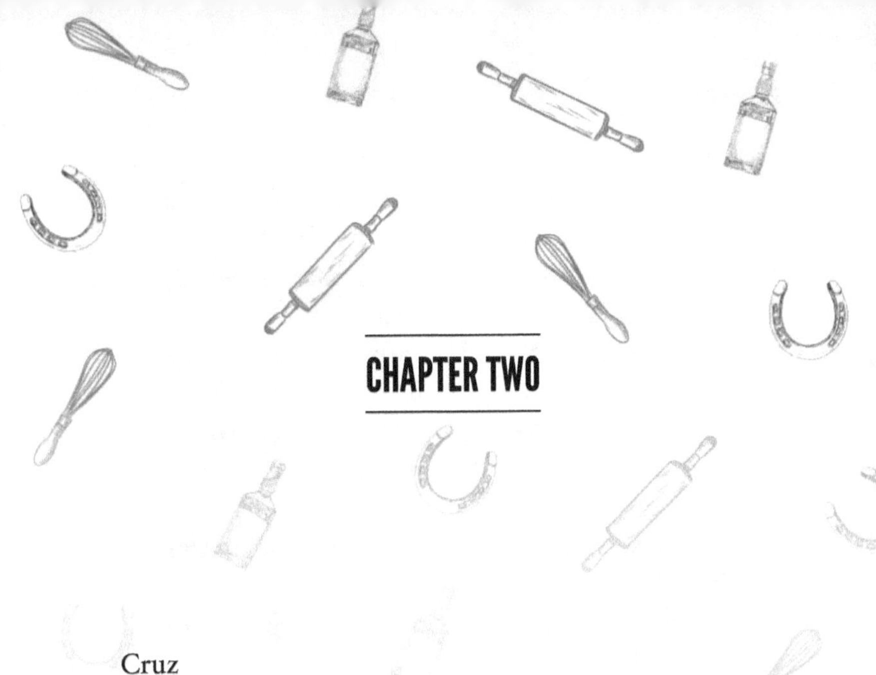

CHAPTER TWO

Cruz

I left the tasting room when I couldn't handle drowning in humiliation. I didn't leave the distillery, otherwise I would've looked really pathetic. Durban was already giving me a weird look for showing up to put in a few extra hours while the crochet club happened to be meeting.

I've sniffed myself at least five times.

Ew, Foster. Ever heard of laundry detergent?

I shake off the playground teasing. I had heard of laundry detergent. Whether my mom could afford it was another story.

I do not smell, and I showered this morning after chores, like always. I only put on aftershave. Lane taught me how to use that and cologne without overwhelming a room like a teen in the throes of puberty.

I've been as nice as possible to my little baker. Every time I try to reassure her about anything, she pulls away so fast and hard my head spins. All I've done is upset her. I just want to get to know her, but I'm the last guy she wants sniffing around.

When she looks at me, she has that knowing gaze. Like she knows I came from the gutter and I'm just pretending to be a good ol' country boy. She looks at me like that grungy kid invited to the birthday party because the rules said everyone had to be invited. All she needs is to give Clem a knowing *hide your purse* glance and I'll be eleven again.

She can see me, and that's why she wants nothing to do with me.

I've spent the last two hours unloading the production line deliveries from the morning, stocking boxes of bottles and labels on the shelving units. When the last box is put away, I rub the back of my neck and eye my work. I just have to haul out a couple of pallets and I'll be done. Maybe I'll mop the floor first. Then I can go home and throw myself a nice pity party.

"Campbell and I are heading out," Durban says from behind me. "The rest of the club is gone or on their way out."

" 'Kay. I'll lock up."

"I left Elodie's baked goods on the counter, but I took one of each to bring home."

"To share with Campbell?"

"I'd be in trouble if I didn't."

I chuckle, and the little bit of humor tamps down the acid in my stomach. We both know that he wants to share whatever he has with his girl. I'd be the same. My stomach clenches. Fucked that up, didn't I?

Expecting him to mosey on his way, I keep working. He doesn't leave.

I'm not going anywhere until everyone's gone. I swore a long time ago I'd never be humiliated about myself again, and I don't need witnesses to my failure. "Is there something else?"

I've gotten to know Durban well over the last five years. He keeps things close to the chest, but he's our distilling wizard. He gets the science behind the product and he likes to experiment. The flavor profiles Durban can extract are admirable, and he's really carved a niche. I like tried and true. I want to stay in my lane and not get kicked out of it.

Indecision plays over his face. "It's not my business, but this thing with you and Elodie?"

I scoff. "There is no *thing*. Trust me. She's not interested."

"Then why did you come today?"

I wouldn't have bought my flimsy excuse of unpacking the shipments either. That's what Tuesday mornings are for. "I thought that, you know, outside of the bakery, maybe it'd be different." I lift a shoulder. "I have my answer. She made it clear."

"Sorry."

I force a laugh and wave him off. "You win some, you lose some."

He doesn't break a smile. "We'll see you, then."

"Have a good night." I stuff my thumb over my shoulder, proud that I can act like my heart didn't get stomped on. "I'll see what we're dumping tomorrow and get the bottling supplies ready."

"Thanks, Cruz."

I complete what I said I would, if only to kill more time, so no one will witness my not-quite walk of shame. Durban might not have bought my excuse, but having done some work makes me feel better. Having followed through also boosts my ego after the dressing-down Elodie gave me.

Yeah, I'm gonna mop up. The dust the boxes left behind might as well be on my skin.

When the boxes for tomorrow are ready and the floor is gleaming, I head out. At the door, I frown at the only other car in the parking lot, sitting cockeyed by the turn that leads to the highway. The hood is up.

Elodie's car.

I might look forward to talking with her again, but I'm going to be the last guy she wants to see. It won't matter. I know my way around an engine thanks to Lane.

I lock up the distillery and trot toward her. The closer I get, the more the smell of burning oil crowds out the distillery's warm grain smell.

She's squinting at the engine. The always-present dismay plays across her expression. "Sorry, I'm blocking the way."

"Ain't a problem." I shove my hands in my pockets and lean over. I don't want to overstep. Besides, any news I give her probably won't be good. The racket her car made driving into the parking lot was foreboding. "Mind if I take a look?"

Her laughter comes out like a shotgun. "I don't think it'll help." She props a hand on her hip and pinches the bridge of her nose, bumping her glasses crooked. She squeezes her eyes shut. "There's been a knocking noise for a while, and I should've taken it in."

"Yeah," I say sympathetically. "A knocking noise isn't good."

"Damn him," she seethes.

Huh? I shake my head. She wasn't damning me. So who's him?

With an abrupt inhale, she blinks her eyes open and straightens her glasses. "You don't need to mess with this. I can call my dad."

"It's no problem, really. I'm mechanically inclined, but I think you're going to need a tow."

"No. I can call my dad."

I suck in a slow breath as disappointment sinks heavy into my bones. She wants nothing to do with me. "Okay." I take a step back so she knows I'm serious. I'm not forcing myself on her in any way. "I'll just wait in my truck, and I know you won't like it, but I'm going to stay here until you get this taken care of."

I pivot on a heel and stride to my pickup.

"Cruz."

I come to a stop. As I look over my shoulder, my chest constricts. She wants me to leave her alone.

She's still in the same spot, but her fraught expression is new. "I'm sorry."

"For what?"

"You just seem . . . I don't want . . . You offered to help and I . . ." She flops her hands against her thighs. "I should've taken it in."

She's really beating herself up about that. As for the rest, she has her baggage, and as much as I'd like to get to know her, I'll back all the way off. "Will you be okay with me helping you if I promise to behave?"

Her gaze turns wary. "What do you mean?"

"You're not interested. I'm not your type. I'll just look at your car, tow it to wherever you want, and drop you off at your place. No flirting, no jokes, no . . . me."

"Can you function without flirting?"

"Oof." I cough out a harsh laugh. "I didn't realize I was that bad."

"God, I'm sorry. I was kidding." Her mouth twists. "Sort of."

It stings worse the longer I think about it, so I cross to the car.

She doesn't go far while she paces. I didn't notice her sandals earlier. In the bakery, everything's covered but her face, and her hair is always secured. Today, her toenails, painted a vibrant shade of lime green, are visible.

My blood threatens to reroute after seeing some skin, so I keep my focus on the dipstick as I pull it out. It's dry. "Shit."

"I just checked it a week ago and added more." She comes closer. Is that what it takes? A catastrophic engine failure for her to willingly approach me?

"Do you get it serviced regularly?" It was really hard to keep that from sounding like an innuendo.

She nods. "Whenever it tells me to, and I add oil in between."

"Then I hate to say it, Elodie, but having to regularly add oil isn't a good sign." I shove the dipstick back into place. "I think the engine might've blown."

She wrings her hands together. "That's expensive, isn't it?" I nod and her eyes get watery. "No. I can't afford this. Not this month. Not next." She lets out a frustrated huff and spins around. I'm still able to hear the "Damn him."

Who is this fucking *him* who's disrupting her life? "Let me call Lane, 'kay? He used to be a mechanic."

"He did?" She sniffles.

"He's still got the tools, and he's got a nice shop. Let

me just ask if he'll take a look when he returns from Denver."

Her hair bounces when she nods. "If you need to be somewhere, I can call my dad or my uncle."

Not a chance. I want to help, and I'm able to. I might also be learning more about Elodie Palmer, but I have more questions too. "The girls I've got waiting at home will be irritated they have to wait an extra hour for their dinner."

"The cattle?" she asks, almost hopefully.

"Kittens. Found them at the end of my driveway last month."

Her eyes go soft. "What are their names?"

"Sage and Basil. They joined Rufus, my dog."

"I always wanted a pet." She pushes her glasses up, discreetly wiping away a tear that slips from the corner of her eye. "Thanks for this. Dad or Uncle Karl would be out here in a heartbeat, but I don't like to worry them."

Nodding, I'd chat more, but she might think I'm coming on to her. Time to get to work. "I'll get my supplies and let Lane know I'm towing your car to his place."

"You haven't talked to him yet."

"He loves getting his hands dirty. He won't mind, but I'll give him a call." I give her what I hope is a reassuring smile and not some creepy come-on leer and head to my pickup.

Elodie

· · ·

I don't ever want to leave Cruz's pickup. It's immaculate. Does he dust the inside every day? He has a cooling option for the seats. I can practically swing my legs while sitting in the passenger side, and the smell—a delicious mix of warm grains and citrus.

We're back in town after pulling my car to Lane's big shop. It was my first time seeing one of the homes of the guys involved in the distillery. I still haven't seen Cruz's house, or any of the others, except for the youngest Hennessy brother's. He lives in the house he and his brothers grew up in. The others have built their own homes since I've moved back here, but I'm too involved in my job to sightsee around town.

Cruz navigates through Huckleberry Springs. A variety of music pours through the speakers—nineties country, early aughts pop and rock, and every so often, I catch an older hair metal song. He's different than I assumed.

The energy he brings everywhere is subdued when he's driving and he seems like he's at peace. When he was hooking up the car and explaining to me what I needed to do to steer behind him, he was locked in. Serious. I liked that side of him. Competent and focused. It was hot.

I don't like the part of him that's been closed off to me since I rebuffed him in the tasting room. A small part of my heart hurts. I miss that lopsided smile getting aimed my way.

We pass the small gas station on the edge of town, and the Chinese restaurant, Wok and Rolls. I stare at the mechanic shop and the insurance agency. He's approaching the bakery.

I should say something, but a thank-you doesn't seem

like enough. All I have to offer are baked goods. Would that be adequate? It's what I would've given my dad or uncle, but it'd be mostly to distract them from being too concerned that I can't afford to fix my car.

Cruz saved my ass. I would've paid a tow truck a lot more than a dozen cupcakes. "Did you try the samples for the Billings street fair?"

He clicks the side of his mouth. "One of each of those has my name on it for breakfast tomorrow."

A warm glow spreads through me. Lots of people eat my food, and I'm proud of it, but knowing Cruz is planning on it flips my belly in all directions.

When he parks in front of the bakery, I don't want to get out. "Do you mind going to the back door?"

"Not at all." He backs out of the parking spot.

The stairs to my apartment are right by the door. It's not like I couldn't walk through the bakery, but it's clean and I'm dustier than Lane's new shop. The guy has his own maintenance bay in that place.

I always thought the Foster brothers sprouted from a ranch, two fully grown cowboys who can make excellent spirits. Cruz has to be about my age and I'm thirty-two. Plenty of time to have a whole life between the childhood years and now. Lane's a few years older than him, but Cruz didn't mention doing anything other than what he's doing now. Did he go to school for something else?

Too soon, we're at the back door. My day of socializing is done. I need to get out more, but I also need to bake even more goodies and come up with tons of gimmicks to increase sales.

Yet I'm not ready to retire to my apartment alone. I'm not ready to let Cruz drive off while I wonder if I'll get more than a polite smile the next time he comes in.

An idea pops into my head, and I go with it before logic interferes. "Want to try them now?" When he turns a perplexed gaze toward me, my heart stutters. "I made a dozen of each, so I have a lot left. They're going to be my breakfast too. I owe you."

"You don't have to," he says carefully.

"You've gone out of your way. It's the least I can do."

"Elodie—"

"Let me pay you back in this small way. It's all I can manage."

I must've said the right thing to persuade him. He kills the engine. "If you insist."

Pleased more than I care to admit, I hop out and unlock the building. I wave to a small table where I have most of my meals, away from the baking area. It's on the other side of the room from where he caught me grinding to one of my favorite wake-up songs. "Have a seat and I'll grab them."

"Mind if I use the bathroom first to wash up?"

"Go ahead." He cleaned the worst of the grit and grease off his hands at Lane's. So did I, but I give mine a rinse before retrieving a serving platter, plates, several forks for sampling, and two of each batch I made.

By the time the table is set, he returns. "Looks good." He presses a hand to his stomach. "I'm hungry enough to eat a bear, but I hope you don't take offense if I only have a taste of each. I haven't eaten since lunch."

He missed dinner because he was helping me. "You can have it all."

He winces, but the corner of his mouth kicks up regretfully. "I hate to pass on the offer, but I need some protein to go with my sweets or I get sick."

"Are you diabetic?" Then I cut my hand through the air. "None of my business."

"No." He chuckles. "Not diabetic, just a hazard of how I used to eat. Lots of heat and serve—if we were lucky. When I went to live with the Baileys, I got quality meat morning, noon, and night, and I just don't feel right if I don't keep that up."

Heat and serve if he was lucky? We? Is he talking about him and Lane? What did he mean *when I went to live with the Baileys*? People talk in the bakery and I've heard about the Foster brothers. I've heard that their oldest brother was an actual foster kid for a time. My curiosity about Cruz is becoming boundless.

He has more dimensions in his story than I assumed, but then I have a whole-ass story I don't want to talk about too. "I can make some eggs."

"I'll rustle up something when I get home. It's not a problem. I don't want to take more of your time."

Irritation at myself scrapes raw against the back of my throat. I don't know Cruz, but I miss the lopsided smile now more than ever. "It'll take ten minutes. Again, it's literally the least I can do." I rush to the fridge before he can argue. "I also have some veggies— An omelet?"

"Really, Elodie, you don't have to."

"I know. Please let me do this." I set a boundary earlier. He respected it. Now I'm regretting what I said. What if he's really a nice guy?

I can't take the chance, but I can show him appreciation for helping me out instead of ditching me. A lot of guys would've passed without the promise of sexual favors.

"All right," he concedes. "An omelet would hit the spot."

He sits quietly while I work. I look over my shoulder, hoping he's got his attention on me, like when he meets the guys at the bakery. They'd all be talking, and out of the corner of my eye, I'd see him studying me, but not in a creepy way. It's made me hyperaware. But my heart drops like a rock. He's scrolling through his phone.

Isn't that what I want?

I whip the eggs extra hard. The omelet's done in no time, and I slide a plate in front of Cruz and set one by my chair. He tucks his phone away, and I search his face as he inspects his food.

"I think you're going to put the café out of business."

"I don't tell anyone I can cook." I twist my hands together. When he looks at me, I shrug. "I went to culinary school." It's not a secret, but it's not something I advertise. Most people toss chefs and bakers into different categories, and I'm happier being classified as a baker only.

"A chef? No kidding?" He digs into his food and shoves a forkful in his mouth. The groan that rips from him is primal and starts a beat right between my thighs.

I shift in my chair. "Is it good?"

He swallows and loads his fork a second time. "It's criminal the public doesn't know how well you can cook." He fills his mouth again.

I beam inside. "Not many people remember what I went to college for, and they assume it was pastry school or something. I only cook for my family. Do you mind keeping it to yourself?"

"Only if you tell me why." He flashes me a closed-mouth grin but immediately turns serious. "Sorry. Of course I'll keep it to myself."

I stab my fork into my food. I've been hard on him and he still made sure I didn't stay stranded. He deserves some form of explanation. "I don't like cooking for others." That's not quite right, and I don't want him to think that I resent making an omelet when I practically tackled him before he walked out the door. "I don't like *feeling* like I have to cook for others."

" 'Damn him,' huh?"

I swallow hard, my mouth going dry. Of course he heard that. Damn me for not keeping my mouth shut. But Cruz isn't probing for more. He's gobbling down my food like he hasn't eaten for days. "Yeah, damn him. Anyway, I like baking. I like making pretty things, and I like being my own boss."

"There's nothing like it. I can't beat my coworkers either."

"You seem like a good group."

"Are you including me in that?"

I can't tell if he's being playful, but I'll be honest. "Yes."

His steady look is unreadable. "Thank you," he says sincerely.

We finish our omelets in silence, and I try not to heave my food back up. The nerves are going to kill me. He's either too busy eating to talk or he doesn't want to chat with me. Another thing I didn't think I'd miss. His chatter wasn't generic. He always asked about me or about something to do with my job. It was personal, and at the time, I questioned its validity, but now I'm more certain he was genuine.

When we're done eating, Cruz looks over the samples.

I push my empty plate away, grateful he's not trying to leave as soon as possible. "I don't have names for them yet. Except I think I'll call the cupcake a Huckleberry Sunrise."

"You name them like we name our cocktails."

"Yeah, I guess I do."

He carefully cuts portions off the cupcakes and the cake and serves me first on a clean plate. He breaks a cookie in half and divides it up.

All the recipes I created are simple and should stand up in the heat of the street fair in a display cooler. Billings isn't far away, but they'll travel well. I've tasted them all, yet I try a bite of each while studying his reaction.

"Damn, that's good," he says about the huckleberry cupcake. "We should make a shot with that vodka that has a dab of whipped cream on top."

"Mmm, sounds good."

His gaze sharpens on me. Heat fills his eyes, but a second later, he skates his focus back to the spiced cake and takes a bite. I slide to the edge of my chair, waiting for his reaction.

"This tastes like Thanksgiving is right around the corner."

Triumph lifts my hopes. I'm the most insecure about the spiced cake. "Do you think it's too heavy for summer?"

He shakes his head and cuts into the gin cupcake. His lips close around the fork and I'm riveted. The shadows of his whiskers have grown darker than they were this afternoon, and it makes his denim-blue eyes stand out more. "That tastes like a floral bouquet but not in a bad way."

"I'll take it."

He smiles and bites into the cookie. His gaze flickers, he pauses, and then he continues chewing.

Oh no. He doesn't like it. Heat singes my cheeks. "That bad?"

"No. It's good."

"But?"

"It's great, Elodie. Everything you make is."

"Don't lie to me," I say harsher than I mean to. His brows pop up. Crap. I overstepped, but he's eating in my kitchen. Other than my part-time staff, only Clem, my dad, and Uncle Karl have been in the back. Cruz is the first man I've had a one-on-one meal with in years. "I can handle a bad review."

"I'm not lying," he says like he's consoling me. "It's good. Oatmeal raisin isn't my thing. I didn't remember that's what you made, and I missed the signs that there weren't chocolate chips. When I bite into oatmeal raisin, there's always the punch of betrayal that it's not a chocolate chip."

A giggle leaves me. The way he explains it is just like him—irreverent and charming. "So you're an oatmeal raisin hater?" I ask lightly. "It's not something to be ashamed of."

His whole demeanor relaxes. Was he that afraid of insulting me? "No, I'll eat them. I'll eat the whole batch. You can ask Mae Bailey. But that punch of disappointment in the first bite is hard to get over."

I bark out a laugh, feeling lighter than I have the whole day. "Well, since I have only a bite or two to hook people at the fair, then I'd better table this recipe."

Cruz's crooked smile is back, only there's something different about it, something softer and personal. Almost intimate. Paired with the two of us together in my cozy dining nook, my guards slam back up.

"I'll figure something else out," I say briskly. "I thought the raisins would work better in the heat since most people will carry them around instead of buying them for an immediate snack like the other stuff."

The aloofness is back in his grin and it becomes the one everyone else gets. "Then go for it. The guys will probably like it. They'll like them all." He pushes back. "Thank you for the amazing food." He rises and picks up our plates. "Where can I put these?"

My heart twists. I want his special smile again, but I'm the one who shrugged it off. Now I mourn when Cruz acquiesces and gives me the distance I insist on. Despite that, he's not forgetting his manners. "By the sink, please. I'll throw them in the dishwasher with my morning dishes."

His broad back is to me as he arranges the plates and silverware by the sink. This kitchen isn't as large as I'd like it to be, but I'm the only baker, so it works. He takes up all the room and fills it with a vitality I've never been able to replicate.

When he's done, he washes his hands. "Lane won't be back for a few days, but I can take a look and talk with him."

A few days. And then the repairs. What if I need a new engine? I could afford one, but I have to pay off my ex.

Shit, shit, shit. I have places to be, money to make, so I don't lose this shop or my reputation. I'll have to ask my parents or Clem, and they'll worry. Acid splashes up my throat. I'm an adult now, but the suffocation of my teen years clings to me. Still, I don't have anyone else to ask for help.

Cruz turns and pauses, concern lining his eyes. "You all right?"

No. "Sorry, I'm just figuring out the logistics of the craft fair in Billings next week." It's one of the bigger events in the area, and with the natural dip in the summer season, I need all the chances I can get to sell my goods. Add in the collaboration with Foster House, and it's not just me who's out more than a little exposure if I have to bow out.

His face lights up. "You can hitch a ride with one of us."

The pressure in my chest returns. Is he always accommodating? Why is an accommodating, nice guy stressing me out so much? "I'll have displays and my tent."

"We have trucks."

"I can ask Clem." It's better than my dad trying to load everything into his SUV. "Wait, no. She's going to be there for the library and help me when she's not with them, but she'll have to drive separately."

He opens his mouth like he's going to insist, then he snaps it closed and heads for the door. "Keep us in mind. Durban has the Rafting and Tasting event, and Iverson's still on reduced hours with the new baby, but Lane, Haven, and I will be working the summer fair." He tips his head like he has a cowboy hat on. "You know how to get a hold of me. Have a good evening, Elodie."

He takes all the air with him when he walks out, just like I wanted him to. I'm left alone with all my problems, and an oatmeal cookie that tastes like betrayal.

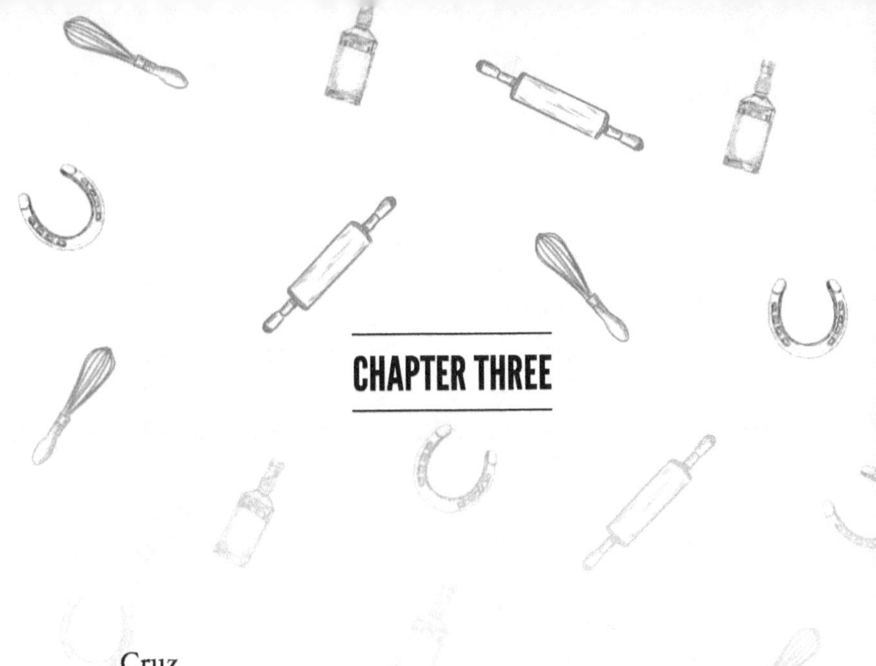

CHAPTER THREE

Cruz

"Yeah, she's gonna need a new engine." Lane's voice drifts out of the speaker I have connected to my phone in his shop. I knew going in that Elodie's car was toast, but I still looped in my brother, though I have to be his eyes and ears. Not that there's much to pass on. It has no oil. "I can get her some times and pricing for shipping. The labor's no issue. I won't charge her."

For Lane, it's like a day of play. He doesn't have to tell me that; I just know he misses being a mechanic. He loves ranching and he enjoys distilling, but his zen is grease-filled hands and engine parts lying around. The pickup he's restoring is parked at the back of the shop.

My happy place is not being a degenerate. I scrub all the grime off my hands. Ranching and the distillery are better than a lot of things I could've ended up doing, and they're both fun while keeping me productive. I like keeping busy, and when one is slow, the other will pick up. I can always count on cows getting out when I think it's time to relax, and the distillery participates in enough street fairs, craft fairs, and holiday shows to fill in the spare time. I wave to law enforcement these days instead of hiding from them.

"I'll let her know," I tell him, and dry my hands, inspecting my nails while I do it. Good. They're spotless. "Hey, you mind if we help her get to Billings and back?"

"Why would I?"

"Just making sure." I cleared it with Haven, and he gave me the look Lane is probably wearing now. Why would we mind helping another business owner, one we like, when we know she's in a bind? "Talk to you later," I say before hanging up.

I'm asking because she may do everything in her power to keep me from lending her a hand. I don't know what I did, but every time I get a glimpse into Elodie Palmer, she slams the window shades down like I'm a Peeping Tom.

Yet the woman still intrigues me. The way her laughter takes her by surprise, her abandon when she finally lets go. Her eyes light up and joy dances across her face. Elodie is one reserved woman, but she doesn't want to be that way. I don't know how I know, but I do.

I try to call the bakery, but it goes to voicemail. Her brusque but chipper voice drifts over the line. It's Tuesday, and after being closed Monday, she's probably busy.

A message pops up on my screen.

Haven: Bootleg at 7?

Durban must be working the tasting room tonight.

The bakery closes at four. I could stop by and talk to Elodie before I jaunt over to Bootleg. Yeah, it's an excuse to see her again. I should quit trying to get a key to those gates she's put up, but I can't. Besides, I'm just helping with her car. Lane and I have been stranded with no way to get anywhere often enough in our lives, I know how it feels.

Cruz: I'm in.

I check the time before tucking my phone away. It's not quite four. I have time to run through the shower, grab a bite to eat, and stop in to talk to Elodie before meeting Haven.

A few hours later, I don't stink like exhaust and grease, and I'm pulling up by the back door of Dee's Sweets. My hair's still damp, but I push it off my head and hop out of the pickup.

I'm almost to the door when it whips open. I have to step aside before I'm run over by an angry baker.

"I heard you the first time." Elodie's livid voice rings out and the screen bashes open. "How long do you think I can sustain this? Oh, you don't care? What about when the well runs dry? Huh? What about that?" Her flashing gaze collides with mine and goes wide. "I've gotta go." Fury passes through her eyes before she spins to put her back to me. "Guess what? I don't care."

She stuffs the phone in the pocket of her loose linen shorts, her oversized shirt getting in the way. I take a step back to admire strong legs that could crush me and make me ask for more. She locks the door so roughly it's amazing the key doesn't snap.

"Didn't mean to intrude." But I'm glad I did. Irate Elodie is a sight to behold. Who the hell is upsetting her? Before she faces me, I yank my gaze off her legs.

She shakes her head to get some hair out of her eyes. "It's nothing."

That sounded like something. "I was headed to Bootleg and wanted to stop and update you on the car."

Her face falls and the stress swelling in her eyes guts me. "How bad?"

She doesn't play games, so I'm blunt. "New engine. Sorry."

She drops her head back, the slender column of her throat elongating in despair. The picture is wrong. It should only do that to let someone in, to make room for a man to lick from her clavicle to her sweet cherry lips.

"Lane's going to do some checking, see how much everything costs and when it'll all come in. Once he has the parts, it won't take him long." I don't tell her he won't charge for labor. Seems like that kind of thing won't go over well right now.

She blows out a breath and looks down the path that leads out of the makeshift alley behind her shop. When she brings her attention back to me, it's on my chest, stroking over my shoulders and down my arms. My skin tingles like a feather is stroking ever so softly over it. That invisible touch travels to other places, like my nosy dick that always stirs when I'm thinking about the curves Elodie hides inside her baggy clothing.

"Right." She nods like she's reconciling something with herself. "I know you gifted the Butter Barrel, but I need the invoice for the spirits you gave me for the fair recipes."

"Those are for a joint promotion." She displays our logo and spirit information with each recipe and we do the same for Dee's Sweets, featuring her baked goods in front of each spirit.

She shakes her head. "No. I'm paying for what I use."

"Should we charge you for our mash bill?" When she

frowns, I want to smooth out the divot between her dark eyebrows. "It'd be weird, right? That's why it's a joint effort."

"Okay. I just need to pay my own way," she says in a small voice.

"I know the feeling." I really do, and this small glimpse into her tells me a lot. She wants to make her own way because at one point, some asshole must've held it over her.

"Yeah?"

I nod.

Her face is tilted up, looking at me. There's a dusting of flour close to her ear. What if I cupped her cheek in my hand? Rubbed that little spot off her velvety skin? Is there a world where she'd let me do that?

It's pointless to go down that road.

Speaking of road, where's she going? "You need a ride somewhere?"

The distance in her eyes is back. This little dance between us is two steps forward and one step back. "No. I'm walking to my parents'."

The Palmers live on the other side of Bootleg Tavern, on the fringes of town. The sidewalk ends a good half mile from the bakery. It stays lighter out longer this time of year, but she still has to walk on the highway for a while or in the ditch, where she'll pick up ticks.

"It's a nice night," she says as if reading my mind.

"I know, but I'm handy. What about the return trip?"

"No. I'll be fine."

I nod and stuff my boot into the ground. She's so damn evasive, and I'm going to worry all night about her walking that highway with no shoulder. There's got to be a way. An idea pops into my head. It'll work for one way only. "It's too bad you've gotta get going. I was going to tell you what the guys thought about your recipes."

Her gaze sharpens. "What did they think?"

I cock my head toward my pickup and shoot her a grin. "Hop in."

She stuffs her hands on her hips. "You're manipulating me."

Shit. I am. Shame burns through me, but it's different this time. She's calling me out for how I'm treating her, and I keep stepping over the line. I'm better than my parents and it's time to prove it. "I'm sorry. They liked them and the oatmeal raisin cookies were a hit. Durban and Iverson of course had to share theirs with Jamison and Campbell, and they gave each kind two thumbs up." I give her a tight smile. "Watch for traffic. Drivers aren't expecting to see pedestrians on the highway."

She doesn't even nod, it's like she's frozen, but I walk away. The last thing I want to be is manipulative. I know exactly what it's like to grow up with someone like that.

I'm about to open my pickup door when I hear a quiet, "Cruz?"

"Yeah?"

She's opening and closing her hands at her sides. "Would you, um, mind giving me a ride home? It'll be after sunset."

I would ordinarily be elated, but I don't want her to think I'm guilting her into spending time with me. "What time?"

"Whenever you're leaving Bootleg. I help my parents with some cleaning and weeding, so I can find plenty to do until you're ready. And if I'm getting a ride, it won't matter if I stay past dark." Her tone isn't quite flat. Is she feeling guilty? Scared? Afraid to trust me?

"Haven and I don't stay out long. I'll text when I'm ready."

"Okay. Thank you." The vulnerability in her voice, in her stance, isn't right. Who put it there?

She'll probably never let me close enough to find out.

Elodie

The sun has barely set and the sky is a blue gradient, growing darker the farther from the horizon it gets. My pulse climbs higher as headlights shine in the distance. I got a text from Cruz a few minutes ago telling me he was leaving Bootleg. I thought he'd stay later.

I thought he'd rather find a woman for the night too, but that's not why I asked him for a ride. The way he shut down on me. His abashed expression when I called him on his tactics. It didn't sit right with me. I was played by a master and that bastard never showed regret. If he did, it was just to manipulate me more.

Dad peers out the screen door behind me. The reflection shows his white T-shirt and scrawny arms. They're getting tan this time of year, but he turns whiter in the winter than vanilla cake batter. "I'm glad you got a ride."

"Yes. Me too." It gave me time to rage clean my parents' place after that phone call. Clementine was here yesterday. Between the two of us, we did the spring cleaning—a few months late—and yard work we don't want our aging parents doing.

"I told Karl you were coming out, and he worried about the same thing. Heard about your car." Dad pats my shoulder like he used to when I was a kid. A perfunctory, reassuring touch. "He's asking around to see if anyone has a beater they're willing to sell cheap."

"I can make do until mine is repaired." I can't afford to buy or rent a car in addition to the repairs. Today, I brainstormed some ideas to pack customers into the place before the end of the month. Doing that without a set of wheels to buy extra supplies sucks. A lot.

"I know you can," Dad says. "Karl will come up with something. He's got more connections than me."

If I don't make bank this weekend at the Billings fair, I'm going to . . . well, I'll keep going. I refuse to let my asshole ex win. I just need time to figure something out.

"I'm sure I'll be fine until Lane gets it up and running," I say lightly, hoping he doesn't hear right through my fake tone.

"Those distillery boys are good people."

A smile plays over my lips. No one calls the Foster brothers or the Hennessy brothers *boys*, but my dad is seventy-two, so to him, they are.

The headlights I've been watching swing down the driveway.

Dad edges around me and pushes out the door, unaware or uncaring that his white shirt is paired with boxer shorts and long white socks. He's stuffed his feet into his green yard Crocs.

"Bye, Mom," I call. She's already in bed, watching the local news. If someone can be addicted to the Weather Channel, it's her.

I pop out the door behind Dad and his slightly bowlegged shuffle. Heat climbs up my neck, but I refuse to be embarrassed over my parents. My ex used to tease me about them even though he'd never met them, and for a while it worked. I was from a tiny town in the foothills of the Beartooth Mountains. He was from the city and had traveled the world. Or so I thought.

Cruz parks and Dad gives him a wide wave like he's outlining a rainbow. Cruz keeps his pickup running, but he hops out and sticks his hand toward Dad. "Evenin', Mr. Palmer. I don't think we've officially met."

Surprised, I stop behind my dad, who's heartily pumping Cruz's hand. He's an extrovert with bad knees who can still socialize like the old days. Cruz is his dream come true—a new person to talk to.

"Call me Bob, like everyone else. Thanks for coming to pick up my girl."

Cruz looks over Dad's shoulder, and instead of smothering the *get a load of this guy* look guys I dated in high school used to give me, he smiles. He appears to enjoy getting accosted by a small-talk-deprived man in his underclothes. The knots across the back of my shoulders loosen.

"Not a problem," Cruz says in the same light tone he uses on everyone else. I held it against him, but maybe it's just the way he is. "How else am I going to sneak a peek at this place?"

Dad beams. "Ain't she beautiful?"

My childhood home is idyllic. We're down in a valley, with pastures my parents lease to local farmers and ranchers between us and the highway. Cattle graze on the other side of the road, and our nearest neighbors are blocked out by trees. We still got to live in a neighborhood, but we had the privacy of a country home. It was something I didn't appreciate enough when I was younger. Back then, it was smothering. Suffocating. The house itself was a marvel of its time, all sharp angles while remaining a homey rambler.

"This place has seen better days," Dad says and strides to the garage, patting the timber accents he and Karl put on years ago. "But she's holding up well."

"I like its vibe." Cruz strokes his gaze over the alpine peak and the porch above us that spans the whole front.

"Dad was the architect," I add, because Dad will never let that fact slip. "Mom too, but Dad surprised her with the house." The builder that Cruz used for his place probably employed someone my mom or dad trained.

"No kidding?" Cruz crosses his arms and the chatting that my dad craves commences. Cruz seems genuinely engaged, and my appreciation grows. I'm in treacherous territory. It was hard enough to resist the handsome cowboy's flirtations, but now that he's not blowing off my dad? I did that enough after I left home; I won't tolerate anyone else doing it.

After a few minutes, Dad holds up his hands. "Listen to me. I'm keeping you kids from your night."

Now I want to groan. He's making it sound like a date.

"I turn in pretty early these days," Cruz says easily. "I learned pretty quick that the animals don't care if I planned to sleep in, so I had to quit planning to sleep in."

Dad chortles, delighted at Cruz's every word. Honestly, I am too. I'm also intrigued. Cruz could've just waited in his truck for me to hop in, and then he could've driven away with barely more than a wave. He's got more depth than I gave him credit for.

I miss the last few words of their conversation. Something about ranching and houses. Dad pulls me in for a hug. "Thanks for everything today, kiddo. Next time, you and Clem need to coordinate so we can have a family meal."

"That sounds nice." It really does, but Clem works the tasting room when the guys are all busy and I'm often baking until it's time for bed. There's no end in sight.

A few minutes and more chatting later, I'm loaded up in Cruz's pickup and surrounded by the same warm-grain-and-citrus scent as before.

Cruz casually drapes his wrist over the wheel. The easygoing smile and the charm haven't been aimed my way. "I always thought your dad seemed like a nice guy."

It's a small town. They probably crossed paths several times, but it pleases me that he has a good impression of my dad. My parents are wonderful people, and they gave me a good life I almost squandered.

"He's cool. Mom too." I wait for him to ask me more about them, or even to talk about his parents, but he doesn't. The silence should be comfortable, it should be what I want, yet it bothers me. "They weren't going to have kids, but they changed their minds in their late thirties. They were always the oldest parents at all the school functions. My mom even went to school with one of the grandparents of my classmates. My ex— An old friend thought I should've been embarrassed about that, but it was normal for us."

"Age is just a number."

"They think so." I chew the inside of my cheek, but

he doesn't continue the conversation. I want to crawl out of my skin. He just talked my dad's ear off. "Did you and Haven have enough time?"

"Oh, yeah. Plenty." We reach town, and he drives straight to the bakery.

My stomach sinks. That's it. I'll never be the recipient of any of Cruz's flirting again.

He parks by the back door. The little light over it illuminates the landing and the inside of the cab. Cruz's profile is strong and the shadow across his jaw is darker. The hair that was damp when he arrived is now dry with a hunk hanging over his forehead, giving him a carefree appeal.

All I want to do is smooth it back, feel the silky strands run through my fingers. How warm is his skin?

"Gimme a call if you need a ride before your car's done," he says, snapping me out of my delusional thinking.

"Oh. Thank you. Uncle Karl is looking for a set of wheels for me."

He shrugs. "My schedule's pretty flexible. Haven said he'll call you about hauling your supplies down to Billings Friday morning."

"Oh, yes. Thanks." Haven's giving me a ride? I might need the cargo space, but . . . Haven? Cruz said he'd be working the Billings fair. "I was thinking of using that whiskey you gave me for an exclusive batch of cupcakes. Who do I have to clear that through?"

"Telling me is fine. I know they won't care." His smile is tight, functional. "But I'll pass it on and let you know that it's all good."

"I appreciate it."

"No problem." There's that professional smile again.

My heart sinks down to where my stomach went earlier. "Well, thank you." I slide out of his pickup, feeling all sorts of rejected, which is ridiculous.

"Night, Elodie." He waits until I'm in the bakery and the door's closed behind me to drive away. I lean against the cool metal and sigh.

I'm *that* girl. I pushed him away, and now I want him close so damn bad.

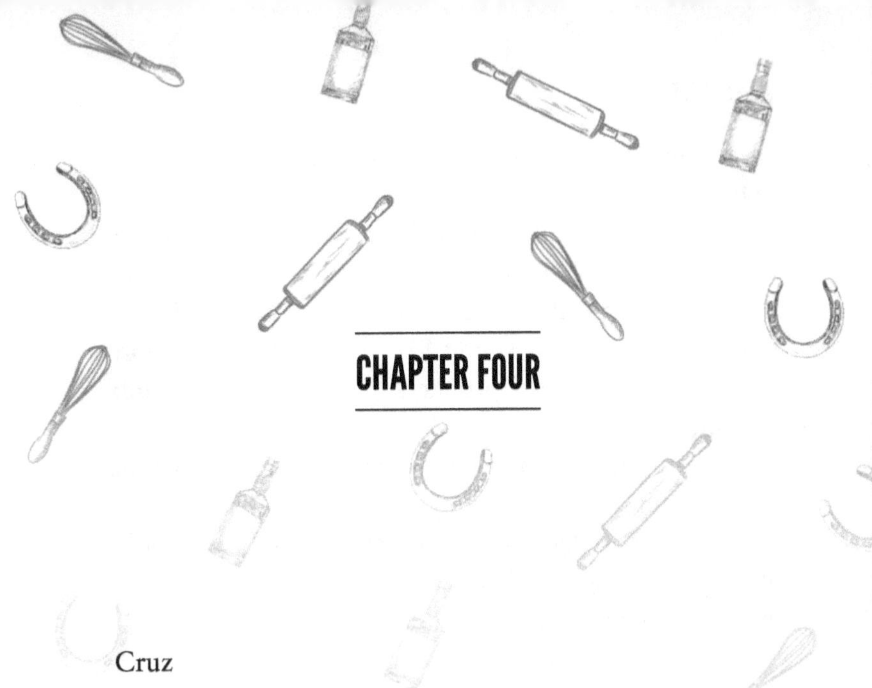

CHAPTER FOUR

Cruz

The crafters fair in Billings is set up over two downtown blocks. Local businesses remain open, using the sidewalk as an extension for their booths, and tents line the middle of the street so people can mill down both sides and shop.

It's packed in the best way. Lane will swing by and help during the busy midday hours, but Haven and I will tackle the whole fair. That way, Lane can work on Elodie's car.

As for Elodie, she's in her element. Her dark hair in a messy bun, wearing a big yellow Dee's Sweets shirt with two cupcakes on the front, she's all business but in a competent baker way that appeals to people. When she smiles and pushes her glasses up her nose, she charms anyone who's talking to her even more.

I've only spied on her twice since the fair started. Once, when I grabbed a bite from a taco food truck, and again when I ran to meet Lane for a case of gin we'd left behind.

Our booth is a block away from Dee's Sweets, but we have plenty of customers stopping by, telling us they have to try our stuff after the sample they had at Elodie's booth. They make it sound like she talked us up more than she did her own products. We're doing the same for her.

Haven pours a sip of juneberry vodka for one of the many people who've been by the booth. This has been one of the best fairs we've sold at to date, and Lane is already planning another run of vodka and gin. Those are a hot commodity in the summer.

"Tell me how that is on the palate." I hand two ladies each a sample of our cask-strength wheat whiskey.

One of the women smiles at me, and I know everything she's inviting in that grin. Her dark hair is in two braids, one over each shoulder, and she has on an itty-bitty camisole top and shorts that show off amazing, bronzed legs. Once upon a time, I'd have taken that invite.

Now, all I care about is figuring out how to get to know a prickly baker who's the most bizarre mix of lukewarm and frigid, yet my brain is hanging on those tepid signs for all they're worth.

The second woman sputters, and the first laughs at her and looks at me, but my attention is yanked away. Behind them, Clem and Elodie are wandering, each with a plate of food.

"Hey, Palmers," I call. Elodie slides her gaze toward mine, keeping her fork poised over the last chunk of her nachos.

Clem waves her plastic fork in the air. "Hey, boss."

"Wanna have a tasting?" I ask, aware I'm ignoring two possible customers in front of me. Damn. I still gotta work. "Haven, you mind taking over for me? Excuse me," I say to them.

Without missing a beat, Haven switches places with me and starts chatting with the women so seamlessly they don't have time to get irritated that I ditched them.

Clem comes over. "What goes with nachos?"

Elodie hovers behind her and glances over our selection, her eyes narrowed like she's studying and designing recipes that would go with each spirit.

"I've got a few that could be considered desserts," I say.

Clem gestures to the lineup with her fork. "I've gotten to taste everything. I'll go back and see how Kinley's doing, El. You stay."

Elodie's eyes go wide. "Oh, I shouldn't."

Clem rolls her eyes. "Of course you should. This is your first break all weekend and only because I made you." She bumps her sister's arm with her elbow. "I don't have to be at the library booth until one. Take your time. It's fun. Let me take that."

She grabs for Elodie's plate, and Elodie scrambles to save her last bite. I fight back a grin. Clem doesn't manipulate. She bulldozes. She has the power only a sibling possesses to get Elodie to do what she wants.

"Byeee." Clem rushes off.

Elodie brushes off her fingers and finishes chewing. "So," she says, crinkling her nose like she's trying to shift her glasses up her nose. She wipes at the corners of her mouth. "What should I try?"

"Of the spirits we gave you, which was your favorite?"

"The huckleberry vodka."

I take out a juneberry vodka, a ninety-proof whiskey with strong notes of cherry and vanilla, and a rhubarb-infused gin. "We've got our own patch of rhubarb growing behind the distillery."

Her soft smile is the biggest one I've seen yet, other than when I made her laugh earlier. "My parents raise rhubarb for me. I saved the patch from weeds when I was over there."

"One time, I thought I killed Mae's fifty-year-old rhubarb plant when I replanted it. I kept trying to snap off a part to plant, hoping she wouldn't notice. Turned out I accidentally grew three more."

Her laughter is another win, but I restrain the force of my smile. I haven't shared this with anyone. I've never talked about my time with Mae with other women, and I don't want Elodie thinking I'm being anything more than real.

Her smile falters, and she chooses the juneberry vodka. After she drinks the small amount, her eyes go distant. She smacks her lips together. "I can tell the difference between that and the huckleberry. Huckle-berry tastes sugary-er, not just sweeter." Her cheeks flush. "That probably doesn't make sense."

"To a guy who peddles fermented and distilled carbs, it absolutely does." I slide a bigger plastic cup of water toward her. She takes a drink and then samples the rhubarb gin.

"Oh." She puts her finger to her lips. "I never thought I was a gin girl."

"It can be like Windex, or it can be a really smooth spirit to relax with, depending on who makes it. Fosters and Hennessys don't make window cleaner. But you can scrub your glass with it too."

She laughs again, catches my gaze, and looks away. Damn, did I sound like I was coming on to her again? I'm trying really hard to . . . not be me. That should be a red flag, but if I'm the type of guy someone jaded like Elodie can trust . . . I'll call that a win. After all, there was a time no one could trust me.

She takes another gulp of water and then downs the scant amount of whiskey we serve for tastings. She smacks her lips together. "That's not bad."

"You don't like it."

"No, it's good." She's aloof again. I'm not getting the real Elodie, and we've come too damn far to backpedal over a tasting.

"You don't want me to lie to you," I say, only loud enough for her to hear, "so don't lie to me. It's an oatmeal raisin cookie for you?"

She nods shyly.

"That's the fun of the tasting. You never know what you're gonna like or dislike."

"You picked it for me to try."

And she was afraid to hurt my feelings? I shrug to make it seem like I'm nonchalant when I'm actually touched. "I help a lot of people with their selections. It's part of the job."

Her expression falls, and she tosses her sample cups in the garbage bin we keep handy for them. "Whiskey isn't usually my thing. Thank you though. Thank you for this."

She's sincere, but she's also rushing off. Was it something I said? All I know is that it's me.

Haven crosses to me just as she's stepping away. "Hey,

Elodie. You mind riding home with Cruz tomorrow? Lane and I need to take the trailer to grab an order from the warehouse while we're in town. Your stuff should fit in Cruz's pickup."

"You mind?" she asks almost cautiously.

Do I mind spending more than an hour in the car with her? Fuck yes. It'll either be an hour of complete, stony silence and I'll lose the urge to continue my dogged pursuit. Or she'll crack and tell me that I'm her dream man, everything she wants, and she can't stay away anymore. It's a good thing I'm not a betting man. "It's fine with me."

"Thanks," she says, and I still can't get a read on her. "Any of my treats left over go with you guys though. It's the least I can do."

Haven snorts. "I'm not going to argue."

The corner of her mouth twitches up before she walks away. Her long, sunny skirt swishes with each step.

Haven's stare bores into me. "Do you want to go with Lane tomorrow instead?"

"No," I say quickly. "Why?"

"You don't seem to like Elodie."

"I like her just fine, but she seems to think I'm some sort of player or something. I'm trying to act trustworthy, and I fuck up every time."

He cocks up a dark brow. "She's been like that for as long as I've known her. She came home to open the bakery, but she's never even told Clem what she did in the years she was away." He rolls a shoulder. "The baker's got a story."

I nod. My story isn't a secret, but not many people know it. Even fewer know about what I was like before I was nineteen. To everyone in Huckleberry Springs, I'm part owner of Foster House Gold and I ranch with my brother. When I lived in Bourbon Canyon, I was one of the two Foster brothers working for Mae. We were too old to be foster kids, but she brought us in like family. No one in Huckleberry Springs knows I wasn't born and raised to do chores in the morning and evening, calve in the spring, and work cattle in the fall.

I owe both my brothers and the Baileys for not being a giant fuckup anymore. No way Elodie went through the type of shit I experienced growing up, not with her folks, but I can understand not bringing up the past. I also get being cynical because of it.

Whatever Elodie's baggage is, it's heavy. It's a good thing I'm a strong guy.

Elodie

If I had a Cruz every time I broke down my booth after an event, I would do more of them. He hauled every-thing and was careful not to bang tables or scratch display cases. All my boxes and equipment are safely stashed in the bed of his pickup, and he even nestled the boxes of extra cupcakes and cake pops in his back seat so they wouldn't get jostled around. Now we're driving back to Huckleberry Springs.

"It was a good weekend," he says.

My weekend is when I'm closed on Mondays, and even then, I'm in the bakery or doing admin work.

"Yeah, it was great." I almost wince at my wooden tone.

My sales were gangbusters. I made enough to pay Lane for my car and fill up the loaner Karl found for me before I return the tiny Ford Focus to him. It was handy around town, but it wouldn't have worked for this weekend. That thing would've been full past the windows just with my cupcakes.

Cruz slides a sidelong glance my way but doesn't say anything else.

He has to have noticed my tone. He seems more sensitive to it than anyone else in my life. More considerate. But then he does that for everyone. Just like he said.

Only he made the claim in regard to his job. He was so animated and knowledgeable when he walked me through the samples, I felt special.

He does it for everyone. At least he's open about it.

I could've been more exuberant about his comment. The weekend was phenomenal. I nearly ran out of business cards. I sold so much on Saturday that I baked over half the night to haul more goods in today. I dug into my stores of frozen cookie dough to sell that too. I ran out.

I'm going to be a baking machine tonight into tomorrow. I'm going to hustle frozen cookie dough hard since it's a proven seller. With those sales, I should have the payment I need for the end of the month.

Nineties country music plays quietly from the speakers. Does he keep it turned down because he's normally visiting with his passenger? The dashboard is still dust-free. Other than the bottle of water in his console, there's no garbage of any sort. Does he vacuum every day too? For a guy who lives on gravel, this pickup is too clean. I've studied everything I can in the cab, but I'm not getting any new insight into him. I could stare at him for the next forty-five minutes, which I'd love to do, or I can gaze out the window.

The silence gets to me.

"My frozen cookie dough was a hit." To think I used to be so smooth I could've sold timeshares along with my cupcakes. I'm not just out of practice. This man scrambles my thoughts. "I was racking my brains last night to come up with more items to sell, or I would've been sitting in an empty booth."

Surprise lifts his brows momentarily and his smile is polite. "Yeah? An unplanned offering?"

"Yes. I keep it for backup when something doesn't turn out or I get behind, but I didn't think of selling it as-is until last night."

"You could offer it for one of those fundraisers, like what my niece's preschool does."

I blink at him. Blink again. I had to peddle cookie dough once when I was in volleyball in middle school. It's easy to make. Quick to package. Just as simple to store if I have enough space. "Holy shit, Cruz. That's genius. I'm sitting on a gold mine."

His laugh rumbles right through me, but there's a slight pink tint to his cheeks. Does my admiration embarrass him? "What do the sellers get, like fifty percent?"

I run calculations through my head. I know how much a batch of each type of cookie costs and what I profit from each one sold, but I wouldn't be baking them. So much time saved. What I get from that, I'd need for mass production and packaging. Then there's storage, but I've been looking at a new standing freezer. "How do I get started in that?"

He lifts a shoulder and turns off the interstate. "I

know it's not her exact area, but Campbell might have some ideas."

"I can't afford to pay for her consulting." I gnaw on my lower lip. I had a bumper of a weekend, but I'm penny-pinching.

He slants another look at me and maneuvers onto the highway that'll take us to Huckleberry Springs. "I can ask around."

He would do that? With his charm, he could get me all the free consultations I want. No, I need to earn this. "You run two businesses already. You're a busy man."

"It's okay to have someone help you." He doesn't say it loud, like he's afraid I'll dive out the car door, roll into the ditch, and take off running at the idea.

I might. I don't deserve anyone's help. A knot tightens between my shoulders. "I know, but it's fine. It's just an idea at this point."

I suck at being nonchalant.

We're quiet all the way to the bakery. He backs the pickup to the door, and with each load he hauls in, I feel worse. He's done so much for me today. I've been weird with him, yet just like the night my car broke down, he isn't ditching me and running.

I hate how he's so reserved around me. I hate that I need him to be, as much as I wish he'd joke around with me again. I hate how much I like him.

He carries in the last of the empty containers that were once full of cupcakes. I can't stand to watch him walk out of here. Our next collaboration is the Taste of Springs street fair. Will he be my contact or give up the chore to Lane because I'm so temperamental?

"Would you like a snack?" I blurt out as soon as he sets the last box down.

"Nah, I'm good—"

"At least a drink." I push my fingertips to my forehead. Has my game slipped that far? No, it didn't slip. I ran from it. "I have that buttery whiskey you brought me."

"You don't like whiskey."

"I didn't like the other whiskey."

He studies me for a moment, a confused furrow in his brow. I have to seem like the hottest and coldest woman at the same time. I am, but only with him.

"Sure," he finally says. "But not a lot. Can't have your cousin picking me up."

My cousin is the area's most well-known deputy. Relieved enough to ignore the anxious knot in my stomach, I grab the bottle of whiskey and a couple of glasses. He takes a seat at the little table, making it look like I'm serving a doll's tea party there.

The man is so pleasingly big. I should be pushing him out the door.

I set a glass in front of him and splash some amber fluid into it, doing the same with mine. I sit and shoot it back, letting the buttery flavor coat my tongue for a second time before swallowing and reveling in the light burn. Then I fill my tumbler halfway.

His steady gaze is on me. "You sure today went well?"

"It's not today that's bothering me. Today was amazing. I wish every street fair was like this one." I put the cork in the bottle and push it to the side. Warmth from the drink fills my chest and tension drains from between my shoulder blades. "It's a whole bunch of yesterdays that are fucking with my tomorrows."

A dark brow of his arches. He takes a slow sip, keeping his gaze on me.

The alcohol hasn't had time to affect me, yet my tongue loosens. "I'm sorry. About how I am." I down another big mouthful. "God, this is good. I could become a whiskey girl if you kept making this."

"Butter Barrel is one of my favorites."

I nod without looking at him. "I didn't . . . There was a guy— You're nothing like him." Have I gotten that lightweight? My whole past is ready to spill out after bubbling away for years, but I only need to explain why I get weird with him.

"What'd he do?" Cruz's tone is low, almost dangerous.

A shiver traces over my skin. No. *No.* I cannot go down this road again. "He was a loser. You clearly aren't a loser."

A ghost of a smile passes over his lips, but there's something slipping through his blue eyes I can't identify. "I'm glad you think so."

"I'm sorry if I made you feel that way."

His dark brows lift. "I appreciate the apology."

My heart twists. He didn't, *nah, you never did.* I hurt his feelings, and he's forgiven me as easy as that. Unless he thinks he doesn't measure up to everyone around him? No, he has to know that the problem is me. Right?

He swirls the fluid in the glass, seeming to study how it rolls along the edges with each turn. "Do I intimidate you?"

I owe him honesty. "You scare me." I toss back the rest of the whiskey. Just like the old days. "But I miss you flirting with me."

Oh god. I said it. That's a confession for the dead of night when I'm alone.

I shoot to my feet and take my glass to the sink. "I'm

sorry. I shouldn't have said that. I must sound unhinged. It hasn't even been that long since I bit your head off." I spin around. He's right there. "Oh my god!"

The guy moves like a panther, and I've never wanted to be prey more. I need to get my wits about me. I'm not losing them over some dude.

Cruz is not some dude, and that's what scares me.

"Now, Elodie," he says in a voice as smooth as the drink we just shared, "you might need to elaborate. Because you fascinate me, but the closer I try to get, the farther away you push me."

He's right, but how do I answer? How do I keep my brain functioning when I'm close enough to soak up his body heat?

He lifts his hand slowly, like I'm a skittish pony he doesn't want to scare away, and slips a few strands of my hair through his fingers.

A low rumble leaves his chest, and he tucks them behind my ear, his rough fingertips brushing against the shell of my ear. "I've been dying to know how soft your hair is. Just like silk."

"I bet you say that to all the girls." *Give me something. Give me a reason to keep shoving.*

"Back in the day, I didn't need sweet platitudes to get a girl in bed with me." A crease bisects his brow just as his own confession sinks in, and it only makes me want to yank him closer. He clenches and releases his jaw. "I might be a flirt, Elodie, but I only ever say what I mean. There was a time I didn't. I've worked hard to be a good man, and I'd like to show you."

My lips part, but no sound escapes. If he tried to convince me what a great man he was, I would've retreated to the corner—after showing him the door.

His admission about his past and then his request to prove he's better?

I want that too. Yet at the same time, it's the worst scenario I could be in. I need to make money and stay under the radar. I need to figure out how to get rid of my financial problem.

"We can take it slow." He moves a step closer. I can't back up, but I don't try. My ass cheeks are brushing the edge of the counter and he's a wall of rugged cowboy in front of me. "Starting with a date. Will you let me take you out, sugar?"

The endearment yanks me out of the trance he's putting me in.

Just as I open my mouth, he brushes his thumb along my lower lip. Desire explodes inside of me. Why is there a direct connection between that and my pussy? I squeeze my legs together as need rides me.

"I knew I messed up as soon as I said it," he murmurs. He drops his head lower, still stroking along my lip with the pad of his thumb. "But I have this feeling that you're just so sweet."

His whiskey-laced breath caresses my skin. I rock forward ever so slightly. Is he going to kiss me?

"What do you say?" he asks softly. "Can I take you on a date?"

"You shouldn't."

The corner of his mouth lifts. "There was a time I did a lot of things I shouldn't."

Confessions are apparently a kink of mine. My curiosity swells as hot as my desire. "You can take me for lunch on Monday. I work every other day of the week."

He lifts my chin higher with his knuckle. "I'll come

pick you up. We'll go to La Taqueria for lunch. See you at eleven on Monday. And, Elodie?"

Our lips are millimeters apart. "Yeah?"

He drops his hand and takes a deliberate step back. "I might flirt a lot, but you'll see that I'm very serious when it matters."

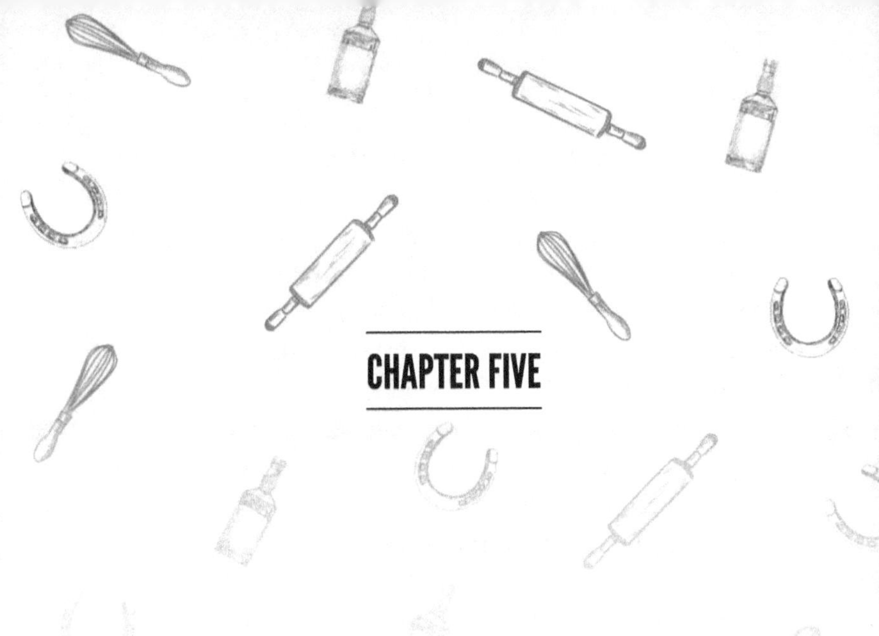

CHAPTER FIVE

Elodie

I stuff all my tubs of cookie dough into the freezer. I have the options uploaded to my website. Checking the time, a full-body zing goes through me. I'm covered in flour dust and I'm in my frumpiest of sweats. I need to go from a chambermaid to a princess as quickly as Cinderella.

The back door dings open, and Clem wanders in, her hands full of envelopes. "Hey, El. I see you have your car back. That's awesome. I came to help."

I haven't had a chance to drive it since Lane dropped it off this morning. Uncle Karl's coming by tonight to get the loaner.

"Hey. Yes. The car is great." I love seeing Clem, and I treasure the times she comes in to help me, but I haven't told anyone about my . . . date.

My belly's going wild, like I turned the standing mixer inside of it to high. I never meant to enter the dating world again. I had too bad of an experience, and I have way too much on my plate. Even more now, thanks to that previous experience. Damn him.

She stops and frowns, glancing around my sort of cleaned-up kitchen. She probably expected a mess. "I thought you'd be a whirlwind in here after how much dough we were moving." She winks.

I ignore one of the many dough puns she's made over the years. "I have something planned." I shove a thumb over my shoulder. "I've gotta go get cleaned up."

Tossing my mail on the table, she very much does not leave. "What's going on?"

"Nothing. I could use your help later though."

She flips a few invoices over and slaps an envelope on top. "Why are you getting mail from Colorado Correctional Center?"

Cold washes through me, and I dig my fingernails into my palms. Damn him. First, his brother calls me and Cruz overhears me yelling. Now he's writing? I thought Dwayne would give up when I never wrote back. "An old friend."

She wiggles her finger at me. "What aren't you telling me?"

So damn much, and I'm not going to start now. "Listen, I've got to get cleaned up. I'm going to lunch with a friend."

"Campbell?"

"I have other friends."

"Jamison."

"God, Clem. Why are you so nosy?"

Unrepentant, she crosses her arms. "Since you cut me off for years. It didn't do any good to give you space then."

It did her a lot of good; she just doesn't know it. Nor does she leave. "It's Cruz," I mumble and only to get her to drop the topic of Dwayne.

She cocks her head. "Sorry, I didn't hear you. I thought you said it's Cruz." When I don't correct her, her eyes fly wide. "He finally asked you out?"

"What do you mean finally?"

"That guy is into you."

"He's into every girl." Just saying it feels wrong. I'm getting to know him and the falsity of the statement bothers me.

"No, he's *nice* to everyone. He *watches* you."

The pleasure that rises like a first proof is embarrassing. "He does not."

"At the crochet club last week? He totally did. Until you kicked him like an eight-week-old puppy."

"I've never kicked a puppy!"

"Where ya going?" she asks in a singsong voice.

"The new Mexican place."

She gasps and claps her hands. "Like a real date!"

"I haven't been on a real date in years," I whisper.

"Then go." She shoos me. "Go get ready."

I start for the stairs, but stop. "Can you come back tonight and help me make tomorrow's specials?"

It was a long weekend and fatigue would bowl me over if my adrenaline wasn't pumping about the date.

"Yes, and you're going to tell me all about it. Now go. Wear something cute that shows your legs."

I start up the stairs and stop. "Don't tell anyone. Okay?"

She scrunches her face up. "What is it about you keeping your life a secret?"

"It's not a secret. It's just not something to be proud of."

"I see," she says quietly. "Seems like that's the stuff you should be able to talk to someone about. I know you're worried about Mom—"

"Exactly. If she thought I was in therapy, she would blame herself just like she did with the accident. Besides, I don't have time." I give her a small smile and rush up the rest of the stairs.

My small studio apartment above the bakery has sloped ceilings and wood floors that echo through the whole place.

I frown at my dresser. It's covered with loose pants, sweats, and oversized shirts. When I moved home, I swung in the opposite direction from the style I'd been wearing.

Should I show off my legs? I'd rather wear something that's halfway flattering, and perhaps I'll catch Cruz looking at them again.

I pick a snug white shirt with a lace bottom. Rifling deeper in my closet, I find a pink pair of high-waisted jeans that should cover what my top doesn't. It's too hot for nice shoes, so I grab some strappy sandals.

Once I'm dressed, I stare at the hummingbirds tattooed across the top of each foot. Tattoos aren't exactly scandalous, but no one's seen mine. I haven't wanted to field any questions about my time away from Montana, and since my ink is tied to a litany of bad decisions, I just keep them covered.

Maybe it was the busy weekend, or the anxiety of the date and what it means—if it means anything—but I'm tired. So exhausted trying to create a clean slate, only for my past to muddy it up again. Clem is right. It's been hard not to talk to someone about everything that went down.

I twist my hair into a clip and take stock of the reflection in the mirror. A woman who looks like the Elodie Palmer from long ago gazes back, and dammit, it's good to see her again.

I rush down the stairs, and as soon as my feet hit the bottom, there's a knock. I almost sprint right back up. Before I can think too hard, I fling the door open. There's no going upstairs to change now.

Cruz, dressed in his normal jeans, boots, and a tight green T-shirt, smiles. "Hey." His gaze lazily runs down my body and heat blooms stronger in his eyes. "Goddamn, sugar. You're looking downright lickable."

Shock hits me just as I want to preen at his compliments.

"Aw, Elodie." He surprises me even more and drops to a squat. He runs a rough fingertip over the top of my foot. "I'm trying hard to be a gentleman, but this is like a peek at my birthday present."

A nervous laugh leaves me. "They're just tattoos."

"That's more skin than you've flashed me since I've known you." He rises, and the smile on his face is nothing like the teasing one he throws at everyone else. It's full of promise. He cocks an elbow. "May I take you out?"

The flirting I got so defensive about? That was some superficial shit. This Cruz? Charming and intense. This Cruz is the one not everyone sees.

But I get to.

I tuck my hand into the crook of his arm, and he leads me out and loads me into his pickup. His cowboy hat is on the back seat, but he keeps his hair neatly combed for our lunch.

"Do you clean this every day?" I ask when he climbs behind the wheel.

He pauses for a moment. "I give it a quick vacuum on most days."

"Most days? You're a rancher. They have dirty pickups."

"This gets dirty." His smile is more distant than I've ever seen. "I just clean it more often. How's your car?"

The subject change is deliberate, but I'm a closed book with him, so I can't call him on it. "I haven't driven it yet, but Lane got it here, so that's a good sign."

He chuckles and drives off. When he parks in front of the new restaurant built on the edge of town, he insists I wait for him to open the door.

My feet hit the ground. "You don't have to open every door for me."

"Mae taught me right."

Mae Bailey. He said a lot in that short sentence, and it wasn't *my mama taught me right*. What happened to his mom?

Like many others in town, I've paid attention whenever anyone talked about Cruz. When he was out of high school, he worked for the Copper Summit Bourbon family, ranching in Bourbon Canyon. Then his oldest brother brought him into the Foster House fold, and now he's here in Huckleberry Springs. Bourbon Canyon's loss is my town's gain.

I push all my questions aside as we walk into the restaurant. Half the tables are full with tourists and locals, and the smell of grilled meat fills the air.

"How ya doing?" Cruz says to a loan officer at the

bank as the hostess leads us to a table. "Afternoon." He nods to a family around the table closest to us.

We're seated in a booth right by the front window. A tendril of dread swirls through my stomach. It's not that I don't want to be seen with Cruz. He seems like a good guy and he's respected in town, but I'm allergic to anyone being in my business.

He's sitting across from me. I'm out with this man. My belly does a dive and swoop. He almost kissed me the other night. I feel like a teen again, experiencing those first heady moments of connecting with a guy.

I'm not an inexperienced girl. Not nearly long enough ago, I was in a committed relationship. But this moment, it's all new again. Scary. Exciting. Unknown.

And that's the part I'm having trouble with.

"Have you eaten here yet?" he asks.

I shake my head. "I don't get out much anymore."

"But you used to?"

I nod and bite my lower lip. "Too much."

"I hear ya."

Before I can follow up with questions, the server swings by, delivering chips and salsa. I order a water, and Cruz gets a root beer. When we're alone again, I study the menu to keep from making small talk. Have I gotten that bad at it?

No. Chatting was always a skill I excelled at until I weaponized it. My dad could talk to an empty park bench and make its day, and I used to take after him.

Cruz sets his menu aside. I knew what I wanted before I stepped through the door. I always order the carne asada if it's available. I set my menu down and brace for the questions.

"You're nervous," he says.

"Yes." Admitting it takes some of the weight off. "But not for why you might think." Well . . . "A little for why you might think."

"I think you've been burned before."

I lick across my dry lower lip and his gaze clocks it. "Yes, but I've also done the burning. Have you ever done anything you're ashamed of?"

He doesn't shrug off my question, nor does he laugh it off. His expression is solemn when he says, "Many times. I was an insufferable dick."

This time, I let out a disbelieving laugh. "Did your flirting get you in trouble?"

"My anger."

Oh. My spine straightens as questions pour into my head. Was he violent? Did he hurt someone? How did he lash out?

"I should amend that," he says and takes the paper holder off from around his silverware and napkin. "My anger made me an insufferable dick. I had a smart mouth and I wasn't afraid to be a pain in the ass with it. Lane was better, but it was also like I had permission to be even less responsible when he was around."

He's not giving me details, but I feel like he's giving me more than he gives anyone else. I need to return the favor. I'll use his same vague storytelling style. "I was a good girl growing up."

His lips curve up. "I'm not surprised."

"I went wild after I left home, but no one really knows. That was the allure, you see. The anonymity. In Huckleberry Springs, I was Bob and Patty's daughter. Pastor Karl's niece. Everyone knew me wherever I went, and they expected the best."

"But you didn't always want to be on your best behavior."

I lift a shoulder. "I guess? Sometimes I can't figure it out, and I've never told anyone the things I did." I roll my lips in. I can't believe what I'm going to say next, but the words push out anyway. "I never even talked to my family about the guy I was seeing, and we were together for years."

His brows lift. "A big part of you must've known he was bad news."

"That was the draw," I say with a sigh. "I was so . . . Ugh. Young and dumb."

A divot forms between his brows. "Don't blame yourself for someone else's bad actions."

I give him a small smile, but my stomach sinks. I might've dated a bad boy, but for a while there, I was also a bad girl.

Cruz

I can't pinpoint when Elodie closed off on me again, but we went from talking about our pasts to idly chatting about our jobs.

It's amazing I can talk at all after seeing her pink-denim-clad legs, and *fuuuck*, her painted toes with the humming-bird tattoos. Her rigid posture is keeping her little shirt from playing peekaboo, and it's killing me. I have to keep focused on our light conversation. Otherwise, I'll do nothing but obsess about that strip of skin at her abdomen.

"So you split equally and there's no arguing?" she asks. Our plates are stacked to the side. While I loved her running commentary of how the restaurant brought out a smoky flavor and pulled back on the heat to create a delectable beef dish, I want to dig into Elodie Palmer. In so many ways.

Only she's been asking about me, and if getting to know what I do each day makes her more comfortable, I'm happy to share.

I'm also pleased that her interest seems real. I've been on dates before where I wasn't the topic of interest as much as my bottom line. I'm doing financially okay now, great even, but for most of my adult life, I wasn't. What I had was someone else's, and I cared for it. Before that, I had nothing.

"There might be some bickering," I say, "but no, we all get along pretty well. The Hennessys are chill. Lane can be uptight with me, but he isn't with them."

"I guess I'm the same with Clem. I'm so glad I have her, so I don't have to hire anyone." Elodie's gaze goes out the window. "I would like to have more than the part-time staff, but it's just not in the cards right now. The bakery's doors are open, so I'll be content with that."

"You deserve to have some help. It's what I learned from my brother."

"Lane?" she asks.

"Myles. He wouldn't have been able to start Foster House without a big investment from Darin Bailey. He fostered with them for a while."

Interest fills her face. I don't normally discuss my family. My brothers, yes, but not like this. It's hard to separate our personal business when it's so entwined. Odd since we'd been separate for so long.

"It's how Lane and I started with the Baileys. We didn't grow up with Myles. He didn't even know about us until our mom died." I swallow hard when sympathy fills her eyes. This part is also hard to explain without airing all my dirty laundry, but then I've never told anyone about it before.

"I'm sorry," she murmurs and reaches across the table to put her hand on mine. My skin warms as energy tingles between us.

"Thanks." Most people know Myles was in foster care. He doesn't keep that part a secret, since it's woven into the brand. Foster House isn't just about our last name. "Myles's dad passed when he was little, and our mom struggled with addiction and would clean up sporadically. She met my dad, and he drove her back to using."

Her brows lift, but her fingers tighten over me. "Shit."

"Yeah. We don't talk to him." I clear my throat before the rest of the story comes out. That my dad and Lane have minimal contact, and he wants to stay in touch with me. I want to tell her how I can't bring myself to talk to him. I blame him for so much. My mom had a metric ton of issues, but the best and worst thing that man did for us was leave. "Mom never married him and that's why we have the same last name as Myles, but we're only half brothers. Otherwise, I'd be Cruz Lawson."

The corner of her mouth tips up and my stomach acid calms down. "From the way you talk about him, you're not half anything with Myles." She draws her hand away, and I wish we were on the same side of the table.

Warmth fills my chest like it always does when I think of the family I never thought I'd have. "I might've been nineteen when I went to work for Mae, but she became the mom I never had. And all the rest of the Baileys kicked me and Lane into shape, especially the guys. It was a weird mix of father figures and bossy older brothers."

She laughs. "I asked my dad once if he ever wanted a son, and he said that Clem and I came out so perfect, how could he ever ask for more?"

"I knew your dad was a cool guy."

"If small talk was an Olympic sport, he'd be a five-time gold medalist."

"Just so happens, I'm a competitor as well. But I liked him."

"He liked you."

"It means a lot to hear that." There was a time I would not have been the man dads wanted around their daughters. I wasn't a cheat, but I could ghost a girl like a haunted mansion. Now's not the time to cop to that. I want her to like me, not distrust me. "I guess you don't grow up with a mom like mine and not have some issues."

"You haven't carried any of those issues into adulthood." She's not earnest, just matter of fact. "You didn't throw away everything the Baileys taught you."

"Once Mae made us dinner, I was hooked. Ain't no way I was giving up three solid meals a day."

I'm chuckling, but compassion fills her eyes. "You weren't getting fed?"

My stomach churns hard around the fajita I just ate.

I opened the door, and suddenly I don't want to go through it. If I delve into my childhood, will the last fourteen years vanish like they never happened? Will I finish scaring Elodie off? If she knew what I was like in the pre-Bailey years, she'd tell me to have a good day and order me not to hit on her again. But in order to keep this thing between us open and growing, I have to share something from the part of my life I don't like to remember.

She shakes her head. "Oh my gosh. It's not my business. I'm so sorry."

"No. It's fine. Food could be . . . sporadic." Low-quality shit that the bugs sometimes wouldn't touch. "Don't worry about prying. I try to be an open book." Mostly.

"I can't say the same."

Damn. She's honest. "I'm a patient man."

"What if I'm not worth it?" She's not asking playfully.

"You are." Who would make her think otherwise? I'm not at all sorry for her to know that I'm not giving up. "I've learned to be patient when it's important, and when you want to tell me something, you will."

"You speak as if we're going to be doing more of this again." There's a hint of a smile on her face.

"I'd like to," I say honestly. "What if I cook for you?"

Her eyes widen. "Cook for me?"

"Yeah. You said you don't like to have to cook for anyone, so let me give it a shot. I have a smoker and I'm not afraid to use it."

"I'm a vegetarian," she says.

Didn't she order carne asada? I'm rolling with it. Whatever she wants. "Smoked eggplants." I'm only half joking. I'll try it. Scouring my brain for nonmeat ideas for the smoker and grill, I snag one. "Grilled pineapple and banana?"

She laughs and her eyes twinkle. "I'm kidding. While that sounds good, I haven't become a vegetarian since we had lunch together."

Her smile is Cupid's arrow straight to my chest. I'm hooked. I made her laugh, and it's going to become my hobby for the rest of my life. I just have to convince her of it. "It wouldn't be a problem."

"Yes, it would. I'm a Montana girl born and raised, and I can't drive past all these ranches and not think about a good fillet and all the things I can do with it. Plus, I can't grow a single vegetable."

This is the most open she's ever been with me. Before, anything I learned about her seemed to be despite her best efforts. "Mae taught me how to garden, collect eggs, and prune the rosebushes. Need any of that, I'm your man."

"Mae sounds amazing."

"She is. I owe her everything."

She leans on her elbows on the table. "You don't strike me as a guy who only takes. What did she get from you? You were more than labor at the Baileys'. I can tell when you talk about them."

She's paid that close of attention?

There's so much more to Elodie, but I wasn't wrong. There's something between us, and she tried to ignore it. I don't want to be a pain in her ass, but I want her. All of her. All the tastiest parts that no one else gets.

That means I should give her all of me, but I'm not ready to give details about what a little shit I was. A kid who had nothing and had to fight for what he did have can end up that way. But yeah, I've learned gratitude since then—because I was overwhelmed with it when I moved to Bourbon Canyon. "I gushed over her food, and for Mae, that's important. Feeding people is her love language."

"She loved your compliments?"

"That and I ate every leftover there was." I think back to my years working for the Baileys. "I was a hired hand, but I lived with Mae. I did whatever she asked me to, and for once in my life, I did it so someone could be proud of me. She expected the best from me and I gave it to her. Before that, no one could get past what my mom said or did to think I was capable of anything. Lane was forced to be more responsible, but we were both rough around the edges. His were just honed a little more."

She contemplates me while chewing on the inside of her cheek. "I bet Mae's really proud of you."

A lump grows in my throat. Damn. That hits me in the feels. "I hope so."

She's looking at me like she's never seen me before. "I was, unfortunately, very wrong about you."

"Unfortunately?"

"For me, yes." A small smile lifts her lips a moment before she shoves her chair back. "I need to get back. I have a lot to catch up on, and Clem's coming by later to help me get ready for the week."

"When can I cook for you?"

She hesitates. Damn. I thought a second date was a sure thing. "I work every day."

But the bakery closes every evening. There's got to be some window of time—as long as she's willing, and that's what I'm not sure of. "Friday at six?"

"Isn't there some big rafting-and-tasting thing this weekend?"

A delighted smile spreads across my face. "Sugar, are you keeping tabs on me?" I drawl.

She rolls her eyes, but a smile dances along her lips. "I have an order for the rafters, but I think Clem's looking forward to the distillery being flooded with strapping men roughly her age."

I shudder. "It's like hearing a little sister is dating someone."

"Now you know how I feel!" She chuckles and falls quiet, lifting her purse to her lap. I'm facing the aloof Elodie who used to wait on me.

She's going to change her mind. She's still not sure about me or about dating. Some cocksucker screwed her over and she's going to continue to be the one paying for it.

She lifts her gaze and shyly meets mine. "It's a date."

CHAPTER SIX

Elodie

The week goes by so slowly. I've counted down each hour of every day. After our lunch, Cruz dropped me off, but he didn't kiss me. I got a sweltering smile as he opened the passenger door so I could get out, and then he made sure I got inside okay before he drove off.

It was the middle of the day! What was I expecting? A smoldering kiss that would leave me in a puddle of need? As if I need a kiss to turn into needy goo. I should gauge my body's reaction and backpedal fast and far. I cannot get swept away by thrill and anticipation and misplaced dedication.

I won't. I'll be careful. There's more to Cruz than I thought, and I can't resist finding out. Nothing might come of a few dates. He might decide I'm not it for him. I might decide he's a batter I want to lick off the spoon.

I puff out a breath. The bakery closed a couple of hours ago, and I'm finishing up the decorations on the order for Sy's Water Adventures. They're offering treats to all the rafters upon their return before they bus them to the distillery.

I made cream cheese candy kayaks to put on the cupcakes, and I'm quite proud of them, but it set me behind. I have to be at Cruz's in an hour. The frosting decoration on the cupcakes is a simple ombre swirl that goes from dark blue to light toward the top. A nod to the river they just explored.

Finally, the last one is done. I whip through cleaning up the kitchen and run upstairs. It's hot today, and he's grilling. That might mean we're outside.

Chewing on my lip, I evaluate my nicer clothing, things I haven't worn for a long time. I like my sweat-pants and loose linen pants, but I also enjoyed the way Cruz's hungry gaze ate up my fitted jeans and sandaled feet. Deliberating, I stand at my dresser longer.

Loose shorts, or the booty shorts I used to wear years ago?

Impulsively, I grab the tiny pair. Other girls with my curves might skip them, but once upon a time, I used to use those same dips and valleys to get free food and drinks.

Cruz is already offering free food and drinks before he saw anything but my makeup-free face.

"Ugh." I'm thinking way too hard about this. I exchange the scrap of fabric for a medium-length pair of shorts, the looser fit easing my mind. I'm not going to think too hard about the pale-blue lace-bra-and-panty set I swapped with my tried-and-true plain-Jane ones.

Instead of putting my hair in a clip, I keep it down, finger-combing the long waves. Having a huge curtain of long hair trapping heat around my neck is a foreign feeling these days, but it's too late to change. I leave my glasses on instead of changing into contacts.

I race downstairs and out the door. I turn to lock the dead bolt and hear footsteps behind me.

Spinning around, my stomach hits my feet and my world stands still. A man approaches. He's only a few inches taller than his brother, my ex-fiancé, and he looks so much like him that I want to run. It's not like I hid after the breakup, and I really should've.

I did nothing wrong. Nothing.

Almost nothing. Definitely not as bad as Dwayne.

Then why is my gut churning enough acid to dissolve this whole town?

His lip curls up when he takes in my half-frumpy appearance, but he smothers it quickly.

My ex's brother flashes the same charming and aloof smile that Dwayne used to wield. "Well, well, well. Long time no see."

A phone call wasn't enough?

He looks the same as when I last saw him, asking me to bail out his brother. Same fake gold watch on his wrist, same most likely stolen designer slacks and dress shirt. His boating shoes make him look like he owns a yacht. He probably can't afford a discount dinghy. "What do you want, Damon?"

"Just making sure you got Dwayne's letters."

"You can tell him to lose my address."

His laugh is barely more than a puff of air. "Sure. I'll let him know." He lifts his chin to the bakery. "Nice place."

"It's a family building," I lie as stomach juices wash into my throat and burn, "so don't think you have any claim to it."

"Then what was the lovely article about how you bought a treasured part of Huckleberry Springs and gave it new life?"

Shit. I have to hand it to my ex and his brother. They always do their homework. Not enough to keep Dwayne from getting confronted and speeding away from trouble right into a life-altering mistake, but I should've taken all that into account when I fled Denver. "What are you doing here, Damon?"

"Looking at the nice place you bought with my brother's money."

It wasn't his. "The account had my name on it."

His face turns stormy, turning his ruddy expression redder. "You're a goddamn thief."

"If you think I took it, why now?" I snap. I've had plenty of time to think about why Dwayne would reach out after so many years. I know too much about all the things he didn't go to prison for, so why risk riling me up?

"I happen to have a business venture, and that capital you stole from my brother would go far."

"Listen, Einstein." My temper's shot. I always thought Damon was trouble, even before I figured out that Dwayne was not my type of bad boy, but they were a package deal. If I wanted to date Dwayne—and I did for no good reason other than I thought he was everything I wasn't—then I had to tolerate Damon. "You two weren't as good as you thought you were. There wasn't much money, and I only put in a down payment on this place. Read between the lines, dumbass—I have monthly mortgage payments. So if you think I'm some gold mine, you'd have better luck digging around these hills."

He crowds closer, but I slip out the side and move closer to my car. He spins with me but doesn't advance. "I came to make sure your payment's on time."

Bullshit. I glare at him.

Smugness fills his expression. "I'd hate for your loved ones to find out what a little thieving whore you were."

I bristle and my gut twists. I was not a whore, but there were times I felt like it. As for the thieving . . . I can't fully absolve myself. There are a few wrongs I can't make right, but I tried.

I can picture my parents' faces when they learn the things I did, all because I thought I was in love. They'd blame themselves, but I flung myself at Dwayne. He seemed so refined and worldly, and I fell under his spell with little more than some flirtation and charm.

Now that I've gotten to know Cruz, I can see how false my ex was from the get-go. If only I'd had the experience to know back then.

He thinks he can make me feel bad for what I already hate myself for every day? I was nothing compared to him. "I'd hate for you to get arrested for blackmail."

His smile is all Cheshire cat. "I don't recall signing any letters. And I'd still hate for you to reassure this town that you won't cheat them out of their hard-earned money."

I work for every cent. "I'll pay before the deadline. So you can kindly fuck off." I get into my car.

"Until next month." His words drift in just as I shut the door.

Spinning out of the alley, I have to force myself to slow down. My night might be ruined before it starts, but if my cousin pulls me over, then my family might hear about it. I don't need them worrying about me. I put them through enough after moving away.

What would they do if they heard about what I was like with my ex? Mom would blame herself and her health takes enough dips as it is. Then Dad would stress about Mom, and no. I can't be the reason they don't enjoy their hard-earned retirement.

What about Cruz? The urge to cry haunts me. I judged him so damn hard, all because I was a stupid, stupid girl.

If the town heard about me, I could lose everything.

Another thought hits me in the sternum. What if Damon fucks with the bakery?

He won't. I can't pay him and Dwayne without it. But what if he tampers just a little? I can't afford a setback.

I punch in my cousin's number.

"Palmer," he answers. Wind buffets across the line.

He didn't answer in the middle of a traffic stop, did he? "Are you busy?"

"Just grabbing a bite before my shift starts. What's up?"

"Do you mind patrolling by the bakery in a few minutes? There was a guy wandering by. He's probably a tourist, but he saw me locking up and looked too interested."

"Got anything else on him?"

"You know the type. Bland. It's probably nothing." I hate lying to my family, but it's better than getting them embroiled in the mess I caused.

"I'll text you when I do."

My stomach finally calms down. "Thank you."

Damon and Dwayne didn't vandalize businesses, but they also didn't blackmail before.

Pushing my hair off my face, I steer in the direction of Cruz's place. I've never been there, but he lives right next to Lane.

Instead of turning onto the road cutting through the trees to Foster House's parking lot, I go in the other direction, where the land spreads out into the valley. Two houses are separated by pines. The shop where Lane repaired my car is visible beyond some of the younger trees. His house is a sprawling log cabin, and it has a statelier presence than Cruz's simpler home.

I coast down Cruz's driveway, and the butterflies in my belly overcome the surge of acid from earlier to unfurl and swirl around, growing frenzied. More dread piles in and my gut squeezes those butterflies until a stone sits heavy in my gut.

After Damon's visit, I really should put my head down and figure out how to get myself out of this mess. I don't need this complication right now—the dating or the blackmail. But I'm tired of missing out on life, and I don't want to miss out on tonight. I was finally looking forward to something that wasn't related to my job.

I was finally wondering if maybe I could find that man who'd change my mind about relationships.

Cruz

As soon as Elodie got out of her car, I knew something was wrong. Rufus got a guarded smile from her, but she dropped her gaze as soon as I grinned. At the same time, my tongue was lolling out of my damn mouth. The woman's got legs for miles. The hummingbirds on one of her feet swirl high enough to wrap around her ankles in a shower of blue, green, and black.

Her baggy shirt only teases at what her top the other day showed me. But those shorts? I've been fighting an erection since she arrived. Elodie in baggy clothing is a mystery I want to unwrap, but Elodie in shorts makes me revert to a teen who can't control his hormones. I have images of sliding the fabric down her legs.

Is she wearing underwear?

The peek of red and pink rose petals outlined in black from under the hem across her thigh is almost my undoing. How many more surprises are there?

She's quiet while sitting on my back deck. The dog is asleep under the table, and I'm prouder than hell of having a girl hang with me at my home while I'm cooking for her. I never thought I'd have a life like this, and there hasn't been someone who made me think that sharing it would be worth it.

After our lunch, I was stupidly optimistic, envisioning a future just because she told me something about herself. Those fantasies are slipping out of my fingers like a handful of grain, several kernels at a time.

I lay the meat across the grill. "Want a beer, a cocktail, or water? Juice?"

She gives me a faint smile. "I'd better stick with water. What can I help you with?"

"Nothing, chef. You get served today."

I'm rewarded with a slightly bigger grin. "It feels weird to get waited on."

I'll make sure she gets used to it if she gives me a

chance. "I called Mae and got a recipe for her pasta salad to go with the steaks. I wasn't sure if you liked pasta salads with mayo, or if you're an Italian dressing girl, so I made both."

Her laugh has a hint of resignation. "You're too good, Cruz. Either one sounds good. You making a whole other salad is not fine."

"It would've been my bad for not checking first. Wait here." Just as I pass her, I lean down. "I like to think I finally got the balance right—I'm not too good but the right amount of bad."

I duck inside to get her water and bring out the tray I have loaded with a pasta salad. The veggies I prepared are already on the grill in a foil packet. When I step outside, she's gazing into the distance with a stricken expression. Damn, her face is pale. If I ask what's wrong, she'll shut down even more. That patience I told her about earlier needs to be in full effect.

"How was your week?" I try to get her talking while I'm grilling, and all I can think of that's safe are the standard questions.

"Good."

"Were you busy?"

"Yes, but a normal busy for this time of year."

I wait, but that's all I get. Short, succinct answers. Whatever tanked her day before she arrived is still sitting with her. "How do you think the weekend is going to be?"

"I'll benefit from the Rafting and Tasting crowd. It helps that the booking office isn't far away from the bakery." She takes a drink of water and flips her hair off her shoulders. The strands fall to her mid-back. She crosses one leg over the other, and her shorts ride up to reveal almost her entire leg.

Now I can't think of a single damn question.

"How about you?" she asks.

It's a good thing I can small talk for hours. "Yeah, it'll be a big sales day."

I have to turn my back to her. Along with seeing more of her leg, a bigger portion of the bouquet of flowers is revealed. I could drag my nose along that creamy thigh, starting at the last hummingbird on her ankle and moving up. She'll smell as sweet and delicious as the real version of those flowers.

"Apparently, there's a rafting crew of just women, and Campbell's warned us that they might be wild." When I turn back, Elodie's gaze is flinty.

"How nice."

I cross to her and squat down. "I might smile real pretty, but that's in the name of customer service. I'm not interested."

"You haven't met any of them." Her throat works up and down, like she's pushing down emotion over and over again.

"Elodie, you can talk to me. What's wrong?"

A shaky laugh leaves her. "I thought I could do this, but I can't." She pushes the chair back and stands so fast I nearly topple backward.

I throw a hand out to catch the corner of the table, steady myself, and rise.

"I can't do this. Trust me when I say it's not you." Her voice breaks. "It's so not you; it's me." She rushes around me to the stairs and stops before taking the first step. "I'm so sorry."

She runs off.

Ditching the steak on the grill, I dart after her, Rufus on my heels. "Elodie, can we talk?"

"No. You're too— And I'm—" She spins, and I nearly run into her. I want to push my hands through her hair and kiss the pain in her features away. "I'm a mess. My life is a mess. I tried to get it together, and it's not there yet. And you've—" Another sardonic laugh leaves her. "Anyone would be lucky to have you, but it can't be me." Tears glitter in her eyes. "I gave away my luck, and I'm still paying for it."

She spins and darts around the corner to her car. I'm frozen in place. Her engine fires up, her tires crunch on gravel, and then the noise fades and it's quiet again. Nothing but birds and frogs chirp around me.

I stab a hand through my hair and look down at myself as if I morphed into that dirty kid right before she ran. Wouldn't be the first date to ditch me because of how I looked. Rufus gazes up at me, and I give him a shrug. What did I do? Could I have done something different? Do I just walk away from years of infatuation? If I tried to pursue it, would that be stalking?

I don't know.

The smell of seasoned meat and charcoal drifts across my nose. Shit. The food. I run back, flip the steaks, and take the salad inside. At least it's covered. Then I plop into the chair Elodie vacated and let out a long, slow exhale. Her glass of water collects condensation next to me.

There has to be something I can do. I'm not too good for her. That's bullshit.

I could call my brother, but he'd probably assume I did something to piss Elodie off. Only she wasn't angry.

She was . . . distraught. Crestfallen. It doesn't make sense.

Dialing the one person I know will be able to tell me exactly what to do, I slump in the chair.

"Cruz," Mae answers warmly. "How are you?"

I feel like I got kicked in the gut by a horse. "I need some advice." I spill everything, from my years of trying to get to know Elodie to tonight, when I thought this date would surely lead to a third and then a fourth and more.

While I talk, I rescue the steaks from the grill and let them rest next to me. They're grilled to perfection and I would've loved to show off my char lines to Elodie.

Mae makes a sympathetic sound. "Clearly, she's had some bad experiences. Perhaps her past is still haunting her, and she feels like it'll either ruin what you two could've built, or that it could just ruin either one of you."

"What do I do?" I'm not a guy who just gives up, and there's a pull between me and Elodie that is special. She feels it too, and she wants to give in. An outside source should not be fucking with us.

"Times like this, she needs a friend."

I don't want to be her fucking friend. But I'll take that over nothing. Something's bothering her, and now that I've got glimpses of the brightness inside of her that she hides, I want to help her. "I can do that."

"Also, Cruz?"

I perk up. Mae's a sweet woman, but she didn't survive fostering so many kids to be merely kind. She had to be crafty, subversive, intuitive, and downright fierce at times. I know. I experienced it. "Yeah?"

"Friends need to eat too."

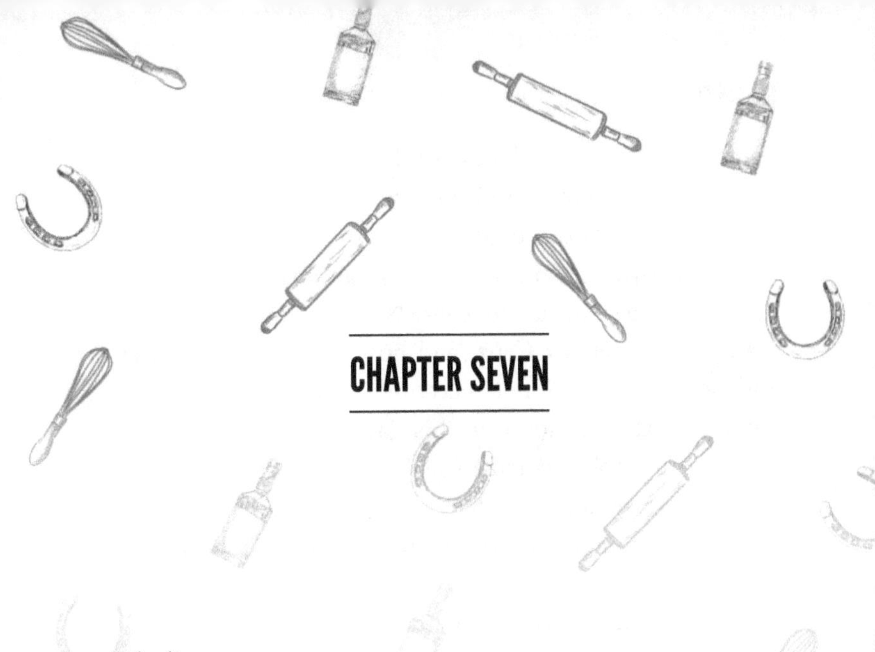

CHAPTER SEVEN

Elodie

My throat is raw, and my eyes ache from squeezing them shut while I sobbed. It's a good thing I didn't go off the road, and my sunglasses hid the worst while I drove through town.

My cousin left me a message that he didn't see any guy hanging around, so I buzzed right into the bakery and collapsed at my little table.

Cruz was cooking for me. Waiting on me. Asking me about my day and my business. He was also holding back. That guy saw right through my defeated demeanor, but he peppered me with casual questions like he knew I'd shut him out and bolt if he delved in further. Which I did anyway.

I wipe my eyes. The skin around them burns like I sandblasted my face. My nose is stuffy, but I sniffle and toss the tissue.

My stomach has the audacity to rumble. That steak I

fled from smelled so damn good. And that pasta salad? I hardly make savory food anymore and he had a whole stockpile just for our date.

I rest my arm across my gut. I can make myself eggs. Tears pop back up in my eyes. No. I'll remember how I made an omelet for Cruz, and how appreciative he was, and how satisfied I felt watching him eat my cooking. The way the muscles in his jaw clenched while he chewed and how his gaze softened with the first bite. I missed a whole night of that.

A hot droplet streaks down my cheek. Followed by another.

Here comes another bout of crying. I should just head to bed and try to get some rest before my alarm goes off at three.

I'm alone instead of sitting outside on a gorgeous night eating damn good food with even better company.

I shudder out a hard breath. That's not for me.

There's a knock at the door.

Fucking Damon. I told him to leave me alone. He's worse than a rotten, stinky egg.

"Go away!"

Another hesitant tap.

Does he think I'm going to tolerate constant interference? I might not have a choice, but he doesn't know that. I rise to my feet and stomp to the door. Whipping it open, I pour all my hostility into my greeting. "I told you I would get you the goddamn money—"

My jaw hits the floor. Cruz's brows are to his hairline, and his hands are full of food containers. My stomach grumbles again, ready to invite him inside while I grab two forks and dig in. I'd eat that steak like a renaissance fair drumstick.

"What are you doing here?" It comes out as more of a shriek. I look over his shoulder and around him as much as I can. No Damon lurking in the corners of the other buildings.

Cruz glances behind him. "Expecting someone?"

Dreading him, more like. "No."

He waits a moment, but when I don't elaborate, he smiles, but his concerned stare brushes over my ravaged face. I must look like hell. "We can at least be friends, right? And friends gotta eat? I brought dinner here."

I fight the urge to grab the food like a feral raccoon and run. The smell of the perfectly charred meat reaches me, and I want to sit with that bowl of pasta salad like it's pudding and keep scooping until it's gone.

He packed all of it like he plans to stay. I'm too wrung out to figure out a reason why this is a bad idea.

"Have a seat." I push the door open farther and go to the counter to grab plates and silverware.

He spreads everything out and a small frown forms on his lips. I set my items down and my heart lurches in my throat. The envelope with the words "Inmate Dwayne Miller" and "correctional facility" on it sits on top of my mail pile. I gather it with the rest of my bills and hide it in a drawer at my island. That letter can get lost among my favorite cookbooks.

"You didn't have to do this." I plop into a seat but dig into his offerings in case he comes to his senses and realizes I'm not worth the effort. I bite back a groan when the burst of perfectly seasoned steak hits my taste buds. I can cook a five-course meal, but it's been forever since I've made a robust dinner for myself. I nibble and taste so much throughout the day, and work even more, that it's not often worth the effort.

He loads his plate before he pauses. "I know you're a private person, but you don't have to go through everything alone."

"I talk to Clem."

"When she's not working all her jobs. Whatever reason you're staying away from me is also putting distance between you two."

I sigh. "I wish I could explain it, but I made a lot of mistakes, and I wish I could leave them in the past."

"Do your parents know what's going on, at least?"

I shake my head and cut off a hunk of perfectly done rib eye. Stuffing it in my mouth, I spin through ways to tell him something he won't understand. We eat through all the amazing food. He lets me ponder as long as I need to before I brave speaking again.

"I'm not proud of what I did," I finally say. "I've tried to make amends, but sometimes it just doesn't feel like it ever goes away. My parents were doting—they still are, but when I was younger, it was stifling. One time, I got into an accident with Mom in the car. She beat herself up about it because we'd been bickering. I broke my arm and cut my forehead, but I healed just fine. But she still gets bouts of vertigo and migraines—and also continues to feel awful about it. So when I left home, I got the freedom I craved. I got more than I asked for, and I spent years evading their calls and avoiding them. They blamed themselves instead of me. Uncle Karl said Dad would start to cry." I won the World's Worst Daughter award. "I can't have them find out how bad things got for me."

I take a steadying breath and gather our dirty plates. He jumps up to do the same with the plastic containers. Pressure pounds at my temples, urging me to tell him everything. I haven't talked to my parents. I haven't opened up to Clem. I work so much that my friendships are as shallow as a kiddie pool.

A dull thud starts at my temples, and worse, the tears are threatening to return. I dump the dishes by the sink. "I'm also afraid no one will forgive me. I did things I'm not proud of and stood by while worse was happening."

I squeeze my eyes closed. God, that was embarrassing. But I can take a full breath again and my sudden headache fades.

Cruz gently turns me around, his fingertips warm, and tilts my chin up. Tingles and heat spread over my skin from his touch. I open my eyes and I'm looking directly into his warm gaze.

"People do forgive and I'm proof of it," he says in a low voice.

He told me about his mom, but her actions aren't his. "You said you were angry, but, Cruz, that's not what I'm talking about. And you were a kid. I mean, look at you. You're a stand-up citizen. A regular Huckleberry Springs paragon."

Emotions play over his face. Deep regret to indecision. The heat in his eyes intensifies, and he lowers his head. Warm, firm lips claim mine, and his warm citrus smell is in my nose.

A surge of desire overwhelms me. I throw my arms around his neck and rise to my tiptoes. Cruz is the best-looking man I've ever seen, and I've thought that since I first laid eyes on him. He's sexy and rugged and that flirting of his worked on me more than I'll ever be able to admit. My attraction has only grown stronger the more I've talked to him.

His hot tongue strokes against my lips, and I open

for him. No hesitation. He delves deep, and I cling to him, letting him do whatever the hell he wants.

My ass hits the counter, and he lifts me onto it. Plates clink against each other, silverware clatters, but I don't care. I wrap my legs around him and hook my ankles together. I taste him, his arms are banded around me, and I want to be swallowed by him. Consumed whole.

He splays his hand across my neck, tilting my head back so he can dominate my mouth. And he does. His tongue dances with mine and I'm struggling for breath. My pulse hammers through my veins and beats hard through my pussy. I'm not snugged up against him like I want to be, but I'm close enough that the monster ridge behind his jeans can't be hidden.

I shamelessly grind closer to him. If I keep doing this, I could come. I've wanted him for too long. Someone who can take charge and make me feel safe.

I'm safe right here, in Cruz's arms.

But he's not safe from the trouble following me.

I stiffen and pull back, but not far enough to break us apart. He kisses a path down my neck while stroking his thumb against my fluttering pulse point. The throb between my legs pounds stronger.

"Cruz," I say with a groan. "We shouldn't."

He lifts his head, taking his lips off me. I feel the loss deep in my bones. "Because we're friends?" His voice is so damn deep. Gruff. I made him that way.

"Friends don't kiss." I sound breathless, and I want him to steal all my air and hold it for me.

"Some friends do." He rests his forehead against mine.

I fist my hands into the front of his shirt. "I . . .

can't." All the air leaks out of me and I slump. My hands fall away from him.

"I understand." He feathers my hair away from my face. "We're still friends though. Right?"

I nod because I'm not strong enough to say no. I spent all of an hour after I ran out on him crying, and I was miserable. I don't care to experience that again.

He takes a step back and adjusts the front of his jeans, wincing. I look away to keep from getting caught staring, but damn. I was so close to getting that. I would've stripped down in this kitchen, hygiene standards be damned.

"I'm here if you want to talk to me about what's going on." When I shake my head, he gives me a quelling look. "I haven't always been this guy, sugar. I might've been a kid for most of my trouble, but I fought, I stole, I vandalized. I thought I was so damn smart and that my cockiness was a good trait." He swaggers to the door while I'm stuck in a puddle of shock. "I was a delinquent, Elodie. I would've stayed that way if Myles hadn't come into my life. The first time I met him, I was being an asshole at the funeral home after my mom died."

Not Cruz. This guy would not be a dick in a funeral home.

He opens the door and pins me with so serious a gaze I have to believe he was once on the wrong side of the law. "The people who love you, the ones who really matter in your life? They'll forgive you."

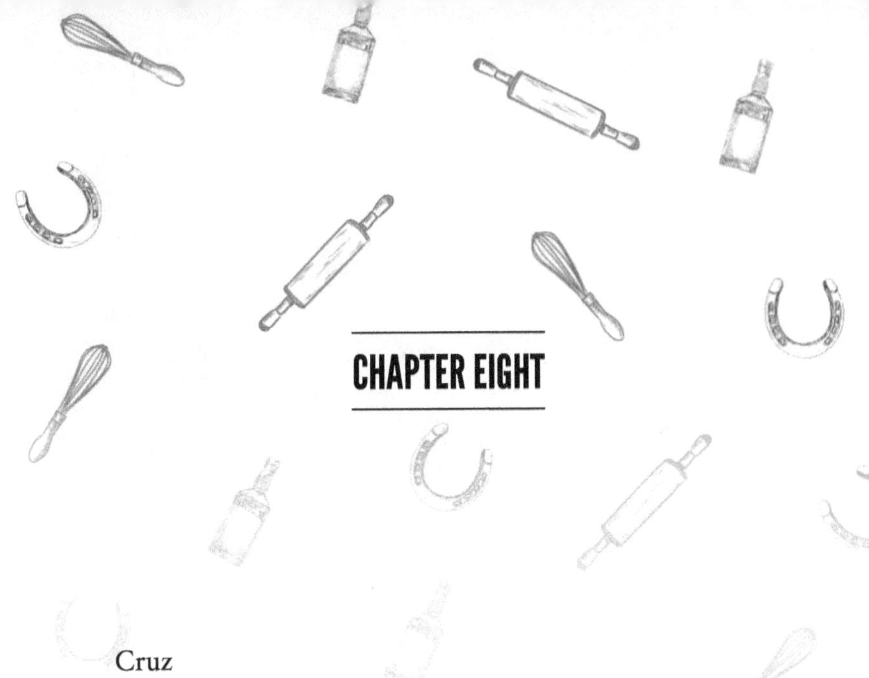

CHAPTER EIGHT

Cruz

I leave the tractor with the sickle mower at the edge of the field between my house and Lane's. He's going to finish, but I have to get to the distillery for the baby shower.

Jamison Hennessy wanted all her friends and immediate family invited to the baby shower for her and Iverson's son, Tavis. That means all the guys at the distillery outside of her husband, her sisters, and her parents. Elodie and Clem were invited too.

So I'm making sure I'm there.

I stride across the yard to my house, fighting a hard-on the whole way. Every time I think about Elodie and the way she responded to my kiss, I get lightheaded. Blood leaves my brain immediately upon remembering the way she ground against my rock-hard dick.

The woman scrambled my brains with nothing but a kiss.

I made the damn thing count though. Best kiss of my life.

I puff out a sigh of relief when I enter my air-conditioned house. After running through the shower, I dress in a blue Dee's Sweets shirt with a clean pair of jeans. It's been three days since I've seen her, and I've wanted to text her, call her, and stop by. But friends aren't smothering.

Friends give friends space. And nearly come in their pants from a kiss.

There's also her reaction after what I said—I never stuck around to find out. I said my piece and left. I can talk about forgiveness, but what if she doesn't want to date a guy who has a juvie record? I've made a lot of changes, and I've worked hard, but there's still lingering insecurity that it won't be enough to erase the little shit I used to be.

I get in my pickup and drive to Foster House. Only Durban, Campbell, and Haven are there. Lane will clean up after he finishes the cutting and Iverson will arrive with Jamison and his kids.

Inside the tasting room, that punch of pride hits me. I helped design the interior, from the types of tables and chairs to the stone under the windows, to bring out that industrial aesthetic. When I stand inside, I feel like I went from the gutter to the penthouse.

I'm never going back there. I'll never be that guy again, using my size to intimidate others. I'm better than I was raised, and I'm a fuckton better than my dad. I might've spent a night in jail, but not the rest of my life.

Durban's behind the bar, digging out glasses and lining up bottles. At the end of the counter is a line of juice and water. Campbell's pushing two tables together by the wall, a bowl with pretzels on one.

"What can I help with?" I ask.

Campbell steals a pretzel and hip bumps a table the last inch, her summer dress swirling around the tips of her boots. "Decorations."

For the next hour, I hang banners and spread out tiny candy pacifiers, line up baby bottles for Durban to fill with virgin mimosas, and tape balloons around the room. By the time we're done, the trendy tasting room is transformed into baby shower headquarters. Lane and I are pros at these after all the Bailey babies born over the last fifteen years.

Haven pops in from the main distillery, where he was checking on the tanks and recording temperatures and pressures. Then Jamison and Campbell's other sister, Avery, shows up with her partner, Thea. Both are walking catalogues for athleisure wear. They look equally ready for a daylong brunch or a hike.

Jamison, Avery, and Campbell's parents arrive next, the picture of lifelong ranchers. Their clothing is nice but sturdy and worn enough to suggest that they don't just oversee the ranch, they're hands-on.

Staff from the ranch start arriving. I've met Chef Cecil, but Durban introduces me to his wife. Then the guest ranch foreman and several housekeepers arrive, Chef's sous-chef, and some of the guys the Hennessys worked with.

A chorus of cheers goes up when Iverson and his family arrive. The tasting room is full of people, and the sounds of talking and laughter bounce off the walls. I make small talk with everyone, but my gaze continuously strays out the window. Clem isn't here yet, so I'm not giving up hope that Elodie's going to show. Several more minutes tick by and my disappointment grows.

Clem pulls into the parking lot and my hope surges. I search for Elodie, but Clem's alone. Fuck.

After half an hour, I step out of the tasting room and into the merch store. The door shuts behind me, muffling the noise. Will I ever quit screwing up with Elodie? She let me close to her as a friend and then I shoved my tongue down her throat and pushed my erection into her.

I shove my hand through my hair just as Lane lets himself into the main entrance of the place. His still-damp hair is shiny and combed to the side, and unlike the rest of us, he's wearing his nicer jeans and a dressier shirt.

His brows rise when he sees me. "What's up?"

I prop my hands on my hips. "Nothing. Just taking a breather."

His gaze jumps to the full tasting room and back. "Lot of people."

"Yep."

"That doesn't usually bother you."

No. It never has. "Elodie's not here. I kissed her the other night."

As much as I'd like to keep my continued rejection to myself, it's always helped to talk to Lane. It's like he came through that entrance because he knew I'd be here, handling my emotions so I wouldn't ask, *Where's Elodie?* to everyone who talks to me.

Awareness fills his eyes. "That doesn't usually bother you either."

I've kissed plenty of women. Had my share of sex. None of them has stuck in my head. If they wanted more and I didn't, I moved on. If they didn't want more, I moved on because ultimately, I never did either.

This time I do. I want it all. "We went on a couple of dates, then she got spooked. I convinced her we could be friends, but then I kissed her."

His brows draw together like he's reading into the definition of that kiss and that it was no mere peck. "She pushed you away?"

"Not really, but I haven't talked to her since then, and she hasn't tried reaching out to me. I stepped over the line."

"Or life just happened. She runs her own business. Things come up. We know that."

Clem pushes into the merch store. "Hey, bosses. I'm taking off. Just wanted to say bye before I relieve my sister."

"Relieve her for what?" I ask so suddenly, Clem blinks.

"She took my dad to an eye doctor appointment in Billings. Mom had a bout of vertigo and couldn't go with him. Elodie said she would take him while I came to the party. I told her to text when she got to town, and I'd go hang with them." She points to her eyes. "He got his pupils dilated, and his vision stays blurry for a while. I'm going to make them dinner, and Elodie can come here."

"Let us know if we can do anything," Lane says.

Clem cocks her head toward the gathering. "Jamison told me to take them some cake, but Elodie keeps our parents stocked in goodies. She's probably getting dinner in the oven even though I said I'd make them some-thing. I'd better get going."

"Nice seeing you, Clem," I say, even more excited that Elodie's arriving soon.

When she's gone, Lane studies me. "I don't have to ask if you're taking off. I doubt we could haul you away before Elodie shows."

I shoot him a scowl. "I really like her."

"I can tell."

"She won't talk about what's going on, but I think someone's hounding her for money."

"She in debt?"

Sure, she could be, but my gut says what she owes is out of the ordinary. "I saw a letter in her mail from a correctional facility in Colorado."

His nostrils flare. "Interesting."

"Isn't it?"

"Dad called me last week."

I stiffen and clench my teeth like usual when I hear about him. "You talked to him."

I'm not asking. He always does. For the kid who was left with a lot of tasks our parents should've handled, he doesn't carry the grudge against our father that I do.

He rubs his chin. "Things are the same for him. Won't be seeing him soon."

"Next time, tell him he can save his ink and quit writing me."

"He won't. Stubborn bastard."

"Yeah." He's the reason why I found the letter at Elodie's so damn interesting. And why I wish she'd talk to me, to someone, but mostly me. I might understand in a way not many others would.

Elodie has me all twisted up. My thoughts are very *not friendly* when it comes to her, but I want to help, and I can't do that if she keeps beyond arm's length. "She doesn't trust me."

"Then try being a friend who doesn't grope her."

Lane keeps up with my subject change. He's used to it when it comes to our dad.

"I wasn't groping." Fondling, maybe. Licking and sucking. She was grinding.

He shrugs. "Never seen you like this, but you've gotta play the long game if she's skittish. For what it's worth—your little baker wants to be more than friends with you."

"She might, but she's decided not to."

"You fluster her like no one else. And when you're not looking at her, she's spying on you. It's like watching two middle schoolers figure out what flirting is."

"Ha ha, jackass. This isn't easy."

"Good. You've worked for all the good things in life. Elodie's no different."

Isn't he a sage old asshole? I don't feel better after our talk, but I could've used it earlier. I should've taken my own advice and turned to Lane instead of spinning myself in circles all night in bed.

I search for a topic that won't twist me in knots, or make me feel like that dirty little kid people loved to hate. "What took you so long to finish cutting?"

"I stopped by Langley's place. He was burning his garbage."

"Goddammit." The last time our neighbor burned his trash, he added way too much of everything and then passed out.

Lane nods. "Damn flames were jumping his firepit and he was passed out next to it."

My stomach clenches. When we bought land from Hutch Langley, we were warned he'd only drink the profits away. People said he'd be a bad neighbor and that his irresponsible ways had cost him his kids when they were young. Langley has no visitors, and his remorse is eating up whatever life he's got left.

I don't have the tolerance for him that Lane does. I try to be a bigger person, but I just see a guy who's so lost in himself that he doesn't have room to care about others. The past rears up and I'm eight again, asking Mom when she'll get out of bed and feed us. I've already watched one adult destroy themselves with some form of addiction. It's hard to do it again.

At least Langley reminds me more of our mom than our explosive, narcissistic dad. Otherwise, I would've insisted we buy land on the other side of town.

As for being a neighbor, Lane and I take turns stopping in to check on him. I do it only because I don't want him falling asleep with a cigarette and lighting up his whole place, causing a fire that could spread to our property. Lane does it out of the same sense of responsibility that didn't leave my petulant ass in the dust.

Lane runs his fingers under his collar. "I called the vet. She'll be out to check his gelding in the morning. And I fed his chickens since I was close."

That's the other reason we both won't steer clear of our neighbor. His animals shouldn't suffer because of him. Sometimes that means feeding the chickens he keeps for eggs that he sells for beer money. Or under-the-table vet care for his horses. The local vets know the drill, and Hutch might get cranky about it, but he waves us off and toddles inside rather than argue about a hoof abscess that needs draining.

Besides, he can still do some farming, growing wheat for the distillery. We're taking a hell of a gamble doing any business with him, but Lane insisted and the

Hennessys don't mind. Langley was a friend of their dad's.

The old man accepts help a whole lot better than a certain pretty baker.

Over Lane's shoulder, Elodie pulls into the lot.

"Let's go in and get some cake," I say, already opening the door.

He flashes me a perplexed look before he sees Elodie scurrying across the lot with a gift bag. "I see. Ditching me for your *friend*."

"Yup."

CHAPTER NINE

Elodie

The bakery is closed, but I'm sitting with Campbell in one of the booths, poring over ideas for a Christmas showcase she wants to throw for local crafters and vendors. She brought it up at the baby shower last week, and I told her to swing by today. When I close on Sundays, it's time for my cleaning and baking frenzy for the week.

"Since the street fair cross-promo was such a hit," she says, looking over my numbers from the event, "I could talk to them about doing it again. Or do you want me to wait until after the Taste of Springs event?"

There's a lot I want to talk to Foster House about doing again. Mostly, there's one man I want to do something with one more time—a lot more times—and it involves his tongue and that hard body. "I can reach out."

"That would be to me." She smiles.

I lift a brow. "You work for them? What about your family's guest ranch?"

"I'm there too, but all the events are smaller scale than what I've done in the past—not as time-consuming. A lot of the wedding parties who've booked with us have their own planners, so I coordinate with them." She props her elbows on the table. "Go ahead. Make me earn my wages."

I snort. "I bet Durban does that." Horrified, my eyes fly open. "I'm sorry—"

She's too busy laughing to see how mortified I am. "Oh my gosh, Elodie, I've missed you."

"What do you mean?"

She sobers. "Sorry, it's just that you've been so subdued lately. Just, you know, different than when we were growing up."

"You were always getting in my business." She's Clem's age, and I'm a little older than Jamison.

"And you didn't put up with it. Clem and I thought you were so cool."

"Well, I'm not."

"You are, and I'm not the only one who thinks so," she says in a singsong voice. "Cruz kept trying to talk you up at the baby shower."

"We're just friends." I duck my head and study the numbers in front of me.

What else can I talk about besides a tall man with a crooked smile who makes my insides melt? Cruz did chat with me, but there were so many people there that we kept getting interrupted. Campbell's dad talked with all the Foster House owners like it was his job. The man always had a gift for gab, and when he used to run across my dad at the farm supply store, we'd be stuck for an hour while they caught up in the middle of the aisle. I haven't gotten to visit that much with Mrs. Hawthorne, or Avery and Thea, because I'm always working.

I had a lot of fun at the shower, and I'm glad Clem and I could split the time helping our parents. I'm also glad I had a chance to tell her that things had gone nowhere with Cruz, mostly. I told her about running out on him. Not about the kiss with a friend I very much do not have friendly thoughts about.

The bakery saved me once from my mess of a personal life. It can do that again. "Actually, can I hire you for something that's not quite an event but will take some coordinating?"

I told Cruz I didn't have the money to pay Campbell, but I also need the cash this venture will bring in. I made July's payment, but August is approaching. Dwayne and Damon won't give up, and I know that making one payment only cemented me into a vicious cycle of blackmail.

I need Taste of Springs to be a success, and I need to figure out the fundraising. Then I'll extract myself from my ex and his brother. Again.

Campbell's eyes light up. "What can I do for you?"

I outline my fundraiser plan, and she's vibrating by the time I'm done.

"That's such a good idea." Her grin is wide. "Everyone wants to support local and get a good product when they do. Do you have the pricing and how much in sales you can handle?"

"That's the hard part." I'd be fitting cookie dough prep into every spare minute of the day. "I'll come up with some numbers, but it'll be limited, and I need to be done before November when holiday orders surge."

"Can you hire more people?" When I wince, she puts her hand on mine. "You realize you get the money first from the orders? So if you need to hire someone just temporarily, you'll have the money up front."

I slowly let out the breath I started holding at the thought of bringing on more people. "Really?"

She nods. "My professor for the marketing class I took used to complain about fundraisers all the time. He'd rant about how they were asking too much money and not offering much quality for a product. Makes the sale harder." She waves her hand like she's afraid of getting too far off topic. "Regardless, you can just hire a couple of people to help package and box, whatever. You have plenty of people who want to see you and this place succeed."

My chest grows tight. I was cheered on so hard when I moved home to open the bakery. On my first day, I ran out of food. For the entire first week, I sold out. It took me forever to figure out how much to prepare because the whole town supported me. I'm a local girl, come home to make good.

If they found out I bought this place with money that wasn't *directly* mine—but should've been—they'd all lose faith in me. I was too close to Dwayne when he stole from others, and worse, I knew about some of it. If that got out, I'd lose my precious business and distress my parents.

Campbell adopts a secretive smile. "I know one man who'll be the first in line to roll his sleeves up."

"Sleeves up, pants off?" I snort-chuckle, but my blood starts to heat. Cruz is a nice distraction from my problems, but he deserves more than that. He deserves a woman without a seedy ex who somehow still fucks with her life from prison.

"I won't tell the health inspector." She covers her mouth like she's hiding what she's saying but we're the only ones here. "The tasting room has seen some action. But we clean up after ourselves."

"Oh my god, TMI." My laughter spills out like a dam broke.

"It's not TMI, but more of a . . . recommendation." She winks.

I laugh harder, but the flush of heat returns. I recommend sitting on the counter in the back with my legs wrapped around Cruz too. "I'll keep that in mind."

When did I last have this kind of girl talk? I instinctively kept Dwayne away from my parents and Clem. I missed out on family time and girl talk. I've pushed Cruz away more than once. Dwayne took so much more from me than I thought.

Maybe it's time to get that back.

Campbell's expression turns calculating, but her smile remains in place. "I think Cruz is working the tasting room tonight."

Cruz

The last customer left ten minutes ago, and I have most of the closing duties done. I leave the door unlocked while I'm in the storeroom. If anyone comes in, I can still talk to them, but I can't serve them.

I grab a new bottle of our juneberry vodka and the

newest whiskey that Haven bottled. Durban's our flavor profile mastermind, but the rest of us still throw out ideas too and make batches. The rye whiskey is cask strength for extra bite, and it's a popular sampler.

Whistling to myself, I start back. The bell above the bar tinkles.

"Hey there," I call. "We're closed, but—" I stop dead at the end of the hall. Elodie's standing just inside the door, looking as skittish as a newborn foal that's found its legs. She's in her usual bakery garb of loose shirt and baggy pants with her hair in a messy bun. A dark tendril curls around the base of her neck, and I'd like to trace the path with my tongue.

"Hi," she says, like she's practiced this a million times and thinks she got it wrong at the last second.

"Hey." I set the bottles down behind the bar. "Come on in."

"I know you're closed." She takes a few hesitant steps, sucks in a breath, then weaves through the tables. "But I won't be long."

That won't do at all. "You have to stay for a taste now that you're here."

"No, I couldn't. I still have some cinnamon rolls to prep for a funeral tomorrow." She stops by a stool at the bar counter. "It's also my breakfast prep. I cook some sausage links so I can chew those cold while I chow down on a roll. It's about the only noncarb I have these days."

"Breakfast of champions." I cross to the door and throw the dead bolt. Whatever Elodie came here for, I'm not letting anyone interrupt. When I return, I pat the seat of the stool closest to her. "Take a seat. Just a quick taste. It won't do more than coat your tongue."

"I don't want to make more work for you."

"It's my pleasure." I grab a tasting glass for her and open the bottle of Haven's whiskey. I splash enough whiskey in to cover the bottom. "Haven named this Haven's Rye because he wanted to see his name on a label."

She smiles. "I can't blame him."

"We have to stay away from using the Hennessy last name so no one confuses our products with the cognac."

"Better safe than sorry." I don't have to give her any directions. She swirls the glass, lifting it to her nose. Her eyelids flutter closed when she inhales. "I almost smell the caramel I make for cupcake filling. Mmm . . ." That sound goes right to my dick. "It's spicy, but also sweet." She takes a sip and rolls it around. "Yes. I can taste it all. Ooh, smoky. I like that." She opens her eyes and I'm captured in her thoughtful gaze. The brown of her hazel eyes matches the drink in her glass. "It'll go well with a fruity confection. Peaches. Cherry? No, I've got it. With a plain poppy seed batter—no almond extract. Nothing but smoky caramel and poppy seeds."

"This bottle is yours."

She blinks. "No, I can't."

"You can, and you're going to make me those muffins. What are you going to call them?" I ask before she can reject my idea.

She studies the label. "Poppy seed cruisers."

My grin spreads wide and my manly pride surges. "Cruisers has Cruz in it."

"I know."

"You'd name them after me when it's Haven's name on the bottle?"

A light pink paints across her cheeks. "Haven isn't the one who kissed me the other night."

"No, he wasn't," I say in a guttural growl. Haven's never shown interest in her, and whether or not it's because he noticed mine, I don't care. The thought of another tongue down her throat besides mine makes me feral.

She pushes the glass away and takes a deep breath. "I came here to tell you that I don't want to be friends, and I'm tired of hiding."

There are two big confessions in what she said, but I'm hung up on the first part. She doesn't want my friendship? I'll honor her wishes, but damn. That's worse than the flirting ban. Am I going to get restricted from the bakery? Will I get escorted out by her cousin like Pete, the guy who berates her for her pricing? "I'm sorry if I did anything wrong—"

"You do everything right, and I don't want to be friends." Her eyes fly wide. "Oh, I made it sound like— No, I treasure your friendship. I'd be sad to lose it, but I want more when it comes to you. I always have."

She punctuates her comment by blowing out a breath. Her nervous energy eases into a steady presence. She folds her hands like she's waiting for my reaction.

When it comes to me, she wants more? She always has? So that whole time I worked to get closer to her, she wasn't cold out of lack of interest? My smile starts long before it reaches my mouth.

"Well then, sugar." I round the counter and plant myself on a stool facing her. "That means I need to take you out again."

She spins to put her knees between mine. "Or you could kiss me now."

Kiss me now echoes loud in my head. That long tendril of hair that's been teasing me is still tracing down her neck. I rub the silky strands between my fingers before sliding my hand around the back of her neck. Gently pulling her closer, I close the distance between us. A little whimper leaves her and she shoves her hands in my hair, less restrained than I am.

The whiskey on her tongue mingles with all the sweetness that's Elodie Palmer. The scent of sugar cookies fills my nose and it fucking fits her. If I could bottle her, I'd drink nothing else for the rest of my life. I'm hard and pulsing behind my fly, and even though nothing's going to come from it tonight, I don't try to hold back.

She scoots to the edge of her stool, but that's not close enough. I don't care how much it pinches my dick, I haul her onto my lap. She straddles me, her legs twining around my waist like the last time I kissed her. In this position, she grinds against my encased erection, and a ragged groan leaves my chest. She echoes with a throaty moan and rubs herself harder against me.

I need to have more of her than this kiss. I line a path with my mouth down her throat and she tips her head back while wiggling her hips with a frantic urgency.

"You're close, aren't you, sugar," I whisper against her throat.

"Yes." She reflexively tightens her legs around me.

If she wants more, I'll give her more. As my fingers tunnel under her shirt, I score my teeth along the base of her throat. A shiver racks her body. My fingertips hit her warm skin, and *fuck*, I'm harder than ever. We're alone and I don't expect anyone, but I can't risk exposing her. "Someday, I'm going to see every inch of you."

She nods, her eyes heavy lidded. The way she's got me in her hold is tempting me to carry us both to the supply room. But when we do it, she's going to be confident that she's good and ready.

"I want to see you," she says as she swivels her hips in a way that elicits another groan from me. "All of you."

"You will." As soon as fucking possible—when I have her in private. I skim my hands up to cover her breasts. They fill my grip perfectly and her tight little nipples poke into my palms.

A whine leaves her and her legs quiver. The hitch in her breath steals my attention from her tits.

"You need to come."

"I'm so close." The more she rubs against me, the stronger my pulse hammers in my cock.

I wedge my hand between us and cup her pussy through her pants. Heat blisters my skin. "You're wet for me? For this?"

I get a moan for an answer.

"I bet that sweet little cunt of yours tastes like honey." She rocks into my hand, but I slip it out from between us. A tremble rolls over her when I slide under her waistband. "I'm going to get your sweetness all over my fingers and lick them clean."

"Cruz."

My name is nothing but a gust of air. I hug her to me, but she's got me in the stronghold of her legs. A tidal wave of desire crashes into me. Fuck, am I going to come in my pants? Elodie's in my arms and she's almost at her peak and we've done nothing more than dry hump.

This woman drives me wild.

The tips of my fingers hit wet heat. "Fuck, Elodie. You're dripping for me."

"Yes."

I circle her swollen clit and she bucks, barking out a cry.

She twists her fingers in my hair. "So good."

"I'll give you better." I tunnel through her heat, needing to be inside of her, even if it's only up to a knuckle. As soon as I hit her entrance, I push in.

"Fuck," she grits out.

I barely get out another swipe around her clit when she stiffens and gasps.

"Cruz. Oh my god!"

My hand gets soaked and she shakes in my hold. Her walls clench around my finger, gripping it tight.

"Ride it out." My cock is throbbing, getting strangled behind my zipper, but this moment is fucking perfect. Elodie coming in my arms? Heaven.

"Shit," she says on a gasp and sinks her butt down as far as my hold will let her go.

I could get her off again. Elodie Palmer has a lot of repressed passion, but I won't push her for more. She's the finest spirit I've ever had on my lips, and I don't rush a good drink. I slowly drag my hand out from her sweats.

"That?" I suck the finger that was inside her into my mouth, loving how her lips puff open and her pupils dilate. "Was goddamn spectacular." The taste of her honeyed flavor on my tongue is better than any whiskey known to man.

A sexy smile spreads across her lips. "It's your turn." She tries to reach between us, but I grasp her wrist and bring her hand to my lips.

I hold her gaze when I kiss her soft skin. "I got what I've been wanting for so long. I told you I'm serious when it matters, and that, sugar, mattered a whole damn lot to me. We'll do more later. I want to savor this."

She runs her hands through my hair, her gaze roaming all over my face. "You're too good to be true."

"Nah," I say with a smile. "I'm a little bit naughty—when it matters."

CHAPTER TEN

Elodie

"It's only Bootleg," I mutter as I fuss with my hair. I've gone too many years just throwing it up and getting only a trim here and there. Now I'm at a loss for how to style it. I meant to tackle my date prep alone, but I texted Clem about how to do my hair because I had no idea. She was here within ten minutes.

She reclines on my bed, her feet dangling off the end. A sandal hangs off the toes of a jiggling foot. "It's your debut. Do a blowout."

Frowning, I flutter my fingers at my scalp. "It's dry."

"Do, um . . . barrel curls? Flat iron? I'm so not the one to ask."

"You do all the cute hairstyles."

She rolls her eyes. "Fun ones. Quirky. Bootleg is the wrong vibe for that." She says that with a wrinkled nose. "I'm a librarian. People expect it."

"What about the cozy mystery writer? What hair-style for that?"

"Usually unwashed and unbrushed."

"And the spicy writer?"

Her smile turns devilish. "Unwashed, unbrushed, and unbothered."

"Unless someone finds out who you are, Cutie Hancock."

Her eyes flare like I announced her secret pen name with a bullhorn in the middle of the street. "You stop that."

"I'd never betray your secret, but you need to tell me how to do my hair." I want to wow Cruz, but I'm not comfortable sexing it up like I used to. Will I ever be again? I don't know. Cruz was after me in the baggiest of clothing, but this is an official, public date. Our lunch out was less formal.

She purses her lips and studies my hair. "Down and curled. So he can fist it."

This time I'm the one rolling my eyes. "It's just a drink."

"It's a *third* date."

"I ran out on the second, so it doesn't count." Not even with that panty-incinerating kiss.

"Still counts."

My belly clenches and a little moan leaves me. He had me twisted in knots and then unwinding until I nearly floated away. I can still feel the steel band of his arms around me. Picture the way he licked his finger clean. The guy hardly touched me and I came so hard I couldn't see straight.

She whips around, her feet hitting the floor, her back

straight. Excitement gleams in her eyes. "Something happened."

"What? No."

She bounces on my bed like she's a kid and not approaching thirty. "It did. This is so fun. You've blocked me out of everything else, so you have to tell me this."

Her words hit home. She said them lightly, but it's a serious topic. I drop my hands from my hair and look at her through the mirror. "I didn't mean to shut you out."

She turns solemn.

"Dwayne wasn't a good guy," I finally admit.

"I know." When I give her a questioning look, she shrugs. "I'm an observer. I watch things, and I know you. You might not think I do, but you're older, of course I've been in your business. When you got that job in Austin, you changed."

Austin. Tulsa. Denver. I moved wherever Dwayne had the urge to go. "I knew I was in too deep and didn't want to drag any of you down."

"What happened?"

Her concern is genuine, and her curiosity has to be eating her alive. Still, I can't bring myself to list my litany of bad deeds. Not only did I nearly cut her off for years after I finished chef school, but I did it for a good-for-nothing man. And that guy is still trying to cause problems I can't solve. "Lots of things. Now help me with my hair."

Disappointment flits across her face. "One day, you're going to realize that you don't have to coddle me. Or Mom and Dad."

"It's not that."

She gives me a flat look.

"I know," I say with a sigh. "I'm ashamed and embarrassed. I walked right into an oven, past a hundred signs that said 'hot.' You remember how Mom was after our accident? I was driving and she blamed herself. I can't put her through that. Or put Dad through Mom going through all that."

"She would've duct-taped you in bubble wrap until graduation if she could've."

"She would blame herself for being too strict after that and claim it's why I got reckless." I flip the end of my hair. "I'm not proud of any of it. Don't take it personally."

She chews the inside of her cheek and nods. "Fine. I'll give you a pass. But I'm here when you're ready."

Forty-five minutes later, I vow to chop six inches off as soon as I can carve out a window of time and brush up on some how-to videos.

Clem gives me an air kiss. Her hair is now styled like mine—shiny with huge curls and pulled back into a clip. We could pass for twins if someone didn't look too closely. Her eyes are a deep emerald green and her mouth forms a cute little bow while mine stretches wider.

"Going with the glasses?" she asks.

"Yes." I might be done up, but it's a tasteful version of how I used to dress. I'm not showing a ton of skin, my hair is down, but my glasses stay on. It's a happy medium. I can be a good-looking Clark Kent and not a sexpot Superman.

"Good. They're cute." She punches me in the shoulder. "This was fun. We need to do it again. You need to take more time off so we can."

"Ow." I rub my arm, but it doesn't hurt. "Says the one working, like, three jobs."

"Writing's for fun. I can write my dream man that's never going to step foot in Huckleberry Springs."

"And then kill him off?"

"Oh no." She fans herself with her fresh bubble-gum-pink nails she painted while I got dressed. "The thrillers are because I listen to too many murder podcasts and get too many ideas. The smut is for the lady who wants the perfectly imperfect man who can give her endless orgasms. It's me. I'm the lady."

"What's this perfectly imperfect man like?" Does he have stylishly long dark hair, dancing blue eyes, a lopsided grin, and a tongue that can make me forget my name?

She smiles dreamily. "He's got to have a rough voice to go with his rough hands. He'll be grumpy but so soft, yet hard everywhere that it matters."

"Where's that?" I tease.

"I dunno. Where's Cruz hard?"

I swat at her, but she dances away, laughing. "Like I said, we need to do this more." She looks me up and down. "The town is going to collectively lose its shit when they see you."

I'm only interested in one man's reaction. She gives me a fierce hug before she leaves.

When she's gone, I inspect myself one last time in the mirror. I kept it modest, but my midnight-blue shirt clings to my torso, and the flirty wrap skirt falls past midthigh. Behind my lenses, my eyes are luminous, almost innocent looking. Without glasses, they used to be a siren for lonely men hoping to get laid.

I almost reach up and muss up my hair. The long strands cascade over my shoulders, and the whole ensemble, paired with my platform espadrilles, propels me back in time. Different faces leering at me, hoping to get under my skirt for nothing but a burger. My practiced flirting and the guilt afterward for milking mostly decent guys for easy money. The pressure to do it again and again.

I should change.

The doorbell rings, and I jump. He's here.

I press my hands against my stomach. I shouldn't have told him I'd go out with him. My quiet, hard-working life was fine without a man. It had routine. I got a lot done. I didn't go out for a drink. There are cupcakes to decorate.

He's waiting.

My excitement to see him wins out. I want to witness his reaction when he sees this version of me. I rush downstairs and open the door before he thinks I stood him up.

His mouth freezes in a half smile. "*Day-um*. You're one fine confection."

I laugh, fighting the urge to do a little curtsy. "Thank you. You look good too. You always do."

He's in a pearl-buttoned, short-sleeved, gray-striped shirt with his hair pushed off his face, sharpening the angles of his jaw and cheekbones. He cocks an elbow out. "Ma'am."

I almost swoon. "A cowboy and a gentleman?"

"On my best days."

I'm a lucky girl, one who might get lucky tonight.

Cruz

I take the smallest sip of my Foster House whiskey. Elodie's having a beer, and she just finished her first. Silas, the owner of Bootleg and an old rodeo bull rider, is irritated that I'm not chugging more, but he's doting on Elodie. I've picked my tongue off the floor a few times since she first opened the door, so I understand his infatuation.

She's not hiding under her mass of hair or swaddled in baggy clothing, and she radiates an energy that draws the eye. A guy can get lost in her big hazel eyes.

"Can I get you another, Elodie?" Silas asks nicer than I've ever heard him take an order.

"Sure. A short, please." She smiles at him, and the man straightens.

"My pleasure."

I gawk at him. I've only lived in Huckleberry Springs for five years, and I don't come here a lot, but he's been nothing but gruff each time.

The glass sloshes a little when he limps over with it. "Sorry 'bout that. Did I ever tell you about how I mangled my leg?"

"I believe so." She gives him a winning smile, probably to soften the way she's letting him down from telling it again. "But you got him for eight seconds."

Silas beams, his ruddy face flushing more. "Sure did." He knocks on the counter as he heads to another guy who just sat at the end of the bar. "Let me know if you need anything."

"Where were we?" She taps her fingers on her glass.

"You being a delinquent. I have a really hard time believing it."

"You'll never know how much of a compliment that is."

Her brow furrows. "Why?"

"There was a time no one could imagine me as the man I am today." I frown into my whiskey. How much do I tell her? All of it would be the right answer, but now that I'm faced with saying it, the truth burns my throat like a strong bourbon. "Lane and I didn't get new clothes before school each year. Our lunch accounts weren't often in the positive, and we were left home alone a lot."

"How old were you when that happened?"

"All ages. I'd be . . ." I swallow hard and my cheek twitches. I take the smallest of sips. The action calms my racing thoughts more than the drink. "Dirty. Our clothes, our bodies, and when puberty hit, a kid with no deodorant? It was brutal. Other kids aren't nice."

"Oh, Cruz. That had to be hard."

"I sharpened my fighting skills." I'm not joking.

Emotions play through her eyes—sympathy, anger for that young boy, and curiosity. Her lips quirk up. "How often did you lose?"

I appreciate that she's trying to keep the topic light. "A few times at first. I was a seventh grader, and I cocked off to some sophomore on the street. Lane had to save my stupid ass. But the time my mom's boyfriend went after Lane, I paid him back."

She frowns and a cute little divot forms between her brows. "Adult men tried to hit you?"

"More than once. She didn't have good taste in guys. Except for Myles's dad."

Her compassion is magnified. "She didn't think she deserved better."

She says it so plainly that I'm ashamed I ever blamed Mom for the way she was treated, but I was young and I blamed everyone. "I know it's not all her fault, but it was hard to see her make bad decision after bad decision."

"Being under the influence doesn't help."

"No." I take a drink of her cold beer and she playfully scowls at me, lifting my glass of whiskey to her mouth. We each take a drink. Someday, I'll get her back on my deck, having a cold drink, and telling me about her day. "I just try not to repeat her mistakes, and I refuse to be anything like my dad."

She rests her hand on mine. "I can already tell you're not, but was he that bad?"

I tangle my fingers with hers. "He was not good. He was in and out of jail for various reasons, and then he went away for a long time. Four counts of vehicular manslaughter."

Her eyes go wide. "Oh, wow. I'm sorry. I had no idea."

"It's because I don't talk about it much. He wasn't a huge part of our life, and now that he wants to be, I don't have time for him." I've never spent this long on the subject of my dad. It's a relief to talk about him. She doesn't have expectations or judgment like Lane, just questions. Lane would argue he's not the same, but the vibe is there. He understands why I cut our dad off, but he's disappointed I'm sticking to it.

"You don't talk to him?"

I drink enough whiskey to coat my tongue. "Lane does, but he's old enough to remember some of the good times between our parents. I just recall"—yelling, pain, and fear—"the bad."

She rests her hand on my forearm. "It's okay if you don't have anything to do with him. You get to be the guy who protects that little boy."

A lump forms in my throat. "Goddamn, Elodie. You can really punch the dough down and get to the heart of it."

"It's a hazard of the job," she says softly. "But you've come so much farther than both of your parents, and I know you'll give credit to Lane or Mae or even Myles, but you did the work on yourself. That's pretty amazing."

I'm not used to someone gushing about the real me. She's pretty amazing. "I don't enjoy talking about the way I grew up, but thanks for listening."

"It helps me to get to know you, and to trust what you say." She says it with such sincerity, I wish I had more baggage to bring up. "But I think it's time we move on to something you do like?"

That's an easy answer. "A sexy baker who has the sweetest little gasps when she comes." There's that blush again. Before I get hard in public, I grasp for another topic. "Tell me about you. What was culinary school like?"

Shadows drift across her eyes. "Lonely. I went to Austin and did a two-year program. I was way too young when I graduated to be off on my own, making decisions away from other adults who cared about me."

She's taking all the blame. "We all make questionable decisions when we're twenty."

"Sometimes the worst one a girl can make at that age is who she's going to date."

"Damn. You're right." When she nods, I stroke my thumb across the back of her hand. "I'm assuming that since you went to culinary school, there was a time you liked to cook."

The corner of her mouth lifts, but sadness fills her eyes. Suddenly I want to return to my fighting ways. "I used to love the rush of a kitchen. I'd go home exhausted and thrilled to do it again. Then . . . it became an obligation. I don't like to *have* to cook." She lets out a small laugh. "I met my ex at my first job, and when you get him, you get his brother, Damon. But not like *that*," she rushes to tack on. "Damon used his own women."

"I can't imagine sharing you." If I had her—if she gave herself to me—I'd make sure she never doubted that she was mine and mine alone, or that she could trust me.

"There's the right thing to say again." She takes a long swig of her beer. After she swallows, she glances at me, then chugs the rest. "I was a good country girl with big plans, but my ex was so cultured, so worldly—or so I thought." There's the melancholy smile again. "For a Montana girl whose dad only took vacations where the fly-fishing was excellent? I was a sucker."

"Don't blame—"

She puts her finger on my lips. "I know."

I lick my tongue out. A light tang of salt hits my tongue, but the hint of sweetness is there from her day of baking. I want her alone and all to myself, but I won't interrupt her when she's actually talking to me.

She traces my lips before dropping her hand. "He took me to London, then Paris. He acted like he'd been there before, and it was to buff up his ego, you know. I had no money for him to scam. I fell further under his spell. Soon, he had this big idea to start his own restaurant, but he needed time to research and raise capital. I didn't know what that involved, so I was charged with paying our rent. Utilities. Food. That was the last two years of our relationship. Before that, he used me in other ways to save money."

"What other ways?" I ask with a growl. A beat pounds in my temples. It's lucky that fucker's in jail or I'd risk being my dad's roommate in prison.

"Not like that." Her gaze jumps around the bar. It's not crowded tonight. There are a few people from around town, and the seasonal workers are easy to tell apart from the tourists, mostly because the tourists don't visit the local dive bar. Bootleg Tavern isn't recommended by the locals, but it's the biggest bar in the area.

When she brings her attention back to me, her jaw is tight. "There was a time I could get us free drinks all night long."

Her bold statement comes out of nowhere. "How?"

"Flirting. Showing my tits. Giggling."

"That usually works on a guy, but why?"

She drapes her long locks over a shoulder and gives me a sexy pout that goes right to my dick. "I could show you."

The lilt in her voice tickles my eardrums and makes me think of an old bombshell cartoon character. A modern dark-haired Marilyn Monroe. But it's not right. It's not Elodie. She's holding tension in her shoulders and the stiff way she's sitting. She does not want to show me. "No, sugar. I'm buying all your drinks tonight anyway."

Her eyes shine, but there's more shame in those hazel irises. "I would order huge meals on dates. I only nibbled at it and took it all to go."

Dates? Wasn't she with that bastard? The con dawns on me. "And Dwayne got a free meal?"

Wetness shone in her eyes. "I would go on three dates in a night so we'd all have a free meal."

Anger pushes at my temples. That's a lot of pressure for a young girl dating her superior. "Did you want to do that?"

She gives me a tiny shake of her head. "I did it anyway. I told you that we worked as chefs together, but his brother also served at the same restaurant. So we ran the con in our workplace. Damon would act like he didn't know me and the rest of the staff thought it was funny."

Ran the con? Something about the way she said it tells a whole other story. "Did you do stuff like that a lot?"

"Yes." She casts her gaze down. "It was just . . ."

I cup her chin and lift her face up. "It's okay, sugar. You can talk to me." We're an oasis in the middle of Bootleg. Even Silas is chatting across the room with some ranchers.

"I've never told anyone about this," she whispers. Her brow furrows and she looks around. "I shouldn't be talking about this in public."

I dig out my wallet and toss down well more than what our drinks cost. "Have a good night," I call to Silas.

He nods goodbye to Elodie, but his attention is on the money.

"Where are we going?" Elodie asks as I help her off the stool.

"We'll drive around. So you feel comfortable talking."

She stops, her hands on my arms. "This is a date. I don't want—I want to have fun."

I asked her to dredge up some of her worst memories, and she did. When the subject of my past got too heavy, she changed it. "I think you have fun when you dance."

That lovely blush dusts her cheeks. "That's private."

I lead her to a small clearing by the old jukebox. Silas doesn't like to have a band, but sometimes people dance. I pull her close to me as I check out the selection. "What should I play?"

"I don't think Silas and I have the same taste in music," she says wryly. The swell of her breasts pushes against my arm, and an electrical current runs right to my dick. "Do some country songs."

"Something with a good beat?" I flip through options.

"No, something slow." She points to "Cowboy Take Me Away."

"Are you trying to tell me something, sugar?" I put money in and a few seconds later, the first notes flow through the speakers.

"There aren't as many about whiskey distillers taking me away."

I chuckle and pull her into my arms. "Even less about vodka and gin distillers."

We move together. She twines her arms around my neck and tucks her face into my shoulder. I'm content holding her. I never imagined how she'd open up to me, and in Bootleg of all places. But in a way, it makes sense. There's no pretense at Bootleg Tavern.

The way her body is pressed to mine makes it hard to

concentrate on our slow two-step. Eventually, the song stops and it's just the two of us by the jukebox.

Silas's lilting steps sound from behind me. "Play a faster song next time," he grumbles as he clears empty glasses from a table near us.

Elodie's chuckle flutters the material of my shirt. "Sorry, Silas. We'll choose 'Goodbye Earl' if we dance again."

"We can still slow dance to it," I whisper in her ear.

She tilts her face up to smile at me. "Or we can go back to my place."

"Say no more, sugar." She doesn't have to tell me twice. I tow her out of the bar and into the parking lot. I'd pick her up, but that might seem too desperate.

When I open the passenger door, she flops into her spot and whips the seat belt across her body. As much as I want to get inside her, I can't have her thinking I'm some sex-starved man and that's all I want out of her.

Leaning in, I cup her face. "Tonight meant a lot." I touch my lips to hers. If I go too much further, I'll drive with the worst erection of my life. "Best date of my life."

"A dive bar and a nineties song?" Still, she smiles. "Mine too."

"Yeah?"

She drags my head down to kiss me again. "Yeah."

I get behind the wheel, throw the pickup into drive, and peel out of the lot. I need a goddamn award for the restraint I have driving the short distance to her bakery. When I park at her back door, she's out before me and is unlocking her door. I put my hands on her hips and nudge her hair out of the way with my nose to kiss the nape of her neck.

A needy moan leaves her just as she pushes the door open. I nearly trip over her in our rush to get inside. Then she swings the door shut and slams her back against it.

"I finally have you all to myself." I line myself up with her, both of my hands on either side of her neck and my thumbs tilting her chin up. I'm rock hard, and I should be used to it by now around her, but I keep from pinning her between my erection and the door.

Our lips aren't even touching, but my tongue is twined with hers. A faint buzzing sound taps at my mind. I forget it in a second when she yanks the bottom of my shirt free. Her fingertips are warm when they land on my stomach. I clench my gut and a groan resonates from me to her.

The buzzing starts again, and her roaming touch stalls. Slowly our kiss breaks and only our breaths mingle.

"Someone's calling you." I'm coherent enough to figure that out. I prop my hands on each side of her head.

"No one usually does."

The bakery phone starts ringing and she jumps, alarm filling her eyes. "Crap. Something's wrong."

She ducks under my arm and covers the distance between us and the noisy phone in three steps. "Hello?"

She stiffens. "No. I'll be right over." She shakes her head. "No. Call them. We'll figure it out later."

When she hangs up, she doesn't turn around. "Mom fell and hit her head. And of course it's after the clinics are all closed, so Dad has to take her to the ER. I told him to call the ambulance."

I tap the fob in my pocket. "Let's go."

"You don't have to—"

"It's late and you've had a couple of beers. I gotchu."

She nods and her eyes glitter. "I didn't even think of that. Thank you."

"Anytime." I'll always mean it.

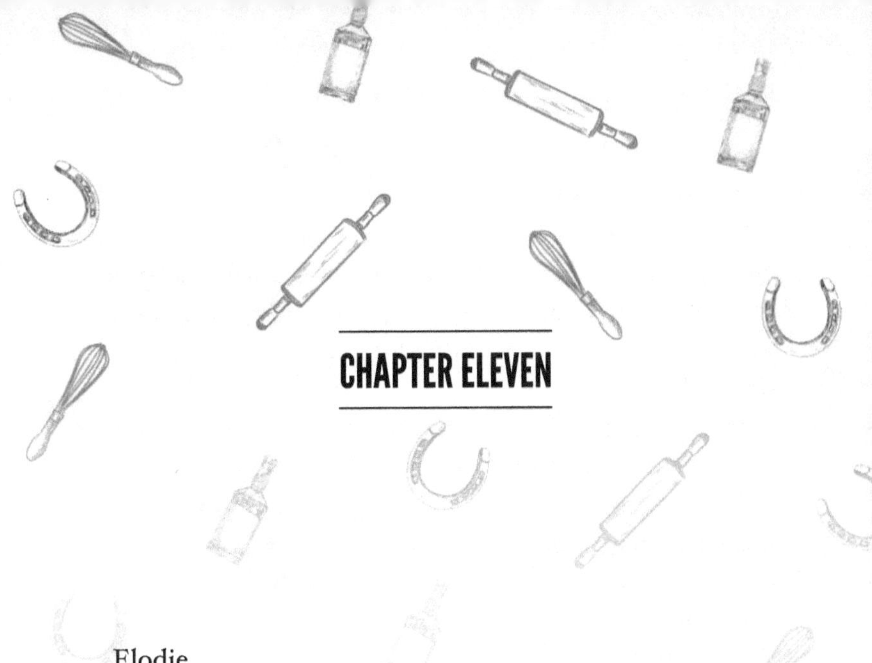

CHAPTER ELEVEN

Elodie

My hands twitch and a little moan slips out before I come fully wake. A hard shoulder is under my cheekbone, and there's a knot in my neck. I lift my head and groan. It's Monday morning, but I'm not in my bed, and I'm definitely not in the bakery.

"Let me get that for you." It's Cruz I fell asleep on. He covers the back of my neck with his warm hand and massages. This man can work his magic in all sorts of ways. I let my eyelids drift shut.

The smell of a sanitized environment surrounds me, and the lights above us shine bright through my eyelids. Mom's in the Billings ER, and Dad is sleeping on an ungodly uncomfortable chair next to her.

I was with them long enough to get an update, then I came out to the waiting room with Cruz. Mom's supposed to get discharged soon, and instead of having

Clem miss work to pick us up, Cruz said he had no issues bringing us home.

A pressure swells in my chest, pushing out and filling all the nooks and crannies. He didn't want me to scam a free drink for him. He acted as if my past experience wasn't my fault. And he didn't leave me when I couldn't sleep with him, again.

Last night was a whirlwind. I fielded calls from Clem. Mom's head hurt and I didn't get much time to talk to her before the doctor stopped in. Dad kept me posted about what was going on. Blood draws, CAT scans, pain meds, and then waiting. Cruz has been by my side through it all, getting me water, snacks, and shoulder rubs.

I should be worried about how much time I'm out for work, but I can't. I'm grateful I could be there for Mom, and even gladder Cruz is with me.

"Can I get you something to eat?" he asks.

I rub my eyes. A raccoon could beat me in a Who Wore It Better contest. Before Cruz and I left the bakery, I changed into a loose shirt and shorts, but I still have my platform espadrilles on. I have to look ridiculous.

I let out a dry laugh. When he looks at me, eyes full of questions, I shake my head. "You're offering to buy me a meal, and I look like hell."

"Are you running a pity con on me?" He smiles as he asks, and he speaks softly so no one else can hear.

How am I at the point that I can talk about this part of my life so glibly with someone? "Most definitely, but I feel like it's too much work for too little payout."

"Pretty bold of you to get your parents in on the scam."

Another chuckle spills out of me. "My bad. I'll work solo next time."

He presses a kiss to the side of my head. "I'll go find a breakfast burrito or something. I can get something for your dad if you want to run one to him."

A message buzzes through on my phone.

Dad: We're almost out of here. Mom's hungry. Can you grab her some food?

I show Cruz the text.

He stands. "Four breakfast burritos coming up. Coffee?"

"Yes, please. That's probably half of Mom's headache if she still has one."

I watch his denim-clad ass when he walks away. He's hardly slept and his swagger makes it look like he's ready to go out and do hours of chores. That man has not given up on me, and I'm so glad I wasn't alone all night.

While waiting, I finger-comb my hair and twist it into a loose braid. By the time Cruz returns with a bag of food and a carrier full of coffees, my mom is getting wheeled out by my dad. A nurse walks next to them.

"I'll get the chariot." Cruz winks at my mom. Her smile is wan, but appreciation shines in her eyes.

The warm pressure is back in my chest, filling every niche possible.

"So that's him?" Mom says when we're outside in the fresh air, waiting for Cruz to pull around. "Your dad's had a lot to say."

"*I* have a lot to say about him." Finally, there's something good I can share with them beyond the bakery. "I'll have to tell you."

"I hope you do."

A few minutes later, Cruz pulls up and helps Mom

into the back seat and I get in next to her. All the way back to Huckleberry Springs, Dad chats with him in the front while Mom dozes. I let my weariness sink in and admire his profile. The way he held me while we danced. There was no hip thrusting or shaking of my ass, and he cradled me tenderly against him.

While I can't take my eyes off Cruz, Dad asks my date all about growing up in Bozeman, and Cruz politely skims over the most dramatic parts of his childhood, dwelling on his time working at the Bailey Beef ranch and learning the ropes of distilling instead.

When we reach their house, Cruz doesn't dump and run. He's Mom's support, helping her inside. She must really be out of it if she's not pestering him with all the questions she slept through Dad asking. Then Cruz waits with me until Clem arrives to stay with our parents, and he drives me back to the bakery.

"I'll walk you in," he says with a regretful note to his voice, "but then I've gotta go. Iverson's covering for me at Foster House."

"You should've told me." I could've figured something out.

"Nope, sugar. The guys and I help each other out all the time. I am right where I want to be."

He says that after being my pillow in a waiting room all night. So much hotter than all his muscles. "I'm glad you are."

When I get out of the pickup, he comes around, putting an arm around my waist. I want to lean back into him, to let someone else carry the heavy load for once, but I don't, or I'll fall asleep. He'd probably stand in one spot and keep me from falling all day too. Is this what being with a real man is like? "Want some cupcakes to take to work?"

"Nah, Elodie. They'd only make me think of how sugary sweet you are, and I can't get my work done when I'm horny as fuck."

The laughter is unexpected. "Fair enough."

"Not fair at all." He tilts my face up and places a firm kiss on my lips. When he pulls away, his eyes are heavy lidded. "It seems to be a condition I've been afflicted with a lot lately."

I rise to my tiptoes and give him another quick kiss. "Me too."

My breath hitches at his smoldering gaze, but I slip into the bakery and shut the door behind me without looking back. Otherwise, I might dive right back into his arms.

Cruz

I'm in the rickhouse with the forklift to retrieve the barrel getting dumped and bottled today. The smell of warm grains, old wood, and musty dirt surrounds me. Only a faint chirping of birds makes it through the walls. This is one of my favorite places to be. It's quiet, and it's tangible proof of my accomplishments.

It's the weekend again, and I've barely gotten to see Elodie. The street fair is three weeks away, and the distillery is in full swing, preparing for the increased tourism load and readying for our booth at the fair and planning out our autumn distribution and cocktail menu.

I brought her dinner two nights ago, the same food she ordered from La Taqueria. She was pale with circles under her eyes. Was she tired? Stressed? She wouldn't share. Her table was scattered with notes and calculations of what she'd need to make for the street fair and when. A large number was scrawled across the top of one sheet and circled so hard and so many times the paper had almost torn.

Something's still going on, and she's not talking.

I told her I was a patient man, and I have to be a man of my word. My pretty little baker is opening up to me. I just have to keep working at it. Unfortunately, I also have to keep working here and at the small ranch I run with my brother.

I locate the barrel I need and double-check the details stamped into the front. Yep, it's the whiskey I'm looking for. I'm about to hop back onto the forklift when my phone buzzes.

Elodie: Can you call when you have a second?

At the risk of looking like I watch my phone waiting on her texts, I dial her up.

She answers with a breathless "Hello?"

"Hey." I'm grinning and I can't even see her. God, I've got it bad, and I don't even care.

"Hi. Um . . ."

I tense. Is she going to tell me that she can't see me anymore? That I'm too much of a distraction, and she's got a business to run?

"My dad wants to invite you to a barbecue Sunday night. He wants to thank you for everything you did."

I grin and lean against the cool metal of the forklift. "I'd love to, but only if you want me there."

"Why wouldn't I?"

My smile stretches farther. That's what I like to hear. "You might be sick of me."

Her soft laugh travels over the line. "I haven't had the time to get sick of you."

"Are you sure? I might need to bring you one more meal to make sure."

"If it's the sesame chicken from Wok and Rolls, that might help me decide."

"Tonight? I have to work the tasting room tomorrow, and Wok and Rolls closes before we do."

"I'm here all night." Weariness pours out of her answer.

"You need some rest."

"I know," she says with a yawn.

"I'm off at five. I'll swing home and do some chores, pick up food, and be right over."

"You sure?"

"One hundred percent. What can I bring to the party?"

"Party's a strong word when it's related to my parents," she says and I love the wry tone in her voice. She's tired but not beaten down by what's been bothering her. "I've got the dessert. How about that pasta salad?"

"You liked my noodles."

"Cruz, I haven't been around your noodles enough to know. We keep getting interrupted."

My laughter spills out of me. "I'll bring so much pasta salad you can't help but be satisfied."

"My parents will really appreciate this," she says softly.

I appreciate her parents for giving me another reason to get close to Elodie when she's neck-deep in work. "It's my pleasure. I'd like to get to know them when they're not worried about their health and safety. I might even have to study up on structural integrity or some other architectural terms."

"He'll be too busy asking you about distilling. Dad loves to learn new things. FYI, if you want to butter up Mom, the new library wing's named after her. It's her maiden name. The Patricia Lang addition."

"No shit? I never put that together, but I'll keep it in mind. As much as I've turned into a good boy, I don't hang out at the library."

"Mm-hmm." It's more of a resigned hum. "Dad donated to the park foundation, so he got a gazebo with his name on it."

No wonder Elodie is afraid to upset them. She says she doesn't want to concern them, but she also doesn't want to feel unworthy. The Palmer who caused problems instead of helping to solve them.

Her parents and sister are that family, the ones who contribute to the community to help poor-as-hell kids like me. I grew up lashing out at kids who had wealth and privilege and the audacity to be nice on top of it. If they'd made a mistake, I would've torn them apart. Socially, at least. "I look forward to the picnic, and I appreciate both the invite and a chance to hang with you again."

"Thanks, Cruz."

"My pleasure." I mean it. Anything with her is.

When we hang up, I stare at the phone until the hinges on the front door squeak loud.

Lane enters, wincing. "We got any lube out here?"

"For him or for her?"

"The stuff that warms when you rub it." He smirks. "I'll remember to grab a can when I come out next." His gaze dips to the phone in my hand. "Talking to your girlfriend? Was wondering what was taking you so long. Haven got tired of waiting and went to lunch."

I didn't mean to hold him up, but worth it. "Elodie's parents invited me out for a meal on Sunday."

He crosses his arms and appraises me. "Hanging out at their house?"

"Her dad likes me, and her mom was concussed." I already told him about the hospital stay and the ride home.

He arches a brow. "You nervous?"

"No."

"You should be."

"Why? The older crowd loves me. I'm a hit at bingo when Edna asks us to go with her." Our part-time accountant takes in every person under fifty as one of her kids or grandkids.

"I was talking about Elodie. You're in love."

"It's too soon." I'm head over boots for her. Wound so tight that I'm afraid to see my water bill after jacking off to her moans and tight nipples against my palms. I can't quit thinking about her and doing everything to make her happy. So, yeah. Maybe I'm boarding the love train. "You don't think I have it in me?"

"I wondered."

"What about you? It's not like you've had a relationship last longer than a pair of socks."

"You gotta specify what type of socks. They aren't made like they used to be." He shakes his head. "I know you have it in you, but you never let anyone in except for me and Myles. And Mae."

"One, I haven't found anyone before who hooked me like Elodie. And two, just because I don't take Dad's calls or write back to him doesn't mean I'm broken. Doesn't mean you are either. Mom didn't love us, and it's not our fault. You can put yourself out there for someone who has their shit together instead of people who are proven to let you down."

He scoffs. "I know."

"Do you?" When he started down this path, I thought he was talking about me. Is he afraid his issue is that he hasn't found anyone, or that he has and passed them by?

"Yes. I also think Mom loved us in her fucked-up way. She kept it together until I turned eighteen."

Then he went from a surrogate parent to a father figure I didn't listen to. He's been putting himself in that responsible role ever since and using it to buffer himself from life. "You'll find someone. You just haven't met her yet."

He scoffs. "Sure."

"Nope. I can see it. She's going to be the one who'll give you blue balls and you'll deal with it for weeks or months or years because you know she's going to be worth it, and if it doesn't happen, you still won't mind because what you got was enough."

Both of his brows tick higher as I talk. "Shit, Cruz. I came in here to see what was taking you so long to get the damn barrel, not to get a life lesson I don't need." He starts for the door, but when he puts his hand on the knob, he pauses. "For what it's worth, I'm happy for you. It makes those years less . . . regrettable."

He doesn't have to specify exactly which years. All of them. He changed my diapers when he was barely out of his. He made sure I had my hat and gloves in the winter, sometimes giving me his own. And he sacrificed his wild teen years to finish raising me and keep me out of jail.

If the only way I can honor him is to fall in love and be a decent partner, it's going to be an easy task. All I have to do is the opposite of what our parents did.

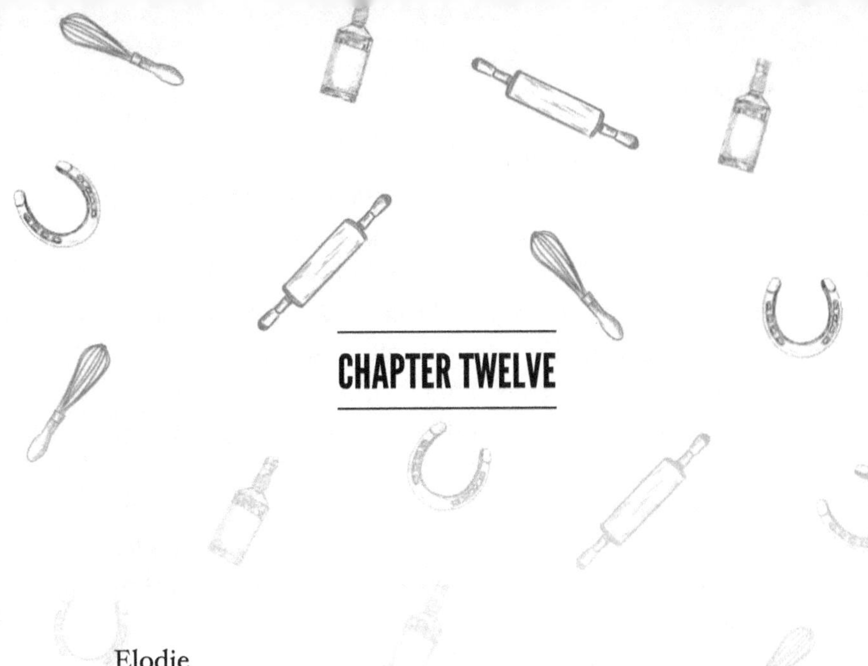

CHAPTER TWELVE

Elodie

Cruz picked me up to go to my parents' place. I stifled yawns the whole way while balancing a tray of salted caramel eclairs on my lap. I liked dressing up for our date, but it's also good to be back in my loose shorts and shirt with sandals. Even nicer that Cruz gave me the same smoldering look.

When we arrived, Clem was already there and so was Uncle Karl. I introduced them, and Dad and Karl have dominated Cruz's attention since we arrived and all through eating. Cruz has probably shared every scrap of distilling knowledge he knows and received just as much gossip about his neighbor, Hutch Langley.

Mom's not allowed to do any work, so the guys are cleaning up the meal too. I'm sitting on a chair beside Clem on the floating deck Dad built behind the house. Mom has her face tipped to the sky.

As if Cruz senses me staring at him, he slides his gaze

over and gives me a little smirk. I pass him an equally sly smile. Does he know how good he looks just standing there? He doesn't have to do more than wake up, run a hand through his hair, and throw on jeans and cowboy boots to get my hormones buzzing. My fatigue isn't as debilitating when I'm admiring his muscles.

"I think Dad approves of Cruz," Clem murmurs.

I push my glasses up my nose and sit straighter. "He should."

Mom chuckles. If I didn't know she'd bumped her head, I wouldn't be able to tell. Her gray hair is pulled back and the pleasant expression on her face is exactly what I want to see. "He's not the hard parent to win over, but I have to say, I agree. Cruz is an open book."

He's been as honest as he can be. Will he and I always be guarded around Mom and Dad? Cruz, because he doesn't want to dredge up a guy who doesn't exist anymore, and me, because I don't want my parents to spiral over something they had no control over.

What if they knew, and we could just be? Would the grief and stress be worth it? Would my parents accept him, so he doesn't hide his past from me? He's a good guy, and he should be accepted for who he is and not how charming he can be.

Cruz's laughter drifts over to me and my lips lift into a smile. The man is easygoing and utterly charming. He doesn't boast. He's not arrogant. He's honest and relatable. And he wants to be mine.

Wouldn't it be nice to fall asleep with him in a bed this time? Sex with him might scramble my brains, but the cuddling would be off the charts.

"I like that I've met him," Mom says, and I'm yanked into awareness.

Was I falling asleep again? With nothing but Cruz and cuddling on my mind? Yes, probably. "I like that you've met him too."

Clem nods. "I even know more than his name and what he does for a living, but that's thanks to working with him."

"You should count your lucky stars you didn't work with my ex."

Both of them look at me. Mom's lips form a troubled line. Damn. My gaze strays to Cruz yet again, still chatting by the porch with my dad and Uncle Karl. I wasn't going to touch this subject, but it slipped out. I cracked open the door, and I want to shut it again.

For years, I gave them the bare minimum—when I actually answered their calls. Guilt chews my insides, but that door is going to stay cracked. I won't shut it completely, not after opening up to Cruz. "I knew something was wrong, and I didn't want to admit it. Now I just want to forget."

"But Cruz?" Mom's approving gaze touches on the group of men. "No history of being bad news?"

I know about the history. That's the difference. "He's not perfect, but he's worked on himself."

"Then save him from another hour of small talk and interrogation." Mom wiggles to get out of her chair, her feet barely touching the ground until she's almost all the way out. "Go get your dessert, and I'll distract your dad."

Laughing, I make my way toward the kitchen to retrieve my eclairs. When I turn from the fridge, Cruz is waiting to take the container from me like my very own dessert.

I could get used to this, to having him there when I

need a hand. "How are you holding up under their attention?"

He flashes his crooked grin. "It's the most fun I've had in a long time. Except for when a pretty girl stopped in at the distillery at closing time."

Tendrils of heat unfurl in my belly, and they only stoke hotter when he gives me a quick kiss. I feel like I'm a teen and I've snuck a date through my window, which is something I've never done.

He carefully tucks the eclairs under an arm. "I've been looking forward to your . . . cannoli."

I let out the girliest giggle. Who am I right now?

He leans against the island and adopts a crooked grin. "Are you ready to go on another date with me?"

I'm ready for so much more than a date. I might be ready to drop, but I'm not missing another chance with Cruz. "How about you come over tonight instead?"

"You don't have to ask me twice." He pushes off the island and leans close enough to murmur in my ear. "And you'll have free rein with me."

My heartbeat thrums between my thighs, and a needy quiver runs down my spine. I have so many ideas about what to do with his hard body and that wicked mouth of his, but my business brain won't shut off. "Whatever I do might be pretty quick because I have a lot of baking to catch up on tomorrow, along with two wedding cakes and a birthday cake."

His grin is unrepentant and full of promise, infusing me with enough adrenaline to chase away a large chunk of my fatigue. "I'm at your mercy."

Cruz

Just like the night we got interrupted by her mom's injury, Elodie and I are all over each other as we plunge through her back door. My tongue's in her mouth, and as soon as we're fully inside, I kick the door shut behind me.

Again, I pin her between me and the door. She kicks her shoes off and I manage to toe out of my boots while keeping our lips locked. The salted caramel flavor lingering from the eclairs is just what she's going to taste like when I get her naked.

I hook my fingers over the hem of her shorts to drag them down, but she shakes her head and grabs my arms. Then she spins me around and my back hits the door with a thump. "It's your turn."

When she yanks my zipper down, I suck in a breath. Having her mouth on me is a recurring fantasy come true, but it can't be an obligation for her. "Aw, sugar, as much as I want you to do that, you don't have to."

"I know." She flicks open the button of my fly.

I'd be all about her pleasure, I'd insist, but my dick has been pestering me for weeks when it comes to Elodie Palmer. And the way she's clawing open the fly of my pants, who am I to deny her something she wants to do?

My brain can be a selfish prick, but all other logic and good intentions vanish as soon as her warm fingers curl around my shaft. A long groan leaves me and her grin is unadulterated wickedness. She tugs the rest of me free and pumps her hand up and down the length. Blistering pleasure sears me behind my eyes. I have to brace myself—against the floor, against the door, fuck, anything. Nothing has felt this good. Ever.

When she drops to her knees, I'm a goner. The sight of Elodie with her big eyes gazing at me from behind her glasses and her lips plump from my kiss is an erotic sight that will never leave my brain. My spank bank has one image in it and it's this.

When her lush lips part and she licks that pink tongue across the crown of my cock, I hiss. "Fuck me, Elodie. You're going to twist me into a pretzel with nothing but that mouth."

"Good. Then you'll feel the same way as me." She wraps her hand around the base of my erection and takes me slowly into her mouth, her cheeks hollowing as she goes.

My desire cranks to infinity, and I fight my way down from my peak. I will not come within a minute of her touching me. This should be an exception, but the night I have planned with her is going to be long, and it's going to start with her coming on my face, and finish with me orgasming inside of her while we come at the same time.

But surely I can enjoy just another minute of this.

Her head's bobbing and it'd be easier on my impending climax if I didn't watch the glistening crown of my cock slip in and out of her wet mouth. When she swirls her tongue around the tip and moans, I gently cup her chin. I'm going to lose it and I have too much planned. She releases me, and my pulse beats through my hard-on, ready to let her resume what she was doing.

My breath saws in and out of me. "I'm not going to last, and I really need to come inside you."

Her eyes are shining when she says, "Let's go upstairs."

"Yes, ma'am." My shirt falls over my dick when I help her up. I'd pick her up, but she takes my hand and tows me behind her.

The stairs are narrow and I duck my head to keep from knocking myself out on the low ceiling. We emerge in a cozy studio apartment. A nightlight glows by a partially open door that must be a bathroom. A bed with rumpled covers is in the middle under a narrow rectangular window with closed blinds. A small counter and stovetop run along one wall and a dresser with clothing piled on top rests against the opposite side.

She doesn't stop as she pulls me to the bed.

"Get on." My command is guttural. The shirt material brushing against my sensitized skin isn't nearly as good as Elodie's mouth, but it's enough to shout loud and clear that I haven't come yet. "I'm going to strip you down."

She gets on her hands and knees on the edge of the bed and casts a glance over her shoulder at me. Then she wiggles her ass.

"Naughty girl." My groan echoes through the whole room. I stalk toward her. "I cannot wait to have you sit on my face."

"Sitting on faces feels like a fourth-date thing." A playful smile ripples across her face.

She flips to her butt just as my knees hit the bed. She sets her glasses on the nightstand, and I prowl over her.

"Lunch, dinner at my house—which one hundred percent counts," I add when she opens her mouth. "Bootleg, and . . ." I grin wide. "Dinner at your parents'. What does that add up to?"

She laughs and fists her hands in my shirt. I let her drag it over my head. I want to get her shorts off, but the way she's devouring my bare chest with her gaze holds me still. I'm caught between wanting to dive into everything Elodie Palmer ASAP and needing to stretch and savor every single moment. She's the finest spirit I've ever gotten my hands on.

She traces a finger over the tattoo on my arm. It's a curving highway circling my biceps with three dots, like three stops on a map. "A road, like the theme of your name, Lane, and Myles."

The warmth blooming inside my chest isn't something I've experienced when I've been half naked with a girl before. "You're the only one who's guessed that other than my brothers. Mom liked the theme and ran with it. Drove with it would be more accurate."

"It's sweet." She runs her fingertip along one of the lanes, then switches to the horseshoe with a *B* inside of it over my heart. "Do you have any other tattoos?"

"I stopped at these."

She returns to the inked highway and trails her index finger along the other side. Threading her hands through my hair, she drags me down for a kiss.

I don't linger long. I'm addicted to her sweet taste, but I have other plans. I kiss my way down her neck as she writhes underneath me, entirely too dressed. For the second time, I dip my fingers underneath her waistband. Just as I'm about to pull down, she gasps.

Half sitting, she props herself on her elbows. "The door? Did I lock it? Shit. Sorry."

She wiggles to get off the bed. Instead of being frustrated, I let out a little laugh and put my hand on her leg until she stops her delectable squirming. "It's not your fault I haven't driven doors and locks right out of your mind yet."

She slaps her hands on either side of her face. "Oh god. I'm so sorry."

Embarrassment floods her cheeks, and it's so damn cute, my brain splinters. She's the perfect mix of adorable and sexy.

A shudder travels through me. Soon. I'll get to have her soon. "I'll go lock it."

Relief and gratitude fill her eyes as she lies back. "Thank you."

"Never a problem." I flip my shirt back over my erection and jog downstairs. I lock the doorknob and flip the dead bolt. She really could do with some alarms and real security, but she probably knows that. Another thing that has to wait for spare money.

To make sure nothing else interrupts us, I go through the bakery to the front door and check those locks. We're secure.

I take the stairs up, keeping my head down. The last thing I need ruining this night is a concussion. When I reach her small apartment, it's quiet and dark like before.

A sense of apprehension descends over me. Nothing terrible, just a notion that tonight isn't going to turn out the way I hoped. I approach the bed and a sprawled-out Elodie. Her limbs are limp and her head is turned to the side. A puff of air escapes her lips, like she just tumbled off a cliff into a deep sleep.

My disappointment is no match for how damn cute she is. I study her, wondering at what point it's creepy to stand by her bed and stare. Her dark lashes are stark against her cheeks. A few fingers twitch a moment before she rolls to her side, tucking her hands under her chin. She curls her legs up.

Her phone is almost falling out of her back pocket, so I carefully slip it out and she stays asleep, which she obviously needs more than an orgasm. I set the phone on the nightstand by a small lamp and a framed picture of two little girls with dark hair sitting on a bench that has their dad's name. The youngest of the girls has a big grin, missing teeth, and the older girl appears to be scrutinizing the camera or whoever is the photographer. A young Elodie was still a serious Elodie.

Next, I take one of the blankets that's not completely under her and drape it over her.

I could leave, but if she wakes up and I'm gone, will she think I ditched her when I couldn't get laid? If I stay and she wakes up to me, will she scream at me to leave because I smashed past another boundary? I don't know. But I don't want to leave.

I'm going to risk her wrath. I'd rather she be angry with me than hurt by me. Besides, waking up beside Elodie won't be a bad way to experience a Monday morning.

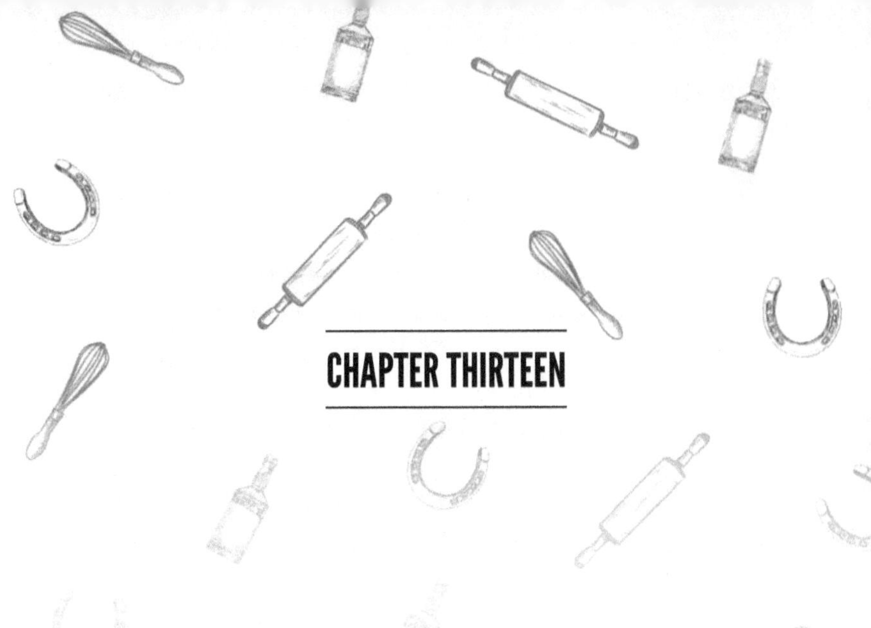

CHAPTER THIRTEEN

Elodie

When my phone's alarm goes off, I bolt upright. My memory's a haze, but the blaring tone keeps me sitting up. What happened? Where am I? When did I go to bed?

A male groan vibrates beside me, and I freeze. Who's with me?

The chimes of my alarm continue to ring as the fog dissipates from my brain. Cruz and my family get-together. Cruz and I making out. Cruz stopping my blow job. Me about to get laid. And then what?

He was over me, and he was going to be *in* me, and then he went to check the locks. Horror swamps me. Did I fall asleep? I pat myself and look down. My shirt and bra are in place and my shorts are still on.

"Goddamn, sugar." His sleep-roughened voice sounds so out of place in my small apartment. "How early do you get up?"

"What are you still doing here? Where's my phone?" My eyes adjust with the nightlight and I find my phone on the nightstand on the other side of Cruz.

He's sprawled on his back with a hand tucked behind his head. His chest is gloriously bare, but thanks to the covers, I can't see the rest. Without opening his eyes, he grabs my phone and hands it to me.

"Early." I silence the alarm. "I usually set a different time for Monday so I can sleep longer, but I have to make up for last night." Speaking of . . . I'm still confused. If I fell asleep, why is he still here? "What happened?"

"You gave me fabulous head and then passed out like a sex goddess who's been up for seven days straight." He cracks open an eye. "I didn't want to leave and have you think that just because I didn't get some, I jetted."

My confused panic fades and my heart rate returns to a normal rate. If he wasn't here, I'd still be fretting about how much I disappointed him. "That's sweet."

"It was a good excuse to get more time with you." He rolls up and his abs crinkle.

My mouth goes dry at the sight, but since I didn't brush my teeth last night before falling asleep, I scoot to the edge of the bed and let my legs hang over. "I seriously fell asleep?"

"A regular Sleeping Beauty."

My cheeks warm. I might've daydreamed about cuddling with him, but not passing out without getting to enjoy him. "But it couldn't have taken you more than a minute to check the locks."

"You were tired. You've been working hard." He sets his feet on the floor. "What are we baking this morning?"

"Cruz!" I twist and prop a leg on the bed. "You aren't staying to work. You have your own job."

He stands and yawns, scratching the back of his neck. His navy-blue boxers don't do much to hold back his morning wood. Ugh. I fell asleep on *that*?

He catches me looking and smirks. "I'm up, and I like the company. Gimme a hairnet, and I'll do the dishes or something. I'll ask Lane to check on my critters. Rufus usually joins whoever's doing chores and gets some treats."

"You haven't gotten much sleep."

"Neither have you. The sooner we get your baking done, the quicker I can finally get you naked." He gives my thigh a pointed look. "I haven't seen those flowers yet."

"It's my mom's bouquet." I lift the hem of my shorts. I never get to show them off, and this one is my favorite. "I took one of my parents' wedding pictures to the artist."

"Got any more?"

"Pictures? Yes." I flash him a secretive smile. "You want to see?"

"All the pictures you want to show me—and any more tattoos."

"Oh?" I say innocently, dragging my hem farther up. "You're asking if I have more tattoos?"

His pupils swallow the rest of his eyes. "Yes." My second alarm goes off and he snaps out of his trance.

I fumble with my phone. "Sorry. I usually set three or four different times just in case. It's hard to get up some days." Most days.

"Yes, it is. So let's get to work."

I'd rather get to showing him where the rest of my

ink is. I'd like to see his horseshoe up closer. I'd like to lick it.

"You keep looking at me like that," he says in a low voice, "and we aren't going to get those wedding cakes made."

We. I like the sound of that way too much. "What about your job?"

"I'm off today and tomorrow, and Lane owes me way more than one day of chores. I'll use the bathroom after you."

I can't resist him anymore, and I don't want to chase him off anyway. To keep me on task, I grab an armload of clothes. "All right. But I need to shower first. Help yourself to . . ." I scan my haphazard apartment. I only sleep here. The rest of my time is spent downstairs, working. He has a nice house. A deck. A backyard. I'm like a ghost in my apartment. "Uh, help yourself to some juice in the fridge. I might have some waffles in the freezer you can throw in the toaster."

"Homemade?"

"If I want a good one, yes." I escape into the bathroom.

I take the fastest shower of my life and get dressed. I grabbed the most atrocious clothing. My baggy shirt is an old one Clem got me for my birthday last year with a cartoon chef on it that reads *I got big buns and I cannot lie.* The leggings in my pile are a welcome sight. With the ovens running all day, I'm going to get hot.

Blow-drying my hair takes way too long, but I get it dry enough. Then I wrap it into a bun on top of my head, roll on a fabric headband, and look into the foggy mirror. Staring back at me is a girl who fell asleep on a guy who can give her the best orgasms of her life.

Way to go.

Yet he's still here.

When I step out of the bathroom, I smell waffles and syrup. He's set my small table with two plates. The brown bottle of Wisconsin maple syrup my parents brought home from their last fishing trip sits in the middle. He's reclining against the island, shirt still off. His pants are on, but the fly hangs open, giving me a glimpse of his navy-blue underwear.

He flashes that crooked grin, and I'm ready to toss my shirt off and tell my customers I got sick and have to close for a day.

Except I have another payment to make to Dwayne.

The toaster pops, and I jump.

"Nervous?" he asks.

"It's just weird. Having you here." No guy has been in this space with me.

"Good or bad?"

I pretend to think. My glasses are on the nightstand, and though his face is fuzzy, I can make out a smirk. "Waking up yet again to a hot man and then he makes me breakfast?"

He grabs one of the plates for the waffles. "Technically, you made breakfast and I heated it up."

"I haven't had this before. It's nice."

His eyes darken, probably because he can read between the lines after our date at the bar. I was taken advantage of, but Cruz is caring for me. "I'm gonna be a lot more than nice to you. I just have to run home and change after I shower."

"Worried I'm going to kick you out for wearing day-old clothing?" I'm teasing, but I catch the way he smothers a wince. "Are you really worried?"

"I don't like wearing dirty clothes."

"But they're not dirty." I don't have to see his shirt to know that it looks no different than last night. His jeans don't have a speck of dust on them and hardly any wrinkles.

"I just prefer fresh stuff."

I trail my fingers through the hair he's already finger-combed. There are shadows in his eyes. The past is haunting him. The kid who was left alone with only another boy to care for him. Two kids doing the best they could with almost nothing. "You do what makes you feel better. Just know that I don't think less of you because you're wearing the same clothes you had on yesterday."

"Noted." His eyes lighten, but not all the way. He's going to run home, and I'll support him as much as he has me.

He pulls my chair out for me like he can't wait to use all the manners he was taught. "There is something you can do for me."

"Yeah?"

He takes a plate, grabs the waffles, and returns. "When we go downstairs, turn that music up loud and shake your ass for me."

I've never had such a fun day at work. Cruz kept the music up, and I tried not to dance like I wanted twenties thrown in my direction, but he remembered the song from last time. His whistles only egged me on.

We baked and cleaned and danced. All the orders are made and in the cooler. I have cookies, cupcakes, cruffins, and trays of chocolate-dipped fruit to put out in the morning. And I dabbled with a new whiskey glaze out of the Butter Barrel that Cruz brought me a few weeks ago for an apricot bread for the Taste of Springs street fair.

The kitchen is now clean. My body is weary, but with Cruz loading and unloading the dishwasher, grabbing supplies, and making runs to the coolers and back, I got more done than I thought. I'm caught up, and I made several loaves of sweet bread.

Imagine if I had help like this most days of the week.

Maybe someday, when I've dealt with the blackmail.

Cruz takes his apron off and stretches his arms. "You ever eat your own stuff?"

"All the time. It's often part of my meals. Like today, I made extra dipped fruit." I cross to the fridge and pull out a plate of strawberries dipped in white and milk chocolate and sprinkled with various nuts. "I have these for breakfast way more than I should admit. There are four more plates in the fridge. Just for me."

"Good." He plucks a strawberry off the plate and holds it up to my mouth. "You need to treat yourself."

"I've treated myself too much."

"If you do anything too much, it's work. Now let me slip something sweet into that mouth of yours."

My lips part on those words and he slides the dessert between my lips. I sink my teeth into the chocolate. It's such an easy thing to make, but I've perfected it, if I do say so myself. My eyelids flutter shut as I chew. I don't always make these. Sometimes I use dried apricots or frozen raspberries. Potato chips, if I can't find decent fruit. I'm picky about the strawberries because they're my favorite.

"Tell me about how it tastes," he says, his voice gruff. We're standing so close together, and his usual citrus smell is tinged with fresh-baked cake. It's like I've imprinted on him.

"I want you to experience it first." I lift the plate from him, take a strawberry, and set the rest on the island behind me. I offer the sweet to him. He opens his mouth. I want to watch him eat not only something I made, but one of my favorites.

His eyes are blistering hot when he sinks his teeth into it, and I'm mesmerized by the bunching of muscles in his dark, stubble-covered jaw. Lust has me in a choke hold. Drawing a breath is difficult, and it's like my skin shrinks while the rest of me expands. I'm restless.

"The sweet chocolate almost makes the strawberry tart, but they balance out." He curls his fingers around my wrist and lifts my hand to feed himself more fruit.

"You have a sensitive palate."

"I know what's good."

Flutters trail through my belly and sink lower. I'm never going to be able to eat these again without getting turned on. "I also drizzled it with white chocolate, so not only do you get the satisfying crunch of the shell and pistachios, the drizzle splinters into pieces that melt on your tongue."

He serves me another bite from the first strawberry and together we toss the green tops on the plate. I think we're done, but he makes his way through the rest, feeding me while I do the same for him. A sensual snack that only leaves my skin feeling too tight from the desire building inside.

Crowding in closer, he wraps an arm around me. "I want to fuck you now."

Please. I'm close to begging. My breasts are heavy and they want to be covered with his hands again. "I want that too."

He pulls me all the way to him with a hand around the back of my neck and smashes his lips to mine. I hook my arms around his neck and devour him just like I did the dessert. He tastes sweet, but there's a richness to him that the chocolate strawberries don't have. He's robust and smooth, like the whiskey he makes.

He breaks the kiss long enough to say, "Wrap your legs around me."

When he lifts me, I do as he asks and he heads right for the stairs. As he's going up, his head scrapes the top and a pained groan leaves him.

"Oh my god, I'm so sorry." I run my fingers over his scalp like I can absorb the hurt. "This building is old."

"Not a problem. I'll risk a concussion to get inside you."

He's barely breathing hard, but he probably lugs bags of grain all over the distillery. I haul flour, but I'd have to rest if I was dragging it up the stairs. I'm attached to him like I'm frosting and he's a sponge cake.

When he reaches my bed, he lays me in the middle and takes my shoes and socks off. Stepping out of his boots, he says, "I'm not wasting any time."

"I am a bit tired," I tease.

He pauses. "Then we'll nap."

I sit up, shocked. "It's late enough to be bedtime. If I fall asleep, I won't wake up until morning."

"If you're tired, we're sleeping."

"You can't miss another day!"

"I haven't missed a day of work since I was nineteen." He adopts a wry grin. "Don't ask me about before that."

He'd put his pleasure aside—again—to meet my basic needs? I'm turned on while being all warm and fuzzy. I rip my shirt off. "I'm not falling asleep tonight."

He sucks air between his teeth and drinks me in. "The door is locked, and I'm ready to explore." He grabs his shirt collar behind his neck and tugs the garment all the way off. When he yanks his jeans down, his erection pushes at the fabric of his boxers.

He withdraws his wallet and takes out some packets of condoms. Tossing three of them on the bed, he grins when I gawk at him. "I'm not going to let being unprepared stop us." He juts his chin toward me. "Take your pants off, sugar. I'm ready to get my mouth on something sweet."

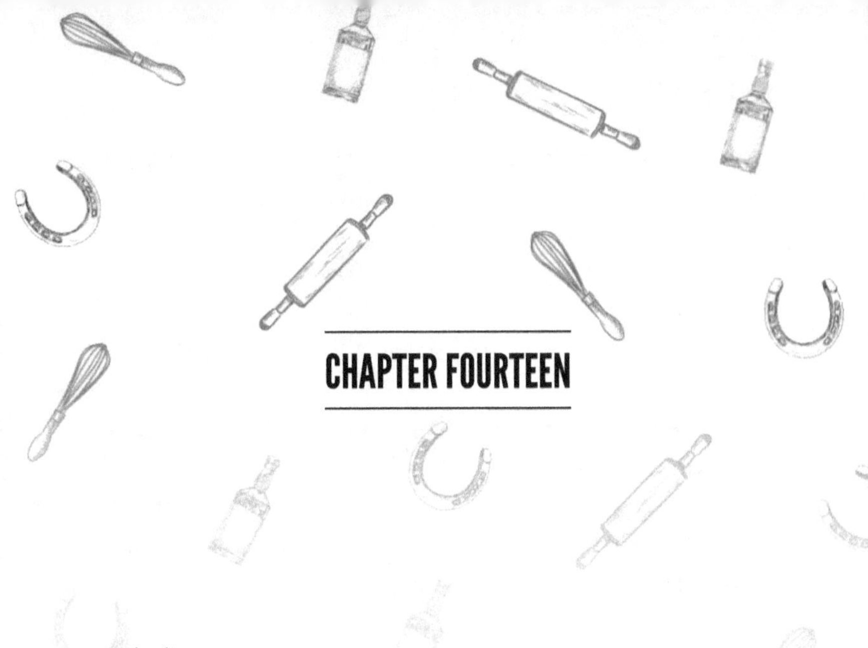

CHAPTER FOURTEEN

Elodie

I wiggle out of my leggings. A sudden bout of shyness hits me and I leave my underwear on.

He cocks a brow and shucks his boxers off. "Keeping something for me to unwrap?"

"It's . . . been a while." I draw my knees up, not caring that it creates a pooch with my belly. It's been years. I've either had DIY orgasms or gone without, and since my schedule is so heavy, I've mostly ignored myself.

"Same here." He starts crawling onto the bed. My heart races, but anxiety starts to build.

"You don't have to make me feel better." Though I do appreciate it.

"If that sounds too pathetic to you, then understand that I didn't want to move to my forever home and fuck around. I wasn't going to run errands while crossing paths with broken expectations and hurt feelings." He pushes me all the way back and lays a kiss on each corner of my lips. "Besides, there's been this sexy-as-fuck baker who'd hardly look at me. I'm not going to be fucking others when I'm trying to get her attention."

His initial confession makes his abstinence more believable, yet I can't wrap my mind around this hot guy, this incredibly sweet and caring man with a good job and ambition, waiting for me. "You weren't even having sex?"

"I've been asked out, but I kept wondering about you. Wouldn't have been fair to them. Didn't feel right to me either, so I played the long game."

I run my hands over his wide shoulders and stuff them into his soft hair. "I can't believe you. All those times you were asking me about the difference between baking powder and baking soda, you weren't just messing with me?"

"I was trying to get to know you, and I enjoyed hearing the frank way you'd explain it all." He grazes my lips with another kiss. "You're cute, and you might try, but you can't hide your sexiness. You own your own business and your friends adore you. The whole town does. I thought you were out of my league, but that didn't stop me from trying."

My heart cracks all the way open. All that time I wasted distrusting him. I'm not going to resist someone who's proven over and over again that he's the real thing. "I need to get my underwear off."

"Let me help you." He drags them down and tosses them aside. Then he settles between my legs, pushing my knees wider with his body. "So fucking wet and perfect. You're just dripping for me."

He has barely touched me, but I arch my back. Need

has been my constant companion for so long that I'm afraid of the explosion. "Cruz?"

"I've got you, baby." He presses a kiss to one inner thigh, then the other. He continues doing that, moving closer and closer to my pussy. "I finally get to taste your sweet cunt, and I'm going to take my time."

A shiver runs through me, and just as it reaches the base of my spine, he spreads my pussy lips and licks across my demanding clit.

The pleasure hits me like a bolt of lightning, and I nearly jackknife off the bed. "Cruz!"

"Let yourself go. I've got you." Another lick keeps my back arched. I have to fist the sheets to hold myself still. I rock my hips with the steady rhythm he settles into.

All the anxious tension in my muscles is replaced by warm relaxation—and tightness in all the right spots. He wraps his arms under my thighs and spreads me even wider for him. The soft lap of his tongue has me transfixed on that point of my body until I'm weightless and floating.

I cartwheel over the edge faster than I've ever climaxed before. I squeeze my legs around his head to hold in the pleasure and ride it out as long as possible. The pure bliss inside of me wipes away years of stress.

I sag into the mattress and relax my legs, then gasp and sit up on my elbows. "I smothered you!"

He props himself on his elbows. "Aw, sugar, that was the hottest thing to ever happen to me."

"No, it's not." We finally get naked together, and— "I crushed your skull."

"One hundred percent not lying." He pushes himself to his knees and holds mine wide, but he doesn't reach for the condoms. "Now that I took the edge off, I can do my exploring."

His cock is straining for me. Tight and pulsing with veins, it looks as demanding as I was minutes ago. "My edge is off. Not yours."

"As long as I'm touching you, I'm doing just fine." Staying on his knees, he lifts my foot. Goose bumps break out over my skin as he traces over the green, blue, and black tattoos. "Why hummingbirds?"

"They like sweet stuff, and they flutter their wings so hard while seeming to be still."

His calloused fingers stroke up my legs to my thighs. "You told me about the flowers." He dances his fingers over my hip bones to the small spatula and whisk over a cookbook on my lower abdomen. His lips tip up. "This is perfect."

"It was a reward for finishing school." I cover his fingers with mine, wishing I could conceal the ink. "It's actually a little embarrassing now."

Surprised, he looks up. "Why?"

"A whisk? A spatula?"

He taps the horseshoe on his chest. "Stuff you care about."

He drops a kiss to the tattoo and continues his trek up my body, skimming his fingers over more humming-birds I have running up the side of my rib cage. "I've got to do something about that bra. Roll over."

I do, growing self-conscious all over again with my ass in the air, but his earlier reassurance runs through my head. He's done nothing but make me feel comfortable. His heat is chasing away the chill of my air-conditioning.

"You were hiding one more." He massages the globes of my ass before working his way up my lower back.

Flattening his hands, he continues up my spine until he reaches the little barn swallow on my shoulder. "What's the story?"

I have to fight to get the words on my tongue when all I want to do is moan. "It's silly."

"Even better."

Always with the right thing to say. "I used to be afraid of spiders. But you know those big ones that build giant webs on the porch? Clem and I call them the big-bottomed spiders."

His chuckle is deep and pleasing. "I've got a few of those. Good bug catchers."

"As a kid, I was terrified. But the barn swallows would fly in and eat them all."

"I can see a little Elodie loving a bird for that."

"I don't hate spiders anymore, but I also don't hate it if a bird eats them all off my parents' house."

He rubs his hands down my back and up again. "I like that story."

"I like that you like it."

"And I like that I finally get to see this ass." He grips my hips and lifts me to my knees.

The bed shifts and the crinkle of the condom packet fills the air. I can't resist looking over my shoulder to watch him roll it on his thick length.

I rock into him, bumping his hands. "I want to do that for you next time."

He gives me a sexy smile. It turns smoldering as he drags two of his fingers through my seam. Slowly, he pushes them inside me. "Are you ready for me?"

So damn ready. "Yes."

He pumps his fingers in and out of me. I immediately clench around him and ride his hand. If this is just an appetizer, how overwhelmed am I going to be with the main course?

"Nice and fucking tight, just like I knew you'd be," he says, working me into a frenzy by barely doing a thing.

He's been imagining me—us—and it's winding me tighter, coiling all that explosive energy inside me.

"Ride it," he orders, and I do.

The pleasure sweeps me away, and the bed rocks with me.

"Still so fucking soaked." He might be behind me, but he's between my legs and his shudder shakes the bed. "Your wet cunt is going to be all I think about all day, every day." He notches his thick head at my entrance and I push back on him. "Fuck, you're so greedy for it."

"For you." Desire has never pounded inside me so hard I'm afraid I'm going to combust and then extinguish like a birthday candle.

With a smooth thrust, he seats himself.

Finally, I'm full. All those empty years. Night after night, going to sleep alone, not believing that someone like Cruz could be real. I groan and stretch my arms in front of me, totally at his mercy. I don't need time to adjust after the way he primed me.

"Christ, Elodie." His fingers dig into both sides of my hips. "Next time is going to have to be sweet and slow."

"Fuck me as hard as you need to." Deep inside, my belly flutters and my walls grip him harder. My pleasure escalates and I race closer to a second peak.

That's impossible. I haven't come twice this close together before.

He withdraws and punches in with a grunt. "Fuck."

Withdraw. "So." Thrust. "Fucking." Withdraw. "Good." Thrust.

He's hitting everything inside of me that needs stimulating. My clit is a happy bystander, getting caressed with each clash of our bodies. I'm loving every stroke. He can take as long or be as quick as he needs.

He collapses over me. Propping his hand on the mattress by my head, he doesn't stop his rhythm. His weight presses me into the mattress, spreading my legs wider, and his hot breath tickles my ear. I'm surrounded by him, caged in the best way, safe. It's everything I didn't know I needed since I came home five years ago.

"So fucking good, Elodie." He kisses the tattoo on my back and winds an arm around me to strum my clit. The wet slap of our bodies fills the room.

The way he's on me, around me, inside me, I can't move. The onslaught of ecstasy hits me and I spasm. My crest is right there, and *ahhh* . . . one more circle of the rough pad of his finger and I'm gone.

"Cruz." Grateful I don't have neighbors who'll hear through the walls, I let out another wordless cry.

"I can feel you coming." His words send a shiver down my back, like adding fuel to a raging inferno. "So goddamn tight."

I split apart. Only he's holding me together.

"Elodie. Fuck." He jerks inside of me. His arm is like a steel band before it loosens and he droops over me, his face pressed against my spine.

I'm nearly flat on the mattress, but I don't want to move. The only drawback of this position is that I can't hold him. Too soon, he removes his hand from between my legs and withdraws with a groan. Rolling to his side, he tucks me into him and kisses the shell of my ear.

Now this is better. I close my eyes, getting drowsy.

"That," he says on a breath, "was worth the wait."

Cruz

I've had the best twenty-four hours of my life. It began in her kitchen, baking, and it's wrapping up there too.

My legs are splayed to the sides, and Elodie is on her knees between them. Her glasses are on the table, and she's got my dick deep down her throat. My brain cells are scrambled.

I can't resist thrusting, but I temper it so I don't gag her. That's about all I'm good for. The *V* of the zipper is pinching my balls, but I don't care. I ran home to touch base with Lane, get an update from him that I didn't want to know, do chores, and grab fresh clothes. When I came back after, she yanked me inside, flipped the dead bolt, and pushed me toward the table.

We fucked three times last night—this morning?— and I was hard as a fucking rock before my ass hit the chair.

I slip her cloth band off and tug the clip out of her hair, freeing those long, glorious strands. She looks up at me and hums again.

"Goddamn, you're killing me." I tuck my fingers into the silk of her hair. The most beautiful sight I've ever seen.

Another hum propels me closer to the brink. I'm balancing at the edge, ready to tip over.

I pump into her mouth, loving how she's working my

length. "Every time I close my eyes, I'm going to see the way you suck my cock so nice and deep."

I don't shut my eyelids now. I'm taking it all in. She's enjoying this, or she's enjoying my reaction, or both. With a swirl of her tongue at the crown, I'm teetering.

I have enough comprehension to warn her. "If you don't want me to release in your—"

She sucks harder and I detonate. I blow my load so hard, it's like it's not my fourth time coming in a day. The heels of my boots grind into the floor as I shudder and jerk through my release. She swallows me down and *fuuuuck*. I'm never going to be the same.

When I go lax, she lets me go with a pop and wipes her mouth. "Finally. I've been wanting to do that."

My dick lists to the side between us, happily exhausted. "Anytime, sugar. I just won't be good for anything the rest of the day."

"Good thing it's the evening."

I lift her onto my lap, and she curls against my chest. My flagging erection is sensitive, but her weight on it is better than nothing.

She brushes her fingers over my chin. "You seemed tense when you first entered."

"Is that what your goal was? To relax me?" I could sleep with her here all night.

"No, it was more selfish than that."

I grin and let my smile fade naturally. "Yeah, I was tense." I don't tell anyone about my dad. When I was growing up, the teachers knew I came from a troubled home, but they never asked about specifics. The older I got, the less they cared. My behavior was on me, not my deadbeat dad or erratic mom. "Lane passed on a message from my dad."

She lifts her head, her concerned gaze stroking over me. I would never discuss this situation with my dick out, but everything with Elodie feels natural. She hasn't run from getting a glimpse of the real me yet.

"He still wants to talk to me." I stroke up and down her back. "That's nothing new. But he wants me and Lane to know that anything we need, we just have to ask."

"Isn't he incarcerated?"

A dry, bitter laugh slips out. "Yes, he is." I'm tempted to ask her how much she knows about the Colorado prison system. She's never brought up the letter from her ex. But she'll tell me when she's ready, so I'll go out of my way to be ignorant. "From what Lane says, he's flourishing. Where he failed on the streets, he's succeeding in the rap sheets."

Her lips quirk, but there's sympathy in her eyes. "Sorry."

"Don't be." I rub her shoulder. "It's ridiculous. He's like a kingpin, or whatever the fuck they call the prison mafia. Might as well make use of his time. He's going to be in there long enough. Which is a good thing. If he got out, he'd be looking for that same power, and he's still got some youth to back it up. He can spout all his family ties and loyalty bullshit, but I don't want anything to do with him." I give myself a mental shake. "Enough about him. What are you doing the rest of the night?"

"I have a few things to get ready for tomorrow, but I want to eat first. Can I make you something?"

"Only if you want to. I can take you out."

Fatigue outlines her smile. We didn't sleep much last night, and she gets up at an hour that I used to party right through. "I should stay in and go to bed early."

"Then that's what we'll do. If you don't mind me sleeping over again."

"No, I like your sleepovers." She gingerly gets off my lap. "Let me wash up and find a clean apron."

I do the same, minus the apron, and grab my overnight duffel from the pickup. I set out a grocery bag of meat I raided from my fridge before I left the house. "I was taught never to go to someone's place empty-handed."

A surprised look crosses her face. "That's really thoughtful."

She's constantly surprised when I do the bare minimum, and it's humbling. I'll be more than goddamn thoughtful. I'll set the bar so high no other guy has a chance of reaching it. "I got all the meat you want."

She rolls her eyes and smirks, but digs through the items I brought, picking out a flank steak. "Don't you miss your house when you can't be there?"

I'm about to say no, but she'll know I'm lying. Earning her trust isn't a one-and-done thing, and I'd like for us to be long term. I want Elodie to be it. I've never met anyone like her.

I have to start opening up more, delving deeper into things I've never talked about. "That house is everything I never thought I'd have. Even after I worked for the Baileys, that's all I thought I'd be doing. It was a huge step up, so I was happy with it. To go from that to building my own home? On my own piece of property? I enjoy my house. I'm proud of it. Yeah, I miss it, but when things calm down, we can take turns with our overnights."

A shadow crosses her face. "Things never calm down, but that's a good thing." She lines up an array of supplies on the island. Some sort of pasta, leafy greens, cream. She digs spices out of a cupboard. "Can you grab the saucepan from the other side of the island?"

"The way it's going, I'm sure you'll be able to hire the help you need in no time."

Her lips thin, but she begins seasoning the meat. "It should be soon. I have some . . . payments to finish before I'll have the funds."

"Mortgage?"

"That's one of them, yeah." She waves to the fridge. "Can you grab the butter?"

As much as I enjoy being her dutiful servant, I don't want to drop the subject of help. There's something she's not telling me about her financial strain, and it's none of my damn business, but that doesn't stop the hurt from worming its way under my ribs. Doesn't she trust me? Surely there's someone she can turn to. Does her sister know, or is there someone else she's talking to?

I retrieve the butter and try to table my concerns. A few orgasms don't mean she has to spill her guts. I've never been in this deep with a girl before, so what do I know about sharing secrets and concerns? I'm thirty-three and just learning how to be a good boyfriend.

What do good boyfriends do anyway?

Take her on dates. We've only gone on one real one. I prop my butt on the counter next to her. She's got a couple of pans on the burners. "Can I take you out again?"

She starts to smile, then freezes. "I have so much to do to prep for the street fair."

"I can help."

"You've been doing too much. Any more, and I'll have to offer you a benefits package."

I lean over to check out her ass. "I've got some bene-fits in mind."

She laughs and uses the back of her hand to push up her glasses. "Yes, to a date, but I don't know when."

I peer out the window. The sun is setting, but I can't see much sky out of the back window. She was up before the sun, worked all day, and she's in the kitchen again. "Sunday. I'm going to abduct you. We'll go to the creek on my property and have a picnic—that I'm preparing—and I'll come back here with you and be an extra set of hands on Monday."

The butter in the pan is sizzling, but she ignores it and glances out the window. A stark look of longing etches into her features for mere seconds before she looks away and it's gone. "Yes, I'd like that."

"Then it's a date."

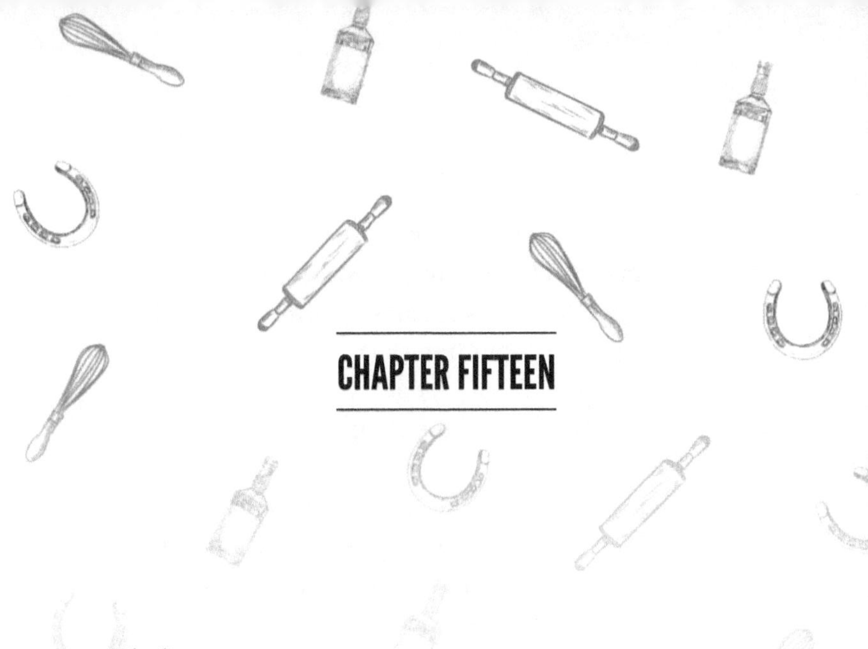

CHAPTER FIFTEEN

Elodie

I finish pulling weeds in my parents' garden and stand up, stretching my back. I'm worn out from a day of work. Saturdays are always so busy, and I'll have more to do at the bakery tonight, but at least I get to be outside. Sighing, I tilt my face to the sun.

Montana summers were something I missed when I was away from home, but since I've returned, they slip by. The page of the calendar changes each month, but my days stay the same. I was almost to the point of hiring permanent staff. Now I feel like I just opened all over again and I'm hustling for a customer base.

I need a break. The knowledge is more acute the more I'm with Cruz.

I'm stupidly excited for a picnic tomorrow.

My exhale is more contented than before. I turn around and Clem is watching me, her arms crossed.

"Something's different about you." She narrows her eyes and stabs a finger in my direction. "You got laid."

I choke on an answer. "N-no." Wait. Why am I lying about sleeping with Cruz? "Yes, actually. Several times."

She squeals and claps her hands. "Mom and Dad have not stopped talking about him since he was over."

I wouldn't stop talking about Cruz either if I was willing to have nosy people up in my business. "You talk to them that much?"

She gives me a *duh* look. "I'm a single woman who works two jobs and writes books, and all my friends are getting married. Yes, I hang out with our parents."

I'm only slightly relieved that they didn't need anything while I was indulging in all things Cruz Foster and only called Clem because they're afraid of bothering me. "I like him a lot."

"You might've had bad taste in men before, but it's good this time."

"It was pretty bad before." I dust the dirt off my garden gloves and slip them off. "I'm not proud of the things I did with Dwayne." I can't believe I said that, but telling Cruz and getting his acceptance opened a forbidden door. Without the pressure of keeping it shut, I just want to talk about it all again and relieve some more of the pressure. "He thought he was—what did Mom use to say? 'All that and a bag of chips.' "

She giggles. "He wasn't a bag of Doritos?"

"He was the generic plain chips that are almost too salty. Even the sex with him was bland." Cruz is like the specialty spirits he distills. I never know how it's going to be, I just know it'll be good.

"Oh, I definitely get that. Why do you think I started writing romance?"

"I try not to think about your sex life."

She throws her hands up. "There's nothing to think about—that's the problem. I don't care if it's missionary for life, I just need it to blow my socks off."

"You also don't want missionary for life."

She exhales a gusty sigh. "I want to be pinned against a wall. Upside down. Spun like a top. I don't care. I just can't take another guy who keeps his socks on during sex."

I snort out a laugh and keep giggling. "You know, I never met him. Jake?"

"Mom and Dad did. Mom faked her vertigo and went to her bedroom to knit. Said he was boring."

Mom has listened to Dad's architecture geek-outs and fishing stories for decades. Jake must've been more than boring. "Oh, Clem. I hope you find your romance hero. No more socks-on Jake."

Her lips curve up. "Me too. But until then, I'm glad we're finally talking about more than how we're going to clean and pull weeds for our parents."

My mood dips. "I'm so ashamed that I've been afraid to talk about it."

Her brows draw together and worry lights her eyes. "Why? It's me."

I shake my head and scan the yard in case our parents snuck outside. They're both usually milling around, doing some extra work, but Dad mowed today, and he's tuckered out. Mom still gets headaches from her fall, so Clem and I chased her back inside. Yet I don't want to sit on the porch and risk them over-hearing.

I plant myself on a big rock that we used to play on when we were young, and Dad was mowing and wanted us out of the way. "I'm the oldest. I'm not supposed to be the fuckup."

She barks out a laugh. "You are not a fuckup. You own a business and everyone adores the work you do."

"I used to scam people. On a small scale. Mostly." My heart pounds once, twice, thumping harder the longer she stays silent.

"I don't believe it," she finally says.

"For drinks and food. I'd go with Dwayne when women would pay for his vacations."

Her eyes go wide. "They do that?"

"There's a lot of loneliness out there. The best thing that happened to me"—until Cruz swaggered into the bakery—"was when Dwayne got arrested. It ended up being for drugs. So stupid, but he was greedy to a fault. Ugh, I should've known better."

She fists her hands at her sides. "Quit taking responsibility for a grown man. Why didn't you tell me?"

"Why didn't I tell my sister in graduate school that her older sister was conning meals out of men who bought me food because I let them think they could fuck me later?"

"Yes! What'd you think I'd do? Cut you out of my life?"

"It's a small town. I wasn't going to tell *anyone*. What if Mom or Dad let something slip and word got around? All they'd have to say is my ex is in prison and people would find out details for themselves. I run a business and everyone trusts me. I was complicit."

"Then why didn't you get arrested?"

"I almost did once."

"Elodie!"

Humiliation burns in my stomach. "Honestly, it's

amazing I'm not in jail, but ultimately, the asshole thought he was so smooth, keeping me so controlled that he didn't let me very far into his life. He had to use his name for the restaurant, but he made me put the apartment in my name. Same with the accounts he hid the retirees' money in, which I sent back." And that landed me in the situation I'm in now, but I wasn't taking anything else from people I didn't earn. "I don't want anyone to know."

"What about Cruz?"

"I told him." Most of it. He's done enough for me. If I tell him about the blackmail, he'll park himself in the bakery every second of every day, with his sleeves rolled up and his apron on. Or worse, he'll track Damon down and revert to the version of Cruz Foster he's ashamed of. I'm not putting him in that position *ever*.

I dig out my phone and check the time. "I've gotta get back and prep for tomorrow." I need to do admin stuff before I can't hold up my eyelids anymore. "I've got a picnic date with Cruz tomorrow night."

She yanks me into a big hug. "You only leave that bakery to do more work. I'm so glad he's forcing you to live again."

I smile and embrace her back, but I can't fight off the melancholy settling in. Cruz is giving me a taste of how much I've been missing, but until I can stop the blackmail, that's all it'll be.

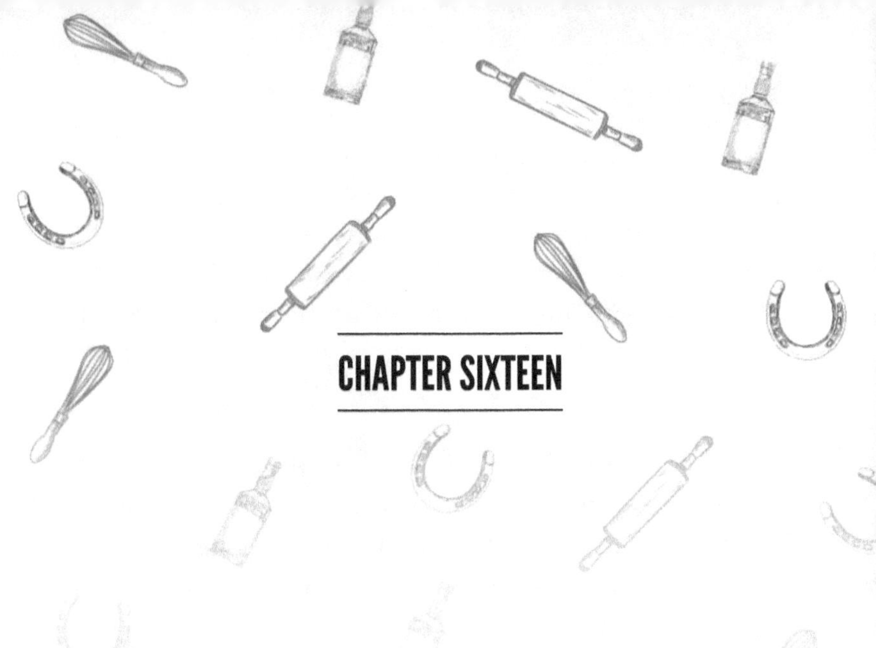

CHAPTER SIXTEEN

Cruz

Haven strolls into the tasting room ten minutes before he said he'd relieve me so I can get ready for the picnic with Elodie. He nods at the few tourists scattered throughout the bar, along with Ned and Isadora, the couple who own the local gas station.

When Haven rounds the counter, I don't leave right away.

"Thanks, man." I give the counter one last wipe after making Isadora's cherrytini. I need to get Elodie out to try one of those—if I can ever get her away from the bakery for more than a few hours at a time. She works too hard, and she's going to drop if she doesn't let up.

Whatever is driving her must be big.

"Not a problem." He flips through the recent orders on the tablet, familiarizing himself. "Got nothing else to do."

"No hot date yourself?"

"Seems everyone's got one but me." He gives me a casual smile, but there's a kinship in his eyes that I recognize from my pre-Elodie days. Since those weren't long ago, I get where Haven's coming from. He's done everything with his brothers his whole life and now they're all living in separate houses. Iverson has a wife and kids, and Durban and Campbell's wedding is next summer.

"I'm sure there's some lucky girl out there for you."

He smirks. "Unless she comes into the tasting room or hangs out at the auction barn, I'm not meeting her."

"You gotta get out more." I'm one to talk. All of us involved in Foster House have sown our wild oats, and the quieter life is more appealing.

"Eh. I'm fine. I went out with Allison a few times last month."

"Allison Johnson? From the vet's office?"

He nods and grimaces at the same time. "I swear I heard her introduce me as her future husband to some friends who came into Bootleg on our second date."

"Oof."

"Yeah. Haven't asked her out since, but she keeps asking what my weekend plans are." He picks up a rag and juggles it from hand to hand. "So if she ever asks, I'm working."

"You do work a lot," I say drily.

"All the time." The corner of his mouth twitches. "I'm not cockblocking you though. Go. Have fun."

I run home and pack the fried chicken I made last night for our picnic. The salad isn't pasta today, but I picked up veggies from the farmer's market. I stuff the special dessert I bought into a cooler with extra ice.

When I drive around the front, the sign on Dee's

Sweets says closed, but Elodie's inside, in front of the window, talking to a man not quite as tall as me. She's got her hands on her hips like she's facing off with him and he's towering way too fucking close to her. Instead of pulling around the back as planned, I park right in front.

They both notice me. Elodie's eyes go wide, and the guy stiffens, but he takes a goddamn step back.

Not going to help, jackass.

There's something about his power stance in front of Elodie that rubs me all the wrong ways. His side-slicked hairstyle and the polo and khaki shorts don't help. It's an absolutely normal look for the beginning of August—and it makes him seem like a giant prick.

Elodie turns to him and says something just as I climb out. His smirk gives me the urge to smear that smug grin all over the sidewalk.

The door isn't locked. I step inside and give him a hard glare before focusing on my woman. "Hey, Elodie. Am I interrupting?"

"No." The word is carefully controlled. "He was just leaving."

"Everything all right?" I ask lightly, but I'm coiled tighter than a rattler ready to strike.

She shakes her head without looking at me and shoves her glasses up her nose.

"Sorry." The man spins around and sticks his hand out. His smile is as fake as the gold watch on his wrist. "I'm Dean. I was just stopping in to ask for directions."

I don't take his hand, narrowing my gaze on him instead.

He drops his arm, and that fake smile of his falters. "I don't come to this part of Montana enough to know where all the good restaurants are. She was nice enough to stay late and give me some recommendations."

The flash in her eyes is enough to tell me he's lying, but I'd know anyway. This motherfucker thinks he's slick, but he's not. He's just like every loser my mom tried to date after my roughneck dad. She thought she was moving up in the world, finding men in suits and slacks instead of my blue-collar father. She assumed their appearance meant they were better men, but the clothes hid the rot. They could be more manipulative and underhanded. Some utterly lacked a conscience.

I get the same vibes from this motherfucker.

"Go to Billings," I say, keeping my steady stare on him. "Plenty of good places to eat there."

"That's what *Dee* was saying."

Elodie's cheek twitches and her nostrils flare.

I open the door. "Better get going, then. Don't want to miss out."

His brows lift like he can't believe my audacity. I have it in spades. Just because I don't use it doesn't mean I won't.

"All right, then." He does a half bow toward Elodie and she gives him an *are you serious?* look. "Thank you for the help. I'll be sure to stop here the next time I'm in town."

"Sure," she says, her tone flatter than cardboard.

I don't get a nod when he passes me to leave. He walks down the sidewalk to the end of the block and turns so I can't even see what vehicle the asshole drives.

I shut the door and throw the dead bolt. She needs a more robust security system. Turning back, I grip her shoulders. "Are you okay?"

"Yes, sorry I'm not changed yet. If you give me a few

minutes, I'll be right back." She breaks out of my hold and tries to scurry away.

"Elodie."

She stops and puffs a strand of hair that's escaped her bun out of her face. "Yeah?"

"What was that all about?"

"That?" She scoffs like the stranger didn't bother her. "You know how some guys get. Waste a girl's time and not care."

"You should tell your cousin." Weird that I'm recommending contacting Deputy Palmer. I used to be the last guy to advise going to the police. I was on a first-name basis with them for a very different reason.

"I will." She flashes a smile as false as Dean's. "Sorry he made me late."

She might want to forget about Dean, but I won't. "You'll tell me? If he becomes a problem?"

"I won't let him become a problem for anyone."

"You don't have to do it alone."

Curiously, she eyes me. "What would you do? Fight him? Run him out of town? You don't want to be that guy again."

The old Cruz never needed a reason. This Cruz will do it for Elodie. "Some people need to be run out of town."

"And what of your reputation? It'll spill over to the distillery if you're driving off tourists."

It might, and I don't want to do anything to risk the distillery's reputation or bottom line. We've worked too damn hard to establish a niche company in the middle of nowhere, and it's not only the Foster House Gold site. I can't tarnish any part of Foster House. I won't do that to Myles. I won't disappoint Lane either. "All I'm saying is that you don't have to deal with asshole customers alone."

"Thank you. I also don't want creepy customers to ruin what I know is going to be a lovely picnic. I'll be right back."

She disappears and I'm left with the last few minutes on repeat in my head. Who the hell is Dean, and why did he target Elodie at closing time? That's shady-as-fuck behavior. Has he done it before?

Would she tell me?

Regardless, she's brushing it off when she was clearly disturbed. What if it happens again? What if I'm not here?

Maybe I need to talk to the deputy.

Maybe I need to track Dean down and teach him a goddamn lesson about cornering women.

I push a hand through my hair. Shit. I'm supposed to be picking her up for a date, not planning my next fight. Whoever he is, he's not ruining today. I stop at the window and fiddle with my hair until I look less rumpled and more like a country Prince Charming.

When she emerges from the back, her long hair is in a ponytail that gives me lots of inappropriate-in-all-the-best-ways ideas, and that's only the beginning. She's wearing athletic shoes, so no hummingbird tattoo today, but her shorts let me see more of her bouquet tattoo than ever. The shirt is going to be my undoing. I want to be a gentleman and give her a romantic picnic experi-ence, but the hem of her shirt brushes the top of her waistband, and the way it hugs her breasts is going to hold my attention far more than the fried chicken I packed.

"You look hot as hell, sugar."

She's put her contacts in, and those big hazel eyes turn shy. "Thank you."

I lead her out, and she locks up.

I nod to the bag. "Were you afraid I wouldn't pack enough?"

"I was also taught not to show up without a gift for the host. I grabbed a couple of cupcakes."

"I have dessert, but we can eat yours."

"We can have both," she whispers, grinning. "I packed a small piping bag of frosting."

"I might have plans for that."

She tosses me a coy look. "I might be interested in what they are."

I'm still smiling when I take off. She's a shit ton more relaxed than when I first arrived. The picnic is already a success. "I hope you like cold fried chicken."

She groans. "I love it. Where did you get it from? The grocery store's bakery makes some of the best. I have it a few times a month since I don't have time to cook it myself."

I clutch at my chest with one hand. "You assume I didn't cook it? Ouch."

"Oh my god, you're right." She covers her mouth, horror in her eyes. "I did assume. I'm so sorry."

I laugh and turn onto the highway to get to my place. "I'm a man of many talents. Mae was so pleased when I started watching and helping her in the kitchen. I even asked to knock off early to catch her prepping some of my favorite meals."

"Did you ask because you enjoyed it? You'd rather fry some chicken than rope some cattle?"

A smile prods at my lips, but the heaviness of the answer keeps me serious. "Uh, it was selfish. If I learned to cook and stayed broke, at least my stomach wouldn't suffer."

She turns toward me. "Like it did when you were growing up."

It's easy to talk to her, and she treasures honesty, so that's what I'll give her. "If she remembered to buy groceries or leave money for us to get food at the closest gas station, all we'd get was discounted cans of whatever. We'd get sent home with backpacks of food from school, and . . ." I shudder. "We survived, but you won't catch me eating a PB and J ever again."

"No one would blame you."

"And it's only fancy white bread for me. Not the cheap, mass-produced stuff." I bypass my driveway and take the dirt road that'll lead to a small access road. From there, we'll do a short stretch of off-roading.

"I'll have to make you bread now."

"You'd do that for me?"

"Why wouldn't I? I wouldn't be a very good baker girlfriend if I didn't bake my guy fancy bread. My sourdough doesn't get enough action."

Does she realize what she said? Girlfriend? Do I dare bring it up?

She looks around. Trees grow thicker and less manicured on one side. Our cattle graze on the other side. "Your property is so beautiful. Where does this lead?"

"A creek. It widens around a bend during the spring, so not as many trees grow there. Lane and I found it when we were out riding one day." I turn onto the narrow road and we bump along. "Last summer, we put a picnic table there."

"You use that line on all the ladies?"

I laugh. "The only female I've brought out there is my mare."

"What's her name?" The tenderness in her question surprises me.

"Catherine."

"For real? Your mare's name is Catherine."

"She's a serious horse."

Her laughter brightens my entire afternoon and chases away the lingering memories of when I was growing up. Back then, picnics were just a frivolous thing mentioned in stories, and I was an angry kid who didn't care because no one else seemed to. Now I'm having a romantic picnic on my property with a local business owner.

She hangs on to the *oh-shit* handle during the roughest part of the ride. Finally, I park in a clearing not far from the creek.

"Wow." She peers out the window at the green trees crowding the shoreline. Weeds and wildflowers are inter-mixed all the way up to the shoreline. The glitter of water peeks through the greenery. "It's gorgeous."

Pride puffs out my chest even though I had nothing to do with how nature carved out this little spot. I'm just lucky enough to call myself an owner of it for this moment in time, and I get to share it with a woman who's becoming really damn special to me.

"You can't hear the highway out here." I kill the engine and open the door. Only the faint trickle of water and the breeze rustling the trees greet us. "I don't come out here nearly enough. Go ahead. Explore while I get everything ready."

"I almost wore sandals. So glad I didn't. The only nature I've gotten lately is weeding my parents' garden."

She scrambles out of the pickup and picks her way through the tall grasses, passing the table, and continuing along a wildlife trail to the water's edge.

I catch myself smiling like a dumbass, watching her frolic in nature. Time for a picnic. I pull out the box of food. I might've learned to cook, but I'm not trained in presentation. An old sheet is going to have to do for a tablecloth. By the time I'm done covering the table and setting out the food, she's wandered back. I wouldn't have rushed her. She needs this, and it's humbling that I can give it to her.

"This all looks so good." She presses a hand to her stomach like it's going to dive for the food. "I'm so stinking hungry, you might have to watch your own plate."

"Each bite you steal from me is going to cost you a kiss."

She smiles. "You're not giving me a reason to behave."

Good. I don't want her to, not with me.

Elodie

Damon's second visit and the reminder that my reputation and, therefore, my business are on the line for thousands of dollars have put a damper on my whole day. Cruz packed the best food. I need his fried chicken recipe like I need to draw my next breath. I've eaten more veggies during this date than the last week. If I wasn't so outraged at the increased amount Damon informed me I now owe, this would be just perfect.

Cruz sets out my lunch bag, but he digs into his tote bag of goodies. What he withdraws shoves the lurking concern of my blackmailer to the dark corners of my brain.

"Macarons!" I clap my hands, suddenly giddy. A row of pristine light green and pink macarons are encased in a plastic sleeve with a tidy little bow. The label reads *Scooter's Confections*.

He grins and pride radiates in his expression. "I have to admit I didn't bake these. Myles was up last Friday and he brought me some from his sister-in-law's bakery in Bourbon Canyon."

The delighted look on his face, all because of my enthusiasm, hits me hard. This guy wants to make me happy. Can it be as simple as that?

It could be, if I weren't getting blackmailed.

How do I keep my shit from affecting him? Do I offer to pay Damon more if he'll never stop by the bakery again? Would Damon even honor that agreement?

Cruz hands me a green macaron. "You like pistachio?"

I'm gladly yanked out of my head. "I fucking love pistachio. And if I don't have to make my own macarons? Even better." I love my job, but this is a treat for me. I don't get out enough to try other bakeries.

He reads the plastic container it was in. "Pistachio with cherry bourbon filling."

I bite into it and groan. The slight crunch of the outer shell is perfection, and the smooth burst of cherry with it gives my taste buds an orgasm. "So good," I say around my mouthful.

The denim blue of his eyes turns to midnight. "Have another one."

I'm not even finished with my first before he hands me a pink macaron. I giggle around the last two bites of pistachio. This is so blissfully romantic, yet it seems normal at the same time. Only Cruz can pull that off, and do it when I'm under so much pressure.

"This one is cherry with pistachio filling." He pivots on the bench seat so his legs are flanking me.

He hasn't taken a bite yet, so I hold the cherry pistachio macaron up for him. "You first." The last time I hand-fed him turned out quite pleasantly.

He holds my gaze as he takes a bite. His lips graze my fingertips and a shiver ghosts down my spine. I have never been so turned on while enjoying all nature has to offer.

A satisfied grunt leaves him and he swallows. "That is good."

I pop the rest in my mouth and my eyelids roll back. "Ugh. I'm never making them again. I'll just buy these. Now I won't want a cupcake."

He cocks a brow and gets that wicked look in his eyes that I've only ever seen him use on me. He digs out the two cupcakes and the piping bag of bright yellow frosting. Nice and summery. Narrowing his eyes as he concentrates, he pipes the frosting onto each cupcake in a sloppy circle. "Damn. You make this look easy."

"It's the technique. You have to gauge that grip strength. Too hard and it all just shoots out." The way his eyes smolder spurs me on. "Too light, and not enough comes out. You might have to keep squeezing and squeezing."

His fingers tighten on the bag and a little dollop falls out. "You might have to show me exactly what you mean."

"We're out of cupcakes." I'm playing with fire, but my belly is full, the day is beautiful, and we're far enough away from town that the worries about my ex and his brother can't get to me.

The gleam in his eye gets brighter, but he gathers all the containers and empty plates. He sets them back in the bag he packed, gently loads the two frosted cupcakes back into the lunch bag, and pushes them aside. Then he pats the table in front of him. "Climb on."

My breath hitches, but I do as he orders. The tablecloth is warm under my shorts, and he spreads my legs until they're on either side of him.

He holds the piping bag and looks at me like he wants to say something.

I sit forward and stroke my fingers down his cheek. "Talk to me."

His dark gaze softens, but there's timidity there. "Earlier, you called yourself my girlfriend."

Oh. Was that bad? "I should've asked first."

"No," he says gruffly. "It's exactly what I want to hear."

"Really?"

"It means you're mine, and now we both know it." He lifts the piping bag. "Take your shirt and bra off. I'm having a sugar craving."

Butterflies explode in my belly and careen back and forth, but I do as he asks. I need to shut my brain off and halt the endless to-do list running through my head and just feel. Cruz will do that for me. He already is—this is just the cherry on top.

Heat licks across my bare breasts with the light breeze, and my nipples pucker tighter than ever. Pure greed fills his face. He stands and rests a knee on the bench. Then he uses the frosting bag to write out four letters across my chest—*MINE*.

"Yours," I say quietly.

"I'm serious about us, Elodie." He puts a hand on either side of me and leans down to lick the bottom of the *M* off. "I'm going to keep showing you that you can trust me."

My nipples are poking into the air like they're trying to get into his mouth, but he's steadily cleaning all the frosting off of me. I tip my head back and enjoy the sensual strokes of his tongue and the low growls that come from him.

When he cleans the last dab off, he pipes a dot on a nipple. "You're so fucking sweet."

Covering the pearl with his mouth, he sucks hard and I arch into him. He's obliterated any logical thinking. I'm just a bundle of nerves waiting for the pleasure he can give me.

He does the same on the other side, flicking my peak with his tongue until I start squirming. Need hammers through my body and pulses between my legs. I want his tongue there. I want his body between my legs. I want him inside me and over me.

"Cruz." His name is a plea. "I need . . ."

I don't finish. I need everything. All of it. I need to forget the stress and the fatigue and the payment hanging over my head that'll only be followed by a bigger one.

"There's no more frosting left, but I've got what you need," he says as he tugs at the waistband of my shorts. "Lift that ass for me."

I do, and he peels the rest of my clothing off me, including my shoes. I'm bare and open to him. Whatever he has in that votive to keep the bugs away is working.

"Already wet for me, sugar?" He takes a seat and hooks his arms under my legs. "Put your feet on my shoulders."

I follow every direction he gives me, trusting him to take care of me. The throbbing between my legs intensifies. If I could, I'd sit right on his face, but I'll take being spread in front of him like his very own picnic.

He gives me a kiss on the inside of one thigh, then the other, before he claims my clit.

I bark out a cry and scare a bird out of a nearby tree. "I'm scaring the wildlife." I roll my hips to meet every stroke of his tongue.

He pushes a finger inside me. "This is all nature right here." Placing his mouth back on my clit, he flicks it with his tongue and I jerk at the rush of ecstasy.

I feel his smile against me before he resumes his rhythm. Forget trying to be quiet. "Cruz!"

I'm flung into a climax faster than I thought possible. Energy unleashes inside me and only part of it is the pleasure he's filled me with. More birds startle and the grasses rustle as I cry out, pouring all of my stress into the release. I'm coherent enough not to crush his head this time.

When I come down, he pulls away and slips his finger out of me. "Goddamn. That was my dessert."

He places another kiss on the inside of my thigh and

rests his cheek against it, rubbing his hand up and down my calf.

He's holding me so sweetly after rocking my world yet again. Cruz Foster is the whole package. He's putting the pieces of me back together.

Fear starts to trickle in, but I put a stop to it. I'm getting ahead of myself. We're enjoying picnic sex. "Does my boyfriend have a condom?"

"Around my girlfriend? Always." He places my feet down on the bench to get his wallet out. After he withdraws the packet, he tosses everything by the lunch bags.

I snatch the condom from him and he rips open the fly of his pants. When I fling the wrapper by his wallet, he pivots to sit sideways on the bench like he did earlier. There's no dignified way for me to put the condom on from this position, but I do it anyway. From the beginning, he's made me comfortable as I am.

When I'm done, he leans back, his erection proudly jutting toward the sky. "How about we celebrate our new status and you go for a ride?"

A relationship. With Cruz Foster. He's mine, and I want to claim him. I want to soak this up every chance I get in case—

I clamber onto him. There's nothing flattering about how I change positions with his help, but I don't care. I need this. I need to feel him against me and in me. In case all of this perfection slips through my fingers.

I link my arms around his neck. With him holding my hips, I hover over him and swivel my hips around, wetting the tip of his cock.

He clenches his teeth. "Christ, I could come just from this."

"You need more." I relax my legs to sink onto him, but he holds me in place.

"Not when I'm with you."

How can he get even more perfect? I kiss him as fiercely as he attacked my clit moments ago. He opens to let me in. I'm desperately ravaging his mouth, and other than having the tip of his erection drag through my pussy, he's not moving, letting me dictate how fast we go. My desire cranks higher and higher. He makes me feel special in and out of bed—or when fucking on the picnic table. Finally, he loosens his hold, and I take him in an inch. He goes rigid against me.

We're hugged together so close that I can feel when he tenses his abs. I rock and take more of him. Then more. My gasp breaks the kiss.

"You're such a fucking tease." He grunts and punches his hips up. I sink down all the way, loving how full he makes me. "I can't get enough."

"Cruz?" I don't know what I'm asking. I need this, but I don't want it to end. When I'm with him, I don't worry about the stuff I should. When I'm with him, I can see how I've put myself in a display case with my cupcakes and locked the rest of the world out. Cruz is opening the lid and crawling in with me. But he's also leaving the display cracked open to give me a glimpse of everything I've kept out.

He kisses my neck. The birds have returned and their singing fills the air.

I still have no words. I want to ask him to stop. To leave me alone so I'm not scared anymore—this time of losing him. I want to tell him to never quit, to keep dragging me out of my cupcake prison. I want all my problems to mysteriously go away.

All I can think to say is, "Fuck me. Hard."

I'm sitting astride him, my leg wedged under the top of the picnic table with his, my other curved around his hip, but he takes over. I'm in his control and that's just the way I need it. My carefully crafted life is at risk, but I need him to take this from me now. To let me just . . . be.

I'm centered on him, stroking in and out of me. The muscles of his arms are flexing against my legs. His clothes scrape against my skin. I'm naked and he's fully dressed. He's got his shit together and my life is a mess.

I tip my head back and he nibbles up my neck. Soft grunts leave him every time I plunge down. A moan slips out of me when he withdraws so far I'm almost empty.

"Cruz. Harder."

"I've got you."

My belly tightens at his deep growl. He does as I ask, but my leg thunks against the table. Hugging me to him, he carefully stands up and moves to the end of it. My ass hits the top and I lie back. Without the interference of the bench, he can thrust without restraint. He pounds into me, just as I asked. I draw my knees up and out to give him as much access as possible.

I'm completely open to him with the sun shining down on us. There's nothing hidden. I can't share everything with him, but I can do this.

"Fuck, sugar." His fingertips dig into my hips.

"Yes!"

He pumps harder. "You take me so well."

"God yes!" I claw for something to hold on to, but the sheet is too loose, so I grip the sides of the table. My whole body shakes, but all I feel is him. So damn good.

I crest and float, riding the high of my orgasm,

arching my back off the surface. "Cruz." It comes out the most yearning, most demanding, most thankful sound.

"I can feel you coming." His voice is tight. "You're fisting me so fucking hard."

His grip is unyielding as he punches into me one more time. He comes on a roar that scares all the birds away. I'm on a cloud of ecstasy. He's filling me, the breeze caresses me, and the heat of the day kisses my skin. It's perfect.

And now I have to go back to work.

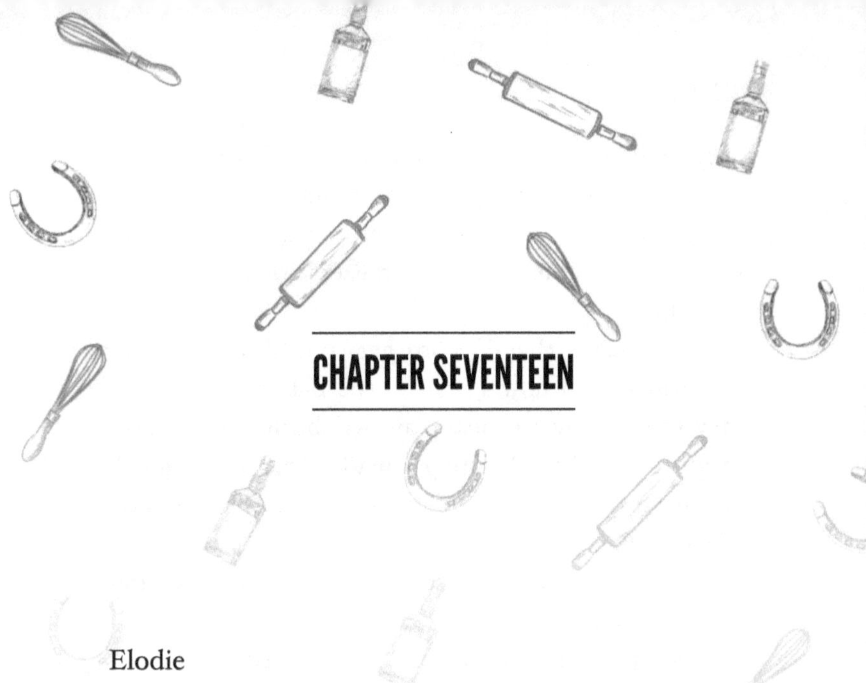

CHAPTER SEVENTEEN

Elodie

It's closing time on Friday. I flip the dead bolt and peer out the window like I have every day since Sunday. *Dean* isn't anywhere to be seen.

Fucking Damon. Like I'd actually talk to someone about him. Fuckwad.

Still, I check the locks again before I finish wiping the tables and running a quick mop over the floor. I shooed away Kinley a half hour ago. I could probably close earlier on Fridays, but then I'd be stuck in the back even longer on my Friday nights.

I could close earlier and just go do something.

My exhale is heavy. Campbell stopped by to talk about future cookie dough fundraisers. The good news is that everyone she's talked to loves the idea. The bad news is that everyone she's talked to loves the idea. Even two sports clubs in the next town over have contacted her, asking about it.

My table in the back is littered with schedules, and I don't know where to pack in hours of mixing and packing cookie dough. It means more work. A lot more. Also, more ingredients, more freezers for storage, and more help.

It also means that if word gets out about my time with Dwayne and how I started the bakery with stolen money, then all my business plans will burn away, like the bourbon I added to the soup I made Cruz last night. It won't matter how much of the money was mine, how much was taken from me too.

As if I summoned him, my phone rings and his name flashes across the screen.

I'm smiling when I answer. "Locked inside, safe and sound."

"Good."

He was with me several hours on Monday to help out, and he's taken to calling every night right after I close to make sure the door is locked. I even saw my cousin drive by in the squad car when Maggie left after her shift.

"Did you ask Callum to look in on me?" I ask.

"I might've mentioned to the good deputy that you had some idiot hitting on you last weekend."

If only that's all Damon were doing. My smile fades. "I told you I would talk to him."

"Did you?"

"Cruz." His heart's in the right place, and he's going to law enforcement instead of trying to track *Dean* down himself, but I can't have him getting my family worked up. "I've asked him once already. Twice is going to make him suspicious, and he's going to tell my dad or Uncle Karl, and then what? That guy isn't a local like Pete."

And Huckleberry Springs' loveable but belligerent Pete is harmless enough.

"This has happened before?"

Shit. "It's tourist season." *Please accept that answer.* "They'll worry. Mom's finally feeling normal again, and she's going to get all worked up."

"Okay. I'm sorry, but I'm worried about you too."

"I've been around creeps like him for longer than I've known you." *I've been around that very creep, in fact.*

"If you'd have known me longer, you wouldn't have had to deal with them."

"That's sweet, but we can't turn back time."

"You actually can. I've been doing it in my head since the picnic."

I bite my bottom lip to keep a groan from slipping through. It was hard to come back to the bakery and dive into recipes and weekly menus. Cruz came with me, but he had to go home soon after so he could get up and do chores. Lane's in Denver again. "It was a nice picnic. We should do it again."

"We should. It's going to be raining this weekend. Can I abduct you after close on Sunday and bring you to my place?"

A rainy day at Cruz's sounds divine. Any day off would be fabulous. "I can spare a few hours."

"I'll help you make them up."

I wish he didn't have to. But not only do I need to be prompt on my next payment, I have to squeeze more golden eggs out of sugar and flour. "I'll see you then."

"Sleep tight."

I will with that voice in my head. I hang up and stuff the phone in my pocket. In the back, I start readying supplies for the cupcakes and coffee cakes I'm going to make for tomorrow. I have two pies that I want to prep and a special-order strawberry rhubarb pie for the birthday party at the senior living center.

I'm in the middle of a yawn when someone knocks. I jump and nearly bite my tongue closing my mouth.

"Who is it?" I call, sounding scared. Damn my ex and his brother. Stupid intimidation tactics.

"Meeee," Clem sings from the other side.

Relief pours through me. I open the door to Clem in linen shorts, socks with sandals, and a shirt that reads *I like big books and I cannot lie*. "You've got bangs."

She huffs them out of her eyes. "Don't remind me. I got so frustrated with a scene last night that I took shears to them."

"You did it yourself?"

She grimaces. "This final look is a la Jess at the salon. She's a miracle worker."

"Good thing you didn't hack them off too short."

She hands me a packet of mail. "I grabbed this for you."

My stomach sinks to the floor when I see the letter on top.

"Is that him?" she asks.

I'm glad I told her, or I'd be explaining it now. A sour taste fills my mouth. I'll still be lying to her. "Yes. He tries to keep in touch."

"Can't take a hint?"

"He just doesn't care."

She comes in and washes her hands. "Mind if I hang out with my big sister tonight?"

"No. Something wrong?"

"I have kids' time at the library in the morning, so the guys don't schedule me for very many Friday nights.

Then I sit at home and write, but I also do that every night. Kind of starts feeling a little, I dunno, lame after a while. You know?"

"No," I say wryly. "I have no idea."

"Sister night!" She flashes me a smile and grabs a fresh apron out of the drawer. "What are we making tonight?"

Giddiness rises inside of me and I shimmy. "This is going to be so fun." I get an evening with my sister, and I have a date on Sunday with my boyfriend. "Go ahead and start on the lemon curd. I know you love to make that."

"Only because I get to eat a bowl when I'm done."

I take the mail to the table and set it down. My happiness dips the longer I look at the return address of the correctional center Dwayne is in. On a whim, I rip open the envelope. I'm not letting him rain on my sister night with Clem.

Who's the new guy? is the first damn sentence he wrote.

I angrily fold the letter up and shove it into the envelope, ripping the side as I do.

That asshole. He also dated it, and it was written before Damon's visit. Damon must've been lurking around town, spying on me, before the second time he stopped in to harass me.

Seething, I turn around. Clem's apron is tied and she's studying me. "That bad?"

Worse. Instead of shutting him out of my life, he's burrowing in deeper. From prison! I struggle to retain my light composure. It's Friday, and I'm with my sister. I just talked to a man I'm crazy about. Fuck Dwayne. He can't get to me tonight.

I aim a broad smile at Clem. "He won't let go. Too much time on his hands, and I'm irresistible."

"Naturally." She does a curtsy. "It runs in the family."

I table the letter and the money I need to raise. One day at a time. First, regular business. Then the street fair. After that, I'll buy myself another month, and then I'll have to face the problem I left five years ago.

Cruz

I knock on the back door, and it swings open to a harried Elodie.

"Sorry!" She gives me a quick kiss and ducks inside. An alarm clock is going off.

I step in and stay on the mat. It's sprinkling out, and I don't want to get her kitchen dirty. She takes out three rounds of cake and tosses the hot pads on the counter before inspecting her work.

I lean against the doorframe. "What flavor?"

She squints and bends, looking for imperfections I can't see. "Chocolate mocha, bourbon chocolate, and cayenne chocolate. All with a simple chocolate frosting."

"Sounds delicious. Wedding?"

She nods and pushes her glasses up. "On a Monday. They're getting hitched at the courthouse, going to the river for pictures, and then they rented the rec room at the senior center to have the reception." She straightens. "I'll put the crumb coat on when I get back."

"What if I tire you out too much?"

"Then you'll have to tell the happy couple that you

fucked me silly and that's why their three-tier cake looks like shit."

"I'll try not to sound like I'm bragging."

She laughs while untying her apron. "I'll run upstairs. I told you I could've driven."

"I get to have you to myself longer if I pick you up and drop you off."

"So damn sweet." She swings by me to give me another kiss, and I make it a much longer one this time before she disappears upstairs.

I keep to the edges of the kitchen on my way to her little table. Pulling out a seat, I spy a return address I've seen before. I pick up the envelope. How often is this guy mailing her? Why hasn't she thrown it away?

Does she still care about him? Are they still in touch?

My fingers tingle to take out the letter and read it, but I won't. She trusts me, and I'm not risking that. I set it down how I found it, push the chair back in, and go to wait by the door so she doesn't have to question whether I looked or not.

The dread still lingers. It's not the same feeling as when I find my own letters in the mail from my dad. A correctional facility in Colorado, but not the same one. What a coincidence that we'd both know someone in prison and that they're in the same state. Does she want to vomit when she sees Inmate Dwayne's letters like I do?

No, this heavy feeling inside me is different. We're more than dating, and we're not just fucking. I care for her. She means a lot to me. I don't want to let her go. But she's still working through some things, and for whatever reason, she doesn't want to share them with me.

The back of my throat aches from something that feels like hurt.

She lands at the base of the stairs. "Sorry you had to wait."

Her hair is still up, and she's kept her glasses on, keeping that cute and sexy mix. She's in shorts again, and another shirt that doesn't reach her waistband. My mouth goes dry and my worries from seconds ago dissipate as quickly as the heat from her ovens. It doesn't take much to undress her when she's like this, but I can strip her out of her sweats just as fast. "Lookin' hot as always."

"Same goes for you. Let me grab the bread I made for you."

"You baked me bread?" She said she would, and I didn't doubt her, but I didn't expect her to make me a priority.

She picks up a small box off the island. "I made fancy white bread, but also a loaf of sourdough. If it's too much, maybe the guys at Foster House will eat it."

They'd gobble up every crumb. Touched, I take the box from her. "Thank you."

"No problem."

It's not for her, but it means a lot to me. She not only remembered my comment, but she cared enough to do something about it.

I load her into the pickup, put the bread in the back, and take off, scanning the sidewalk for a guy in golf clothing and a smug expression. I haven't seen Dean again, and she hasn't mentioned a problem customer again. He must've left town by now.

When I pull up to my house, I park outside the garage since there's a lull in the drizzle. Rufus is on the porch in his little igloo doghouse. He waddles out, his corgi butt wiggling, barks once, and goes back in his hut. A small sigh leaves her. I cast a questioning gaze her way.

Her expression is at peace. "I just love your place. Rufus is adorable."

My chest puffs out like I'm a kid and she told me I run really fast in my new shoes. "Rufus knows he's adorable, but the cows disagree, and you get to see the inside of my place this time."

"Can't wait."

Neither can I. All the guys I work with have seen the house, but I haven't brought a woman home. Not even the Hawthorne sisters have been inside, and I'd consider them in my friend circle.

I have a friend circle. Another one I built outside of the Baileys. Moments like these show me how far I've come.

"What's wrong?" She must've sensed the shift of my thoughts.

I blink. I've been staring at the sweeping arches and looming picture windows on this side of my house. "Just marveling over how much has changed. I used to stay home alone in a dirty apartment in filthy clothing. Then I moved in with the Baileys, and I dunno, maybe deep down I thought they all just tolerated me because Myles married into their family. Lane earned their respect, but I was respected only by proxy."

"You underestimate that charm of yours." She reaches over the console and squeezes my hand. "And how likable you are when a girl is trying really hard not to notice."

"You made it look easy," I say softly with no blame in my voice, and stroke the back of her hand with my thumb. "But then I moved here. My last name is Foster, but I'm only part owner because of Myles. We have an understanding about our rank at the Foster House Gold site. Lane's the top, under Myles of course. Then it's Iverson, because he was in charge of the Hennessy trust that Myles bought the land from."

She tilts her head like she's working through the information I just gave her to see my point.

When she doesn't respond, I continue. "They're my friends. Jamison and Campbell are too, and while it's because I work with their guys, they don't have to have anything to do with me. Then there's your sister and Edna. I work with them, and I'm sort of their boss, but at the same time, they're friends. Edna doesn't have to take me to bingo. I have people. That kid sitting in his underwear, eating stale, dry cereal before school, where he'd get teased, has his own crew now."

"Oh, Cruz." She clambers over the console and into my lap. "You're breaking my damn heart." She runs her fingers over my scalp, and I hum at how good it feels. "If I could go back to my childhood and give you half the love and support I got, I would."

"I never felt sorry for myself." I stroke a finger along her jaw. She's on my lap, and blood is rerouting. I'm almost fully erect, despite our heavy conversation. "I was just angry. Then I didn't care."

"You care a lot."

"Now I do, yeah." I trace her lower lip. "I care about you. And if we keep going like this, I'm not going to get to feed you." Stroking my hands down her arms, I eventually release her to open the door. I climb out with her in my arms.

She giggles but clings to me. "You can put me down."

"I know." I like the idea of walking into my house with her in my arms too much. "I'll come back for the bread."

I unlock the front door and toe it open. Going through the entry with a mat for shoes and a line of hooks for coats and hats, I'm careful to keep from hitting her limbs as I carry her into the main room.

She looks around, a small gasp leaving her. "It's gorgeous."

"Lane says I should put a picture up or something."

"Why?" Her wide eyes take in my arched ceiling, the massive panes of glass, and the clear walls. "It's so simple and beautiful."

"It's open and clean."

She wiggles to get her feet on the floor. I set her down, but I don't let her go. "That's important to you. It's why your pickup is spotless, and you're always freshly showered. You leave to do chores, but you never come back dirty."

"Am I getting called out for having good hygiene?"

"It's just a thing for you. You're not compulsive about it. Meanwhile, I'm often dusted in flour and my main style is sweats."

"I like you in sweats." I wish she wasn't in anything at the moment.

She catches the gleam in my eye and smirks. "Give me a tour."

"This is the living room." I snicker when she shoots me a *ha ha, smartass* look.

"I like your furniture." She tows me to the plush, earthy-brown couch flanked by a matching chair. Red plaid throw pillows are some of the only color besides the wood in the room. "It looks comfy."

"I've taken a few naps on it." I lead her to the kitchen. "This is where I don't make as much magic with eggs as you."

"I can make you eggs. You make me whiskey to bake with."

"It's my favorite of what we produce."

"Why?" She crosses her arms and her eyes twinkle. "It's my turn to ask about your job. What makes whiskey different than gin or vodka?"

"I've never thought about it." I scratch my chin, enjoying her real interest in my world. The guys and I discuss what we make and why, but not like this. I treat all three spirits equally when it comes to my profession. But personally? "Whiskey is an all-in-one. It's like a meal in a glass. Vodka, to me, is more of a starting point. You can drink it straight, but people rarely do. It's an excellent canvas to paint with other flavors. Gin's not quite the same. I like it best straight because its flavor profile is often more delicate than whiskey. I like a simple life and a complex drink."

"And I like your perspective." She breaks away from me to wander around the space. She peeks in the oven, checks out the microwave, and opens both doors of the fridge. "You have nice appliances."

"I just told them I didn't want shit that would break down in five years."

She leans against the counter and traces my chocolate-brown farmhouse sink. "Whiskey's your favorite to drink. What's your favorite to make?"

"Whiskey wins again. Durban likes to play with the flavor profiles and mess around with the infusions, aging times, and barrel types. I like to straight up make a damn good whiskey."

She tips her head to the side. "And when you find a recipe you like, you don't mind making it over and over and over again?"

"Not one bit." We share a smile, and I close the distance between us. Propping my hands on either side of her, I stay nice and close to her. "What's your favorite thing to make?"

"Muffins."

"Muffins? Not some fancy cake?"

"I like the challenge of some of the wedding and birthday cakes I make, but muffins are easy. I don't mind decorating, but it can be stressful. After I've been burning through the kitchen at a hundred miles an hour, holding still enough to pipe the perfect rose can make me cry." She gets a faraway look. "Muffins are reliable. I don't often put icing on them or anything. I just get to throw things into the mixer, pour it into cupcake tins, and then I have a breakfast that's basically a dessert."

"Favorite flavor?"

"Sour cream almond poppy seed."

I kick a foot out behind me to lower me enough that our faces are level. "How often do you make it?"

"Once a quarter."

I straighten. "Why not once a month?"

"They aren't a big seller."

"Can't you just make them for your enjoyment?" She pours herself into work out of necessity, but is she actively depriving herself of pleasure?

"I could, but it's a whole batch, and it's easier for me to eat what I make to sell."

"Damn, sugar." I feather my finger down a free lock of hair. She kept the messy bun from when she was working, but a few tendrils have escaped. "You need more pleasure in your life."

"I happen to have had more of it lately." Her voice becomes a sultry purr, going straight to my dick.

My pulse hammers behind my zipper, and I haven't even started cooking yet. "We should do tonight backward."

"Yeah?"

"I'm going to fuck you right here." I drag her shorts down, dropping to a squat to help her get them off. Her bare pussy is inches from my mouth, and I start salivating. I take her sandals off too, and run my fingertip over the polished blue toenails on one foot. Goose bumps explode over her skin. "Then I'll cook for you, feed you, and after, we're going to your place, and you're going to make those muffins."

She tenses and tries to shrink away. "I can't. Every dollar counts right now. I don't know if the street fair will be a boom or a bust and I have . . . bills."

I run my hands up and down her thighs. If I could help obliterate each penny she owes, I would. I look up her body. Her chest rises and falls, softly rustling the fabric of her shirt. I wrap my hand around her calf. "Make a whiskey icing for it, something that'll help move them, but leave some uncovered and all for you."

Her eyes lighten. "A whiskey icing would go really well with the muffins. I sell more whenever I use a Foster House product as an ingredient." Heat blends the brown and green of her irises and she pushes her hands through my hair. "I like a guy with a big brain."

"No one's ever been with me for my brains."

She cups my chin and prompts me to rise. I hate leaving my vantage point, but determination lines the set of her mouth. When I stand, she rubs her thumb across my lower lip. "Your brains, your body, and your booze. I'm not a picky hussy when it comes to you."

"You're my hussy."

"Just for you."

Just for me. I lift her to the counter and unzip my jeans. This guarded woman gives herself to me over and over. Yet as I roll on the condom and plunge into her, and when she wraps her legs around my waist and hooks her ankles, as she lets me do what I want to bring us both to our peak, she's still holding a part of herself back.

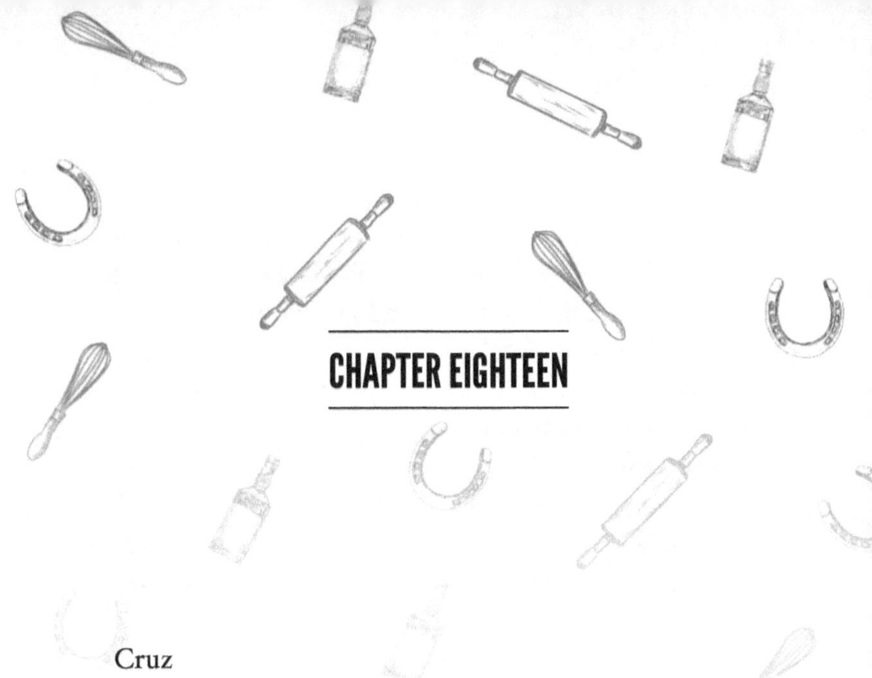

CHAPTER EIGHTEEN

Cruz

My Friday night in the tasting room is bustling, and Lane stopped in to help. The end-of-summer tourist season is booming, and in one corner, there's a table full of rafters. In the other is a group of trail riders. A few general tourists doing a weekend of distillery and brewery crawls fill some of the other seats. And at the bar are two women working really hard to get me and Lane out alone with them for the night.

My anxiety rises by the minute. I didn't ask to get hit on. It's worse that there are witnesses. I'm used to rumors and speculation. As a kid, I hated it. I would succumb to the fury of knowing that the other kids were right or that teachers talked about my home situation. After living with the Baileys, the gossip turned to who I was seeing and for how long. Then there were comments about me and Lane pushing Myles out of the business. It didn't matter if what they said was false. Nothing seemed as bad as where I'd come from.

But this? If the story swells and bloats until people are saying I actively flirted back, or worse? Went home with one of them? I've never had anyone on the other end who cared what was said.

I've made a lot of progress with Elodie. I can't lose it now just by doing my job.

"The cabin we're staying in is so nice," one says in a throaty purr. She pushes her long, blond-highlighted hair off her bare shoulder. If her other strap falls any lower, the integrity of the top will be at risk, and I'll get flashed. That might be the goal.

The table of rafters stands up. One of the guys gives us a big wave. "Thanks for the drinks. Damn good."

"Appreciate it, man." I see my reprieve and rush around the counter to clear their table. "Enjoy your river cruise tomorrow."

They file out and I collect their empty glasses and napkins. I breathe easier getting a break from the incessant flirting.

Lane appears behind me. "Chicken."

In this? Yes.

"I've got a damn good thing," I mutter only loud enough for him to hear. "But I'm not sure if Elodie will think so if these girls go to the bakery tomorrow and boast about how into them I am." I give him a flat look. "I'm not."

An amused grin tugs at his lips. "Oh, I know. You're ready to crawl out of your skin, and I'm enjoying the show."

I glare at him. "Those two are thirsty as hell and it's

not for water or alcohol." I stuff a finger at the dirty table. "I'm wiping this off."

He brandishes a dishcloth I didn't notice. Dammit. "I got it."

"Jackass."

His laughter follows me back to the bar. I juggle my armload to the dishwasher and take my time. Anything to keep from having to attend to the women and their cleavage.

One of them slides off the stool and tries to scoot around the bar. "Let me help with that."

Alarm spikes my pulse. I spin around, a glass nearly slipping out of my hand. "Whoa, whoa, whoa. Only staff are allowed back here."

She pouts but doesn't move away. "I used to bartend. I can help."

"That's what Lane is here for."

Lane returns and she has to move to let him through. He gives them a charming grin, and I think I hear the one still sitting moan. "Don't want us to get in trouble with the boss, do ya?"

Lane loves to use that line. He rarely identifies himself as the one ultimately in charge, and he definitely doesn't out himself as an owner.

The almost intruder sits back down. "Invite him too. Our cabin's big enough."

Her friend nods. "We can pick up some drinks, and y'all can stay until morning. I hear there's an excellent bakery we can try."

"The bakery is the best," Lane says with a shit-eating grin. "You've had some of the best desserts of your life there, right, Cruz?"

"Without a doubt. My girlfriend knows what she's doing." I didn't know I'd been waiting to use that line forever.

The girl with the boob nearly spilling out doesn't rearrange her shirt after my girlfriend announcement. Damn. I dump the remnants from the glasses into the dishwasher and load them.

When I turn back, Lane's preparing a new cocktail for each girl. Fuck, that means they're going to be here longer. I've never been this stressed before, but this is the first time I've been blatantly hit on in a long while. Usually, a little charm goes a long way. The other party puts out feelers, I wave them away, and we all go about our business.

I haven't been seeing Elodie for that long, but I didn't think to talk to her about these situations. I was too worried about her getting creeped on by the Deans of the world. Guys can flirt with her from dawn 'til dusk, and I know she won't be seduced. She fended me off for years when she was interested. It's different on my side. I'm the flirt she didn't trust, and I don't know who she'll believe.

Can I call her now? Tell her the details before I get screwed by how small this town really is?

The woman with the loose top leans over the counter, and a whole tit almost dumps out of her collar.

My stomach acid is going to chew through every organ in my body. I beeline to the table of trail riders to see if anyone needs refills. They're just talking about leaving. Dammit.

The distillery crawlers are also calling it a night so they can hit up at least one distillery in Billings before they quit serving for the evening. We're open for two more hours, and the barstool stalkers aren't leaving.

This has never been an issue. I never went home with people I met here even before Elodie started giving me the time of day, but that's not what the gossip says. None of the guys did either when they were single. In fact, hitting on us at work was a sure way to get our rejection. All of us are dedicated to Foster House Gold. Doesn't stop people from talking, but with five of us, it was never clear who was the root of the talk, so it didn't matter to us that there was talk.

I should ask Iverson and Durban what they do. My situation isn't quite the same, but if any of the other guys were working, these two would be all over them too.

A couple comes in, and I shoot Lane a glare before he even thinks about greeting them and taking their order. I head there before my brother can fuck with me. Spending a few minutes chatting gets my pulse to settle down.

When I return to the bar to make their drinks, I go straight to the shelf of bottles.

He appears next to me and tips his head close to mine. "You've gotta relax. It's going to be okay, but the customers are going to sense your mood."

"What if it's not okay?" I whisper back without turning my head. "There was nearly nipple action, and it wasn't an accident. I don't need that getting around town."

"I can ask them to leave."

I let out a long breath. The distillery's reputation could take a hit. They're nothing but flirty girls. They aren't the first and they won't be the last, and I need to get over it. If only I could talk to Elodie, calm my anxiety down, and be my normal, flirty but aloof self.

I'm not doing anything wrong, and I'll have to trust that Elodie knows me well enough to realize the truth over rumors that haven't even happened yet. "I don't want to fuck this up."

I don't have to specify what I mean.

He slaps me on the shoulder. "I've got your back."

Now both of the woman's tits are on the countertop. She's bellied up to the bar so close that her ass can't possibly reach the stool. I'm not going to be the one to check.

The glint off a car window in the parking lot catches my eye before I spin around to shelve the bottles I took out for the couple. Thank fuck more customers are arriving.

The door opens. When I turn back to make sure Lane knows I have dibs, my tongue sucks back into my throat. Fuuuck.

A woman struts in, all legs and abs and full, lush tits. Her long, glossy dark hair flutters behind her, and her shrewd hazel gaze sweeps the room as she makes her way unhurriedly toward the bar. The denim shorts she's wearing reveal her entire bouquet tattoo, which means half her ripe ass cheeks are sticking out. One humming-bird is visible along her rib cage thanks to the scrap of a top she's wearing. The sky-high red stripper heels unlock a million fantasies I didn't know I had. She moves like she's on a runway, and I'm stuck in the tractor beam of her sex appeal.

"Whoa," Lane breathes next to me. "Didn't see that coming, and I'm the one who called her."

I don't have time to be confused. Her gaze collides

with mine, and the air sizzles between us. The corner of my mouth tips up. Elodie's here. Sexual tension replaces all my earlier frustration. She clears the counter without slowing down, heading right for me. When she reaches me, she throws her arms around me and gives me the biggest kiss. I hug her to me, bending her back, though not far. Those heels are throwing off my perception of how tall she really is.

"I thought no one was allowed behind the counter?" the almost intruder complains.

"She works with us sometimes," Lane lies easily. Sometimes our old habits come in handy. "Besides, she's his girl."

I let Elodie up for air. My hands are at her waist, but I'm touching mostly bare skin. She's hot as fuck, but this outfit puts a big ol' spotlight on it. "Sugar, you're so damn hot you're gonna combust all the liquor in here."

She grins. Her red lipstick is smeared. Half is probably on my lips, but I rub at hers gently with my thumb instead. It gives me an excuse to touch her. I don't know what Lane did, but he must've sent an SOS on my behalf. And she's here when there's a ton of baking she's got to do for the street fair next weekend.

Eyes burn into us, and likely into Elodie's ass cheeks, but I haven't been gifted with that view yet. I tuck her into my side. My smile has to be as goofy as it feels, but I don't care. My relief leaves me as relaxed as drinking a few shots in a row.

I stroke my thumb up and down the bare skin of her side. "Our two guests here heard about your bakery. They want to visit it tomorrow." Did Lane tell her about them? When did he have time to shoot her a text?

I don't care. She's here.

"That's so amazing to hear." Her smile has a hint of wickedness. Turning around, she reaches into her back pocket and pulls out two business cards. How'd they fit in that teeny pocket?

Again, I don't care. The sight in front of me strikes all thought from my head. The curves of her ass cheeks top long, smooth legs. Those heels . . . Lust pumps steadily into my veins.

"These are for a free muffin or cupcake," Elodie tells the customers. "Our special this weekend is sour cream almond poppy seed with a Foster House whiskey glaze, but I'll have more options if that's not your thing."

"Thank you so much." The girl with the near wardrobe malfunction stuffs the card into her purse. "I love your shoes."

I fucking do too.

Elodie's smile is serene and a touch vapid. It's disarming and endearing. No wonder men bought her whatever she wanted. "You're so welcome. I really hope you stop in. I'll even get a load of Foster House whiskey–glazed apricot bread ready."

Appreciation simmers in the other girl's gaze. "That sounds delicious. Everyone in town has been so nice."

"Well, you make it easy." Elodie gives them an alluring pout. "It's easy to see how much you enjoy the place we love. I hope the rest of your trip goes well. If you have any questions, just ask these guys—or me. I'm happy to help."

The other women blush and nod at Elodie's gushing compliments. I'm not a gambling man, but I would put money down that these flirty customers would buy Elodie drinks if she slid onto a stool next to them.

"If you two need to go talk, I'll cover for you," Lane offers, running the wiping rag through his hands.

"Thank you." I say it with enough inflection that he knows I'm thanking him for so much more. I take Elodie's hand and lead her out of the tasting room.

In the main distillery, by a rack of Foster House ball caps, I pull her into my arms again. "I've got to thank you too."

"You're welcome. Lane made it sound like you were going to have a breakdown."

"I was. They were bold. What if word got to you and you didn't trust me?"

She frowns and runs her hands down my shoulders. "I do trust you."

"Not with everything."

She opens her mouth. Shuts it. "There are some things that aren't important enough to drag you into."

"Everything about you is important."

She feathers her hands up my arms and cradles my face again. "I promise I won't think the worst of you." She winces. "I don't like people telling me they promise something and here I am doing it."

"Would you have been upset? If they'd come in talking about how much fun they had with the guys working in the distillery, and you knew one of them had been me?"

Her white teeth dig into her ripe lower lip. "I would've been upset at first, but I hope I'd realize that it's you. You flirt, but it's your way of making everyone feel good." She runs a fingertip down my nose. "You get a special look when you're talking to me. It's all mine."

It'll always be hers. "Just don't throw me away."

Understanding fills her eyes. "Cruz. You're definitely

worth keeping, and you always were. If anyone tosses you aside, they're the problem. Not you." She gives me another kiss.

I delve deep into her mouth with my tongue and she meets it with hers stroke for stroke. With her body in my arms and that vision of her entering the distillery like sex on a cloud in my head, I'm hard as a rock and aching so bad I might come in my pants.

"I need to get you to my office." It's up a flight of stairs. One wrong wobble and her ankle is toast in those shoes. I pick her up.

She laughs. "I can walk, Cruz."

"The way you walk in those shoes is obscene, and I can't risk fucking you right on the stairs."

I take the steps two at a time, reaching my office faster than I ever have from the ground floor. When I get inside, I kick the door shut behind me. The only windows I have in my space face the parking lot.

She looks around. "It's nice. Very clean." There's not even a notepad on my desk. A box of alcohol samples is under my desk, and the laptop is closed and in the middle. I'd probably store that somewhere else too, if I could. "It's the size of my bathroom."

"I didn't want a big office." I set her ass on the edge of my desk. "If I'm spending too much of my day in here, then it's time to find a different career."

She leans back. I can't see the swells of her breasts, but her shirt teases them. I skim my fingers along the hemline. "If you wore this all the time, I'd be your biggest champion, but I'd also have a million heart attacks."

"I'll wear it just for you."

"Nah, sugar. You wear this for you or not at all." I lift

one of her legs. My gut clenches harder to see her foot tucked into a fuck-me shoe. "You're going to leave these on, and I'll strip down the rest of you. That'll be for me."

"Now?"

"Lane's covering for me." I release her leg to kiss her. Then I draw her top over her head. Her tits bounce free and I almost choke on my tongue for the second time tonight. "Fucking hell. No bra?"

"It's built in." She reclines back and shimmies her shoulders. "Guess what else I'm not wearing."

My groan rips out long and ragged. Two articles of clothing and she's naked? "You want me dead at your feet, don't you?"

I drag down her bottoms and she lifts her ass for me. I have to take a step back and evaluate my handiwork.

"Put your heels on the edge of the desk." I don't recognize my own voice. It's thick. Guttural. Straight up caveman.

"I might gouge the surface."

"Worth it. Now do it and spread those knees wide."

She first lifts one leg. Then another. The tips of her sharp heels hold her feet in place. My blood is thumping at my temples and pounding against the zipper of my jeans. She's wet and glistening for me, such a deep pink, it's become my favorite color.

I rip open my zipper and free myself. I get a condom on in record time and toss my wallet who knows where. "There's one thing that I want to commemorate this moment with."

I stoop carefully to keep from strangling my erection in my fly and grab a single-serve bottle of Buttered Cob. I twist off the top and take a drink.

Her lips part as I lean down to kiss her. She opens

for me, drinking in the warm whiskey, and she moans, her lips vibrating against mine.

Her mouth is wet and shiny when I pull away. I take another drink, almost finishing it off and sink to my knees. I swallow and claim her clit, swiping my alcohol-soaked tongue across her swollen nub.

"Cruz." She rocks her hips up.

I blow across her hot flesh.

"Oh my god." She leans back farther, shoving my laptop to the side so she doesn't knock it off the desk.

I finish off the rest of the small bottle and cover her clit with my mouth, plying the bud with my tongue until she's writhing. I swallow everything down that didn't escape to drip to the desktop and rise. Her eyes are half-lidded when I push into her. They roll all the way back and she drops her head back.

She surrounds me and all my worries wash away. The women in the bar. The secret she's not telling me. How much she works. All of it vanishes as soon as I'm buried inside of her. "That's it. Just relax and let me fuck you."

I put one of her heels on my shoulder and pump away. She scrapes at my abs with her nails, undulating her hips with my thrusts. My climax is roaring down on me like a coal train. Her walls are gripping my cock, but I need her to topple over the edge with me.

Her clit's wet enough, but I lick my thumb anyway and strum the swollen nub. She's the only instrument I've ever played. Her hands fall away to catch herself on the desk, and she arches her back.

Fuck me. I'm never going to forget this sight. So many beautiful images of her in pure ecstasy are seared into my brain. I'm one lucky bastard.

"Cruz!" She grips me so fucking tight I can barely

move. Her walls convulse, rippling over my shaft with blinding pleasure.

I pound into her and slam into my orgasm. My ass cramps as I come, punching into her one last time before I release.

I squeeze my eyes shut. "Fuck, Elodie."

Whimpers and moans leave her as we both try not to yell through the building.

Once we both finish grunting and shaking, I peel my eyes open. She's sprawled across my desk with a dreamy expression. Her foot is hanging off my shoulder, and her other leg is dangling off the edge of the desk.

"It's amazing I'm still standing." And that her heels are still on.

She smiles at me. "This wasn't part of the first tour I got."

I smooth my hand up and down her leg. "It'll be a part of them for you from now on."

Elodie

I wipe the back of my wrist across my forehead. The weekend has been a flurry of baking. Now it's Monday and my final push for the week. All my notes are spread out on the table, and I'm checking off each batch I've got done.

The street fair starts Friday evening and goes through late afternoon Saturday. Clem hasn't been able to help. The library needs her to prepare a booth and set up an area for kids to play. The main part of the fair will be a block away from the library, but people will be roaming all over our small town.

Cruz comes through the back door, a bag in his hand from La Taqueria. "Carne asada, just for you."

I groan. "That sounds so good. I'm starving. I've been preparing cookie dough and making extra apricot bread and whiskey glaze in case I sell out. What if I'm making too much?"

I'm planning less than what I had for the Billings fair, but I took on a last-minute anniversary cake order, another round of cinnamon rolls for a funeral, two birthday cupcake orders, and a family reunion. Everything's getting celebrated this week while so many people are in town.

"You'll sell them Sunday." He almost sets the food on the table, but he jerks it back.

All my notes. He must be afraid to mess them up.

I rush over to gather them all into a pile. "What if people are sick of baked goods after the street fair?"

"That'll only happen if they buy so much from you on Saturday that they can't possibly stuff another bite in their bodies."

I need Cruz and all his optimism in my life. I grab for another stack of mail I had pushed toward the wall. The return address for the correctional center Dwayne is in slips free. I scramble to stuff it under another envelope. When I peek at Cruz, he lifts his gaze from the stack in my hands. His smile is small but understanding.

I do not deserve him. I transfer everything to a clean edge of the island. "Have a seat."

Adrenaline, like I've been caught doing something wrong, pumps through my veins, but I grab us a couple of bottles of water like the mail is nothing out of the ordinary. For me, it's not.

I'm fine. It's fine.

Totally okay that I'm hiding a secret from Cruz and he's been an open book.

It's for his own good.

I hang up my apron and join him at the table. He's already set out the chips and salsa. I ignore my food container and dig into the chips. He does the same. The crunching fills the silence between us.

"How was work?" I ask. I haven't seen him since last night.

He went into work today for Iverson since Jamison went back to work and Cruz didn't want her to worry about juggling a baby on her first day back in the office. He went home after to feed his horses and do the rest of his chores. Naturally, he showered before he picked up our dinner.

"Good." He opens his to-go container and steam escapes. "I like Mondays when we're closed and I can just do work without having to put on a show."

"Clem said tours go through the distillery several times a day in the summer. I can't imagine the kitchen being open to public viewing."

He nods and keeps eating. Am I imagining the awkwardness between us?

"Cruz . . . about my mail."

He stuffs his fork into his rice and inhales. "You don't have to tell me."

I wipe off my mouth and take a drink of water. How can he be so accepting? He knows I'm keeping something from him, and he's trying to act like it's not bothering him.

I want to spill everything. Tell him every single detail. I stuff a chip into my mouth and bite down. A sharp point stabs me in the gums, and dammit, I deserve it.

What if I spilled the ordeal to Cruz? He's a smart guy. Maybe he'd have ideas on how to stop my ex and his brother. I let my gaze drift over his still-damp hair and his clean T-shirt. He was so stressed that I wouldn't trust him about the interested women that come and go from the distillery, and it's because he can sense that I'm still walled off.

I open my mouth and his words from weeks ago filter through my head.

No. I can't be a tell-all right now. I can't risk putting Cruz on alert and doing something he'll regret.

I chug another drink of water. But I can say some things. "Dwayne writes me sometimes."

He abandons his fork loaded with his own carne asada. "I have to admit that I've seen his letters before."

"You have?"

Guilt passes through his features, but he nods. "I didn't read them. But I saw the address."

Of course that's the mail of mine he sees, and not my invoices for my flour shipments and the standing freezer I just purchased. "It must look so familiar."

"Different place, but same thing basically."

That sums up how I feel about the letters. Same feelings, basically. "What are the odds?" My half-hearted comment lands flat between us.

He smiles anyway. "Seems to be a hundred percent. It's just one of the many things that drew me to you. Like you had things in your past you didn't want held against you. People who did bad things that you want nothing to do with."

There's always been a connection between us. I fought it for too long, but I'm glad he didn't give up on me. I need his patience just a little longer. I'll tell him everything once I get rid of my Damon-and-Dwayne problem. "I don't reply. I don't email him, and if he tries to call, I don't answer."

"My dad does the same. Why do they keep trying?" He grabs his fork and stuffs his food into his mouth. "I mean," he says around the mouthful, "we're not reciprocating." He sits back, embarrassment filling his eyes, and he brings his napkin to his mouth. "Sorry."

"For what?"

"Talking with my mouth full."

That hurt little boy makes appearances at the most startling of times. Talking about guys in prison must do that to him. "I'm honored you felt comfortable enough around me to do it."

"Thanks for trying to make me feel better."

"It's the time," I say, tilting my head toward the stack of mail. "They have nothing else to fill every facet of the day. For Dwayne, it used to be how he could swindle money and resources. How to make a quick, easy buck. It was a game. Constant mental stimulation. Now . . . he's cut off. The same for your dad?"

"I'm sure he'd disagree."

"Do you . . ." How do I even ask this? I haven't been completely honest, yet I'm going to prod at a deep wound. How much has he stuffed away about his dad? How bad is it for him? I used to struggle with what was real between me and Dwayne, and it's easier to assume nothing was. But for Cruz, it's his dad. The prison situation has to be harder for him. "Do you have good memories of him?"

His brows pop. "Good? Of my dad?" Disgust drips from his tone.

If I could claw the question back, I would, but it's out there. If I explain more, will that help? "I dated Dwayne for too many years, but once I learned of his true nature, it was easier to divorce myself from him, if that makes sense. Your dad is an awful person, but he's . . ."

"A part of me?"

"I think you got the best of him. You and Lane are what he and your mom could've been."

His features soften. "Never thought of it that way." He pushes his food away and crosses his arms.

Did I rob him of his appetite? I should've kept my mouth shut, but discussing how he handles a person in jail who used to be close to him is soothing for me. It shows that it's not just me. A good guy like Cruz has done bad things in his past. He was mostly a kid, but the parallel makes me feel less foolish.

"Lane has more memories," he finally says. "It's one reason why he still talks to Dad. The guy walked out before I was three. When he tried to come back into our lives, it got ugly, and then he was in jail before I got out of high school."

"It's valid. However you feel? Totally valid."

The corner of his mouth lifts slightly. "That's what my school counselor used to say. I thought he was full of shit."

A giggle bursts out of me.

He laughs, his Adam's apple bobbing. "I can see now I might've been wrong about Mr. Bauer."

Scooting his food back in front of him, he eats some more. Good. I didn't ruin our meal together.

When we finish eating, I start to gather our empty containers. "Thank you for dinner," I say as I rise.

"He used to bounce me on his knee." Cruz doesn't look at me.

I slowly sink back into my chair.

"I thought for a while I was just making shit up. Wishful thinking of a kid, you know." He rubs the back of his neck, and his gaze touches on my stack of mail. "Then Lane said he used to bounce us each on a knee like we were racing on horses side by side, and we'd laugh so hard we almost fell off. He, uh, wrote me about that story after Lane told him we rode our first horses at the Baileys'."

"Did your memories become clearer after you read that?"

His nod is jerky. "I remembered more too. Like when he would take me and Lane to get a burger and fries. We felt like fucking kings." He runs his hands along his thighs. "Mostly because Dad would call us out of school to do it."

It's a sweet memory, and unlike mine with my ex, it was likely genuinely a dad who wanted to spend time with his kids while he was in a decent place mentally. No con. No scam. Cruz and Lane's dad wasn't using them. "I imagine you thought you were a big deal."

"So fucking big." His smile fades. "When he didn't stand us up. But, yeah. There were some good times, and I think that fucked with me more than anything. I know he can dangle a solid father-and-son relationship in front of me and yank it away at a moment's notice. I don't have anything to do with him, but I'm forever tied to him, as much as I don't want to be."

I get up and cross to sit on his lap. We end up like this a lot. I set my glasses on the table and wrap my arms around his neck. "Thank you for telling me."

"And thank you for telling me," he says solemnly.

My dinner threatens to heave right back up. "You're welcome."

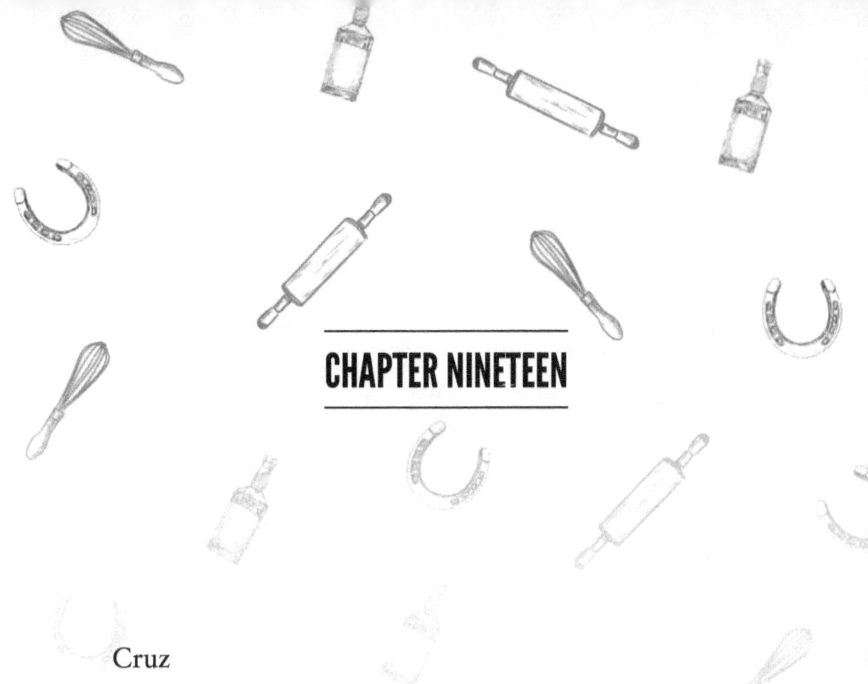

CHAPTER NINETEEN

Cruz

The first day of the street fair is hot enough to melt frosting. Elodie's freezer must be pumping away. A Friday evening fair still puts us in the sun, but the most brutal strike of the rays is over and some shade from the buildings creeps over us.

Elodie's booth is set up right outside of the bakery, and our booth is a half a block down in front of the insurance agency. All the agents from inside came out to get samples after closing time.

Haven's working next to me, selling three bottles of juneberry vodka and two liters of Golden Nugget whiskey that are going to be future Christmas gifts.

I line up two small plastic cups for a couple. Only the wife is drinking. I splash some lavender gin in one and huckleberry vodka in the other. I run through the script of each spirit, how we make it, and what notes they'll taste. I can recite the details in my sleep.

She wrinkles her nose with the whiskey, but smiles after the vodka. "Much more my speed. I'll take a bottle of that."

"Absolutely."

"But it's Foster House."

I pause while reaching for the bottle. "Excuse me."

"You said 'absolutely.' Absolut Vodka? The brand? Bad joke."

Chuckling, I shake my head. "It can't be bad. I plan to use it myself someday."

I package her purchase, and just as I hand it off, a guy gets in line behind her. He's wearing aviator shades and an arrogant smile. When he sees me notice him, he smiles, a slow, sly spread of his punchable lips.

Fucking Dean. "What do you want?"

Haven's busy with the girls from the tasting room the other night. They're sampling everything we have, but they mostly want a taste of Haven. I saw Allison, the girl who's maybe stalking him, walk by a few minutes ago, and the women scared her off. Good.

Dean's smile gets even bigger and more smashable. The sun gleams off all the product in his hair. "A taste. What do you recommend?"

He takes off his sunglasses and tucks them into the pocket of his polo. He's wearing khaki shorts again and resembles the insurance agents more than the tourists.

I grab one plastic tasting cup and barely cover the bottom with a splash of gin. I should be nice and ooze the charm Elodie used to hold against me, but there's something about this guy, and it's only gotten worse since I first saw him looming over Elodie. "Here."

He throws back the sample, and his brows draw together. Shaking the cup, he tries to get the two drops I poured out. When he does, he smacks his lips. "Gin was never my thing." He narrows his eyes. "How 'bout some whiskey?"

I give the same amount of the cheapest whiskey I brought, which is still a damn good product.

He rolls the tiny amount on his tongue. "Mm. I have to concede. You know what you're doing."

"And I know what you're doing."

One golden brow arches. "And what is that?" He looks around the booth. "You're Cruz, right? The founder's brother?"

I don't answer him. People like to use personal details as leverage. No part of my life has that sort of power and he needs to know it.

His smile fades, and a hard glint lights his eyes. This is the real Dean. "I'm going to stop by and see Dee."

The way he uses that name rankles me. "It's Elodie."

He cocks his head. "Is it?" He gets a faraway look in his eye. "I feel like I've met her before."

Again, something in his tone settles like lead in the gut. Does he know her? Does she know him? "And I feel like you're messing with her. The folks around here won't let you do that."

"Nah, I'm not messing with her. I'm just a fan of that apricot bread. The whiskey glaze is new. Are you the inspiration for that?"

I don't give him an answer.

He rubs his stomach. "I might just have to go get some now. Do you know if she's single?"

Anger sears across the back of my neck. "I can't see where it's your business."

"Eh, I can ask her."

Dean is being a dick because he can be. He wants me

to be flustered, get angry, and damage my own business. Anything I do will spill over to the Dee's Sweets booth.

I flip out another tasting cup. "You say you're not a gin guy. You've gotta try this." I ooze some of that charm I'm known for.

This time, I fill the damn thing with our strongest gin. The botanicals slap a person right across the palate. Only major gin lovers will enjoy it. I packed it today because a few people in town are gin aficionados and will be stopping by.

Distaste turns down the corners of his mouth, but he's not backing away from the challenge. He shoots the whole thing and his mouth twists. "It's like drinking a juniper bush," he wheezes.

"Ain't it great?" Elton, one of the mechanics who likes to come into the tasting room and geek out on engines with Lane, lets out a guffaw. "Is that the Dry?"

"Foster House Dry," I tell him. "Just for you."

Dean shakes his head and tosses his cup in the trash we keep by the booth. "You can have it." His expression darkens like he remembers he stopped by to get me worked up. "Well, I might have to save the sweet treats for tomorrow." He smirks. "Can't wait."

He strolls away and I glare at him.

"Who's Slick?" Elton asks, jerking his thumb over his shoulder.

"Some guy who thinks he's being smooth."

"And what do you think?" Elton's eyes are shrewd. He's barely over five and a half feet tall, but he's got swagger and arms as thick as the barrels in our rickhouse.

"I think he's going to bother Elodie."

A low growl comes from him. "I like her cannoli."

To anyone else, that'd sound like innuendo, but I've chatted with Elton enough—and I've tasted Elodie's cannoli—so I nod.

"Tell you what." He knocks on the tabletop. "I'll go see how the Dee's Sweets booth is doing. Why don't you package up my order of Dry?"

"Will do. And thank you."

"Those city boys gotta learn they can't fuck with us." He swaggers away and the crowd parts for him.

I have no idea if Dean is from a city, but he's got the same *I'm better than you* attitude that I encountered a lot growing up. Nor is he an overt flirt who can't take a hint like the girls in the bar last weekend. He's the type to corner Elodie after close. He didn't stop by the Foster House booth for the samples. I was his target. Why? Because I confronted him with Elodie? The guy waves too many red flags for me to relax while he's in the state.

The asshole mentioned tomorrow. He's staying somewhere close enough to return to Huckleberry Springs, and he's planning to come to the Taste of Springs tomorrow.

I'll be watching for him.

Elodie

I'm packing away my goods for the night when a shadow falls over me. Before alarm can spike in my veins, Cruz takes one of the cases I loaded the cookies in. "I can haul this for you."

My grin has to look as tired as I feel. "Thank you. I just have to get these inside and tie my tent shut."

"In the back?"

"Yes, please."

I admire the width of his shoulders as he holds his load. He makes it look easy. I catch his eye in the reflection of my window, and he smirks. Doesn't stop me from staring at his tight ass in his blue jeans. The denim is a darker blue, like his eyes.

He ducks inside and it's me staring back at myself. I'm wearing my cupcake shirt and skirt, and my hair is in a sloppy bun. Comfortable enough clothing. Loose and airy to keep me as cool as my cupcakes. He fucked the sex siren in the distillery, but he wanted this first. Shoving my glasses up with a satisfied grunt, I finish my closing duties.

Once I'm done securing my little stand, I heft two totes loaded with more sweets and my tablet and cash. Cruz appears and grabs those from me too. "Some of the booths are still shutting down. Want to walk around and see them?"

My excitement surges. "I'd love to. I was hoping to go around when I had Kinley here to help, but we were too busy to leave her alone."

"Be right back, and then we'll take a stroll."

After he returns, I lock the front door. He slips his hand around mine and we start down the sidewalk.

The couple who owns Wok and Rolls are kicked back in their camp chairs with a plate of food in their hands. A platter of my lemon drop cookies is between them on a small table. We exchanged a serving of lo mein and sweet-and-sour chicken for my cookies and two cupcakes. The portable buffet they set up is empty, and steam wafts from the open settings. They wave, unsurprised to see me holding Cruz Foster's hand.

People have seen him coming and going from Dee's Sweets for weeks. And there were our two dates outside of the bakery and his place.

I smile. "See you tomorrow." And I hope we can make the same food swap.

In between them and the corner is a booth for a butcher from out of town. They have packs of frozen steaks and hamburgers to sell, but they've already loaded up and cleared out for the evening.

Cruz continues to lead me the long way around. Most booths have their shades drawn for the night, but I get to see the setup and what's available. It's exactly as Campbell said. A small but busy affair. She thinks more visitors will be here on Saturday. All the cabins and rentals in and around Huckleberry Springs are full. Our lone motel is booked out, and I had one couple stop by from Texas. They're escaping their heat for ours.

This is what I want. A quiet evening with my guy, enjoying our small community and the people in it. I have connections with other business owners. They trust me—as long as I keep giving them a reason to.

"How was your day?" Cruz asks.

"It was good, but I hope it's busier tomorrow. How was yours?"

"Fine."

I glance at him. A five-o'clock shadow covers the hard slash of his jaw, but there's an ominous glint in his eyes. Everything was not fine. Will he talk to me when we're alone?

We reach the Foster House booth. Their sign with

the yellow logo is eye-catching and inviting. The whole tent is yellow and three times the size of mine.

Haven and Durban are packing up crates.

"Was it a good night?" Durban asks, leaning over the counter. Haven joins him. Two dark-haired country boys who happen to run a distillery.

I should take a picture of them like that and send it to Campbell. If all five of the guys lined up for a photo shoot and we put it on the flyers for next year, attendance would triple. "I moved a lot of cookies, but it was mostly one-off desserts. Hopefully, tomorrow there'll be orders by the dozen or half dozen. You?"

Haven grins. "Whiskey was flowing."

"And gin and vodka." Durban squints up and down the street. When his eyes fill with heat, I don't have to look to know Campbell's heading our way. "I expect tomorrow will be slower until the evening."

Campbell's skirt swishes a little harder around her knees when she notices Durban and she rushes over. He pushes back to wrap an arm around her and plant a big kiss on her.

A strong tug jerks my heart. The way Durban looks at her? That's the smoldering gaze I get from Cruz. How did I ever think he was messing with me? The heat has always been in his eyes, but now it glows.

"There's the lady behind the event," Haven says.

Campbell laughs but stays tucked into her man's side. Her bright gaze lands on me. "I was just coming to check on you. Need anything for tomorrow?"

"Nothing comes to mind." Other than more customers. Sell everything. Make it last forever so I don't have to pay off my ex and his brother and then figure out how to extract myself from the mess. "See you tomorrow."

Cruz and I resume walking. I have one more fair in Bozeman next month, and then it's holiday baking. But I can't keep up this breakneck pace. Cruz is going to get tired of my limited time. He hasn't said so, but the worry is in his features. I want to hire a full-time baker and give someone else in the area a chance to work a job they love instead of having to move to a bigger town. I want to do cookie dough fundraisers and help the community.

I want to give back, and I can't while my ex is still taking from me.

I took from him first.

No. That money was *mine*. Dwayne used me to pay his bills—and Damon's. All I did was take it back from him. He had such a big stash because he was living off me.

After waving goodbye, Cruz stays with me all the way to the bakery. I turn at the front door. This is a lot like getting dropped off after a date.

I'm anticipating a goodnight kiss—a long one—but his troubled gaze creates a lump in my throat. "What's wrong?"

He scratches the back of his neck. His hair is pushed off his face and there's no hat crease since he wasn't wearing it while working. I want to ruffle my fingers through it, but I stand still. "Did you get another visit from that guy Dean?"

A pit forms right in the middle of my stomach. Shit. Why would he ask that?

A chill drips into my veins.

"No." Horror almost chokes me. There's no other

reason Cruz would ask, or why he'd have that worried and pissed-off expression on his face. "Oh god, was he here?"

"You didn't see him?"

I look up and down the sidewalk. Where is that bastard? Did he harass Cruz and not me? Why? What game is that asshole playing?

There's no trace of Damon.

I dig into my pocket for my keys, unlock the door, and haul Cruz inside. "What happened?"

He gives his head a small shake. "So he didn't bother you?"

"Not today, no."

Relief smooths the crease on his forehead. "Good." He frowns. "He said he'd stop by tomorrow, and I'm not sure he just told me that to fuck with me."

A knot yanks so tight in my chest that I can barely breathe. Damon's lurking around. He's bothering a guy I'm seeing. When will this end?

"I think we should find Deputy Palmer."

I'm shaking my head before I open my mouth. "We can't."

"Elodie, something was seriously off with this guy. I think he might be stalking you." Concern is scrawled all over his handsome face, and it's for me. I'm a terrible person. I said I wouldn't be like my old self and here I am, justifying how what I'm doing isn't lying.

I let out such a long breath it's a surprise I'm not a deflated mess on the ground. "His name's not Dean. That was Damon, my ex's brother."

My gut twists in a hundred different directions when realization plays across his face. Disbelief. Understanding. Betrayal. That last look is like a physical slap, but I don't deserve any less.

"Like your ex who's in jail, Damon?"

"I'm sorry I lied." My voice is hoarse and hot tears fill my eyes.

"Why didn't you say anything?" He's not raging at me, but his pupils are big and it's not from desire.

"I don't want to drag you into it."

"Into what, Elodie?"

My lungs freeze and I can't inhale. I went too far. "Nothing." I squeeze my eyes closed. "No, it's not nothing. He and Dwayne want their money back."

"What money?"

"The stuff he put in an account with my name on it to hide. I paid his victims back and used the rest to buy my bakery." My vision gets blurry as tears crowd my eyes. "It was mine too. I-I paid all the bills. They lived off me and I supported those selfish pricks. It wasn't stealing." I swallow hard and a hot tear rolls down my cheek.

He brushes it away with the rough pad of his thumb. "It wasn't stealing," he repeats softly.

"I'm sorry I didn't tell you who he was the first time." Another tear falls and he catches that too, and I sniffle. "I thought that I could deal with him, but he just keeps asking for more."

Confusion dulls his eyes. "That's why he's in Huckleberry Springs? To bully money out of you?"

My heart pounds. I could leave it at that. If I can't tell my boyfriend I'm getting blackmailed, who can I tell? But Damon's starting to harass him. What if Damon goes after my family next to milk more pennies out of me? "He's . . ." Ugh. Do I have to do this?

"Yes?"

I lace my spine with steel. "He's blackmailing me."

The air gets sucked out of the room, and it's like a thundercloud builds right in front of me. A mass of swirling, boiling anger. "He's who you were on the phone with that one day?" His voice is cold, even. "When you were shouting about money? How long has he been harassing you?"

He's too smart and caring for his own good. I don't answer.

Cruz paces a few steps to each side before stopping in front of me. He props his hands on his hips. "What're the terms of his blackmail?"

"I pay him each month," I say hoarsely, "and he won't spread the word about everything I did."

"Everything you—" He tilts my face up to him. "You did nothing."

"I was—"

"Young. Scared. Getting conned."

"I would pretend I lost my wallet so older people would buy me a coffee." I wince at how absurd yet callous it sounds.

Incredulity screws up his face. "And if they'd heard what you were going through, they'd probably have bought you a coffee anyway."

I grip his wrists. He has to see what's at stake. "My family will learn what happened, and it'll stress them. Their health isn't the best. Huckleberry Springs is a small town. I'm asking the public to spend their money on me. They won't do that if they don't think they can trust me."

"You're underestimating just how highly everyone regards you."

My heart expands until it hugs my ribs. "I can't take the risk. If the bakery fails, I'll have to move to get a job to support myself. My parents need me. I lost too much time with them and Clem."

Some of the fury drains out of him. "Damn, Elodie. How many times have I told you that you don't have to do it all alone? You're worried about everyone but yourself, and trust me. I can handle that asshole." He growls the last part.

I'm worried about him too. "I know, but you have to respect me on this. My worst fear is that I'll drag my past into my present. You can't interfere, you can't call Callum, and you can't engage with Damon if you see him again."

He doesn't agree, but he pulls me into him. My cheek is tucked against his broad chest as he wraps me in his arms. I hook my hands around him and soak up the strength.

Fucking Damon. Fucking Dwayne. Fucking Dee Palmer, who wanted to live on the wild side.

"They used to call me Dee," I murmur against his shirt. "I hated it, but I named the bakery Dee's Sweets as a small fuck-you to both of them. I just never thought I'd be worth their time again."

I was once more a naive girl. It wasn't like they didn't know where I came from, but it's easier to link an entire business to me when I name it after the nickname they used to call me.

"That man isn't going to leave you alone," he says, the words flinty.

"He will. I'll figure it out."

"Not on your own, you won't. I'll help him figure out it's in his best interest to leave you the hell alone."

I yank back and spread my hands on his chest. "No, you won't. Damon is not going to interfere with you or the distillery. He's not going to be responsible for any bad rumors or gossip or whatever. Please don't engage with him."

"I'm not going to let him harass you."

"Cruz, please. I just need to get through the weekend."

"And after the weekend, you'll let me help?" Energy ripples under his skin, like if I let go, he'll bolt out the door and hunt Damon down.

I nod. Anything to make sure he doesn't get caught in Damon's snare. "Please. Promise me that you won't get involved."

He cups my chin and brushes his thumb across my lower lip. "I don't make empty promises."

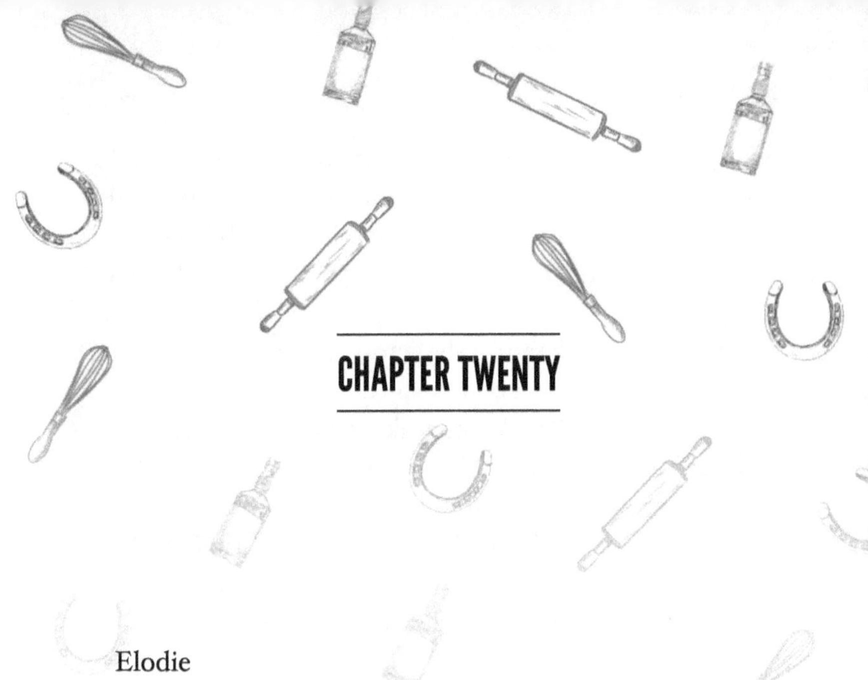

CHAPTER TWENTY

Elodie

The way my conversation ended last night with Cruz hangs over me like a rain cloud on an otherwise beautiful summer day. He didn't placate me. He didn't brush me off. His charm was gone and he was serious. I've been strung tight all day and flinching at shadows.

Someone grabs my elbow and I jump.

"Sorry!" Clem rips her hand off me. "I didn't mean to startle you."

"No, it's me, not you." For all his many faults, Damon is smoother than grabbing someone. He'll come back, act like a customer, hang around until I reach peak discomfort, then leave, letting me subtly know that he'll be back. I shouldn't be so skittish, but it's not me I'm concerned about. "I didn't sleep well."

I had Cruz's firm response to my begging playing on repeat in my head. He gave me a kiss and went to his place, like he knew that I'd keep on him until I got that fake promise I was demanding. It was for the best. I was too anxious from learning that Damon had confronted Cruz using the same method he's been using on me. What next? Dwayne starts writing Cruz letters too?

"Stressful weekend?" She crosses her arms and it crunches the pinwheel on her shirt.

I've got a different cupcake shirt on today and another long, loose skirt. "How're the kids' games?"

"Also stressful." She flashes me a grin. "But empty right now. Seems to be a lull all around and I thought I'd come to say hi."

"And refill the mini cookies for the kiddos?"

"For me." She peruses my selections. "I'm loving the crossover with Foster House. The shortbread with gin-soaked raspberries is orgasmic."

"I'll write that on the description."

"Your silent auction donation is up to a hundred and fifty bucks. That white chocolate cake is getting people in a choke hold."

Cruz is probably driving up the price, and he'll pay as much as it takes. I grin.

Clem rolls her eyes. "Your boyfriend is buying it? Ugh, that's so sweet."

Another wave of customers is making their way up the street. My breakfast of those very cookies curdles in my stomach. Is there a medium-height guy in the bunch who looks like he's going to the golf course after?

If I lean over far enough, I might get a glimpse of the Foster House booth, but I'll never see the guys through the throng of samplers. Their booth is one of the most popular, constantly surrounded by people, just like it was in Billings.

Nerves cartwheel around my stomach. That's been happening all day.

Clem finds my container of minis and tucks it under her arm. "I should get back. Is Kinley helping out today?"

"She's out getting a bite to eat. I traded again with the Huangs for some more sesame chicken. I wanted to stick around the booth, and they have their grandkids tomorrow and wanted some extra treats."

Clem groans and holds her stomach. "I wish I could trade the library's books for food. Actually, I'm just going to head there and bring a plate back with me." She's about to cut through my tables to weave between the back of the booths where most of the vendors walk, but she stops. "Are you okay? Is it just the sleep?"

Do I look like hell? I slept horribly last night without Cruz next to me.

"I'm fine." A guy walks past, and I do a double take. He's wearing wraparound sunglasses and has a long dark braid down his back. Nothing like Damon. Dammit. "I'll be fine. It's just . . . everything's catching up with me, and I'm worried it'll interfere with the important things."

"Like your boyfriend?" Her light teasing hits home.

"Yes."

It's her turn to look surprised. "Oh, Elodie. That man is not going anywhere."

"It's . . ." I wave a hand in front of my face. The group of tourists is coming closer. "I'll talk to you later." And I will. I'll tell her about how Damon keeps stopping by, and hell, maybe I should tell her about the blackmail. More minds can help me figure this mess out.

The next few hours fly by. We get another couple of

rushes, and I sell more than singles of cupcakes and cookies. A few people order a dozen, several that live in nearby small towns take my card, and there's a lot of gushing about the Foster House collaboration. Kids are happy to get in on the baked samples when they can't sip and sample with their parents.

Best of all, my day was Damon-free. I just hope Cruz's was too.

I don't have much to pack up. I let Kinley go since the cleanup won't take long. Is Cruz going to stop by again?

What will I say? We didn't exactly part on a bad note, but it wasn't a good one either.

I bring a folding table inside the bakery and push back out onto the sidewalk.

Damon's standing at the corner of what's left of my booth, his arms crossed, and an arrogant twist to his lips.

"Ugh." I was stressed the whole day because of him and he shows up at the end, and he likely did that on purpose. Damn him! "You're like a turd that won't flush down."

His anger is immediate, darkening his eyes. "Do you have my money?"

Cruz's reassurance from last night stays with me. "Do you mean more of *my* money that you're blackmailing from me?"

His shocked expression gives me a short moment of satisfaction. He looks around, and so do I. I should've done that before I cocked off. No one's close enough to hear, and anyone who saw us would think he's just a latecomer.

I prop my hands on my hips. "It's not the end of the month."

"Close enough."

"Fuck off. I still have time."

"I'd hate for someone to hear about how you used to whore yourself—"

Damon flies to the side and slams into the wall of the bakery, thankfully missing a window.

Cruz steps onto the sidewalk, his features livid and his hands balled into fists. "Shut your goddamn mouth."

"Cruz! Stop." I don't know whether to run or laugh or cry. I could've handled Damon, but I also loved seeing him go flying.

Damon shakes his head. "What the hell—"

Cruz shoves his finger in Damon's face, crowding him toward the buildings. With more size and experience—and fury—than Damon, Cruz has no problem intimidating him. "If you don't fucking listen, you're going through the window this time. And then I'll stand on top of you and make you glue every goddamn piece back together."

Damon backs up so far, he hits the building again. "Get out of my face."

"Get out of my town," Cruz says through gritted teeth.

"She owes me money," Damon shoots back.

Dread fills me and I have the urge to sprint again.

Cruz looms in front of him. "She doesn't owe you a goddamn thing."

I've never seen him like this. All charm is gone. There's no humor. His eyes are almost black. He's in cowboy boots, but he stands ready to chase Damon down. His arms are out and ready, and his hands are clenching and unclenching into fists.

"Cruz." I creep closer to him. The angry kid is now an irate adult. "Let him go."

Damon slips out from between the wall and Cruz. Cruz pivots to make sure he's blocking me from Damon. I scoot to the side to peer around him.

Oh hell. The sidewalk is lined with everyone who's still here. Worse, the three Hennessy brothers and Lane are flanking Cruz. Of course this is the moment all of them are together.

Damon looks behind him and grimaces. He must've spotted the line of tall, dark men with menacing expressions. His mouth curls into a sneer and he pins me with a glare over Cruz's shoulder. "The due date is soon. Don't be late."

Cruz steps to the side to block his glare. "Start walking, fuckface."

"You need to stay out of this." Damon's menacing voice has nothing on Cruz. "She doesn't want people to know about her criminal back—"

The punch is so fast, I jump back and gasp. The smack of Cruz's fist against Damon's face is louder than I could've ever imagined.

I dart to the side to see better. Damon's stumbling around, trying to keep his balance. Cruz is flexing his hand.

"What the fuck!" Damon's working his jaw around and shaking his head. A trickle of blood escapes from the corner of his mouth.

"Start walking." Cruz's steel tone makes a shiver whisper over my skin.

Damon spins around but spots the men glaring at him. Even the Huangs are standing guard between the booths like they're making sure Damon can't hide anywhere. He pivots toward me and Cruz.

"Boy, you'd better start running." Cruz stalks toward him.

Damon takes the advice, tucking his head down and doing a lurching jog. At the last second, each of the Foster House men moves out of the way, but not enough that Damon doesn't get jostled going through them.

Satisfaction fills me, but the ramifications are right behind it.

Cruz whips around, and he's back to being my Cruz with a concerned blue gaze and a softness just for me. "Are you okay?" He rushes to close the distance between us, but I scurry backward.

His boots skid to a stop. "Elodie."

I shake my head. Dismay fills me so full. My temples ache. "You weren't supposed to do that."

"The shit he was spewing was wrong."

"He's going to tell everyone," I say in a strangled whisper. My pulse jumps and lurches. God, what a mess.

The attention of the onlookers burns into me. My skin shrinks tight while my insides expand from all the fear and anxiety. I can't stand this. I rush into the bakery.

Cruz is on my heels all the way to the kitchen. "Look, I'm sorry—"

"Are you?" I yell and throw an arm in the air. "Are you really? I asked you not to confront him."

"He called you a whore!"

"That's *my* problem." My hands flop down and hit my thighs. Stress is a vortex in my belly, making it clench to heave the lunch I had hours ago. "Now I'm going to have more."

"We'll deal with him."

I draw in a shaky breath. He's so sure of himself. So resolute. He doesn't know what's at stake. How could he? I didn't talk to him. "He's going to ruin my business, Cruz. This is a game to him."

"A game you don't need to play."

"But I do! He doesn't need the money. He'll use it, but he doesn't need it. He wants to see me panic. He wants me to scramble to pay him. And when I fail, he's going to have just as much fun telling everyone about me and watching my business disintegrate."

"No one's going to believe a cocksucker like him. Huckleberry Springs loves you, your family, and the bakery."

Misery sets in. Love isn't enough. "They didn't scam thousands of dollars because they sucked. The only reason they didn't do millions was because they wanted to stay under the radar. If Dwayne hadn't gotten into drugs, he would still be doing it. I would've wised up and left, but I'd be broke as hell." Anguish twists in my chest. So many problems; all my fault. "I can't lose this bakery."

"You won't."

"I know. Because I'm going to figure a way out of it." I poke myself in the chest. "*Me*. I know how to deal with them. I know how their brains work. I'll take care of it myself."

"You don't have to." Worry lines his face and he crosses to me. I want to lean into him as much as I want to push him away. "It'll be two against one."

"It's my mess. You made it worse."

He rocks back on his heels, and I regret what I said and the tone of it, but I can't deny the truth. Maybe I would've had one or two payments to make before I figured out what to do. It could've been three or four more months. Hell, a year. But I'd have my bakery in the end. My parents wouldn't make themselves sick with sorrow. My sister wouldn't be ashamed of me. Now? I don't know.

"You need to leave." The words hurt to say, but it's for the best. For him and for me, even if it feels like the worst thing I could do to myself. "You need to leave me alone."

He stares at me for a moment, working his jaw back and forth. Then he pivots on a heel and storms out.

Cruz

My house is dark. I sat outside with Rufus until the sun sank below the horizon. The wind picked up and rain spat in my face, driving me inside with my conflicted feelings.

I prop my feet on the coffee table in front of my couch. My gaze bounces off the bare walls. Elodie said the space doesn't need added decoration, but as I sit here, wondering if she'll speak to me again, the emptiness isn't helping me. It doesn't matter how clean my place is or how much I shower; I ended up alone because I stepped in with my fists.

I don't regret it. That fucker. How long had Dean—*Damon* been stalking her?

Was she scared to tell me, afraid I'd make it worse?

Or worried that I'd revert to a part of myself I'm ashamed of?

I proved her right.

I push a hand through my hair. Basil jumps onto the couch with a little mew. He stomps onto my lap and curls up. Sage does the same. The center of my cold chest warms. I never had pets of my own before my kittens and dog. They help a lot when I'm sitting and berating myself.

I rest my head on the back of the couch. After several moments, headlights swing across the window, and hope sparks hot in my chest. Disturbing the kittens, I sit up straighter and they readjust themselves. A sigh leaves me. It's a pickup, not Elodie's car.

Since my door's unlocked, I stay where I am. Another set of headlights swings in.

There's a knock and then nothing. The door cracks open. "Yo, Cruz?"

"I'm here."

More footsteps than just Lane's pile in and the light flips on. I blink against the onslaught.

The scrape of their boots on the rug fills the air, and then some muttering. Clothing rustles and there're a couple of grunts as they take their boots off.

I tuck my finger into Basil's soft fur. "How many of you are there?"

"All of us." Lane comes out of the entry, shoving his hair off his face. His black T-shirt is sprinkled with wet spots.

"Why?"

Iverson pushes past him. "We wouldn't leave Lane alone about you. He swore you'd want some time to yourself, or we'd have brought dinner."

I haven't eaten, but my appetite is gone. "I'm not hungry."

"I brought some leftover pasta." Durban shoves a container into my hands and sets a plastic fork on top of it. "Campbell made extra, so I brought you some. Haven's got your win from the silent auction."

Haven holds up a decorative box with a cake inside and baking supplies. Elodie's donation, which I made sure I won.

"You can put that on the table. Or take it to work tomorrow and eat it." When he puts the reminder of Elodie on my kitchen table, I frown at the food in my hand. "You didn't have to ditch your home for me." He didn't fuck up his relationship.

"Campbell wanted to know why the hell I came home in the first place." He sits across from me on the love seat and Haven drops next to him. "We're not the ones Lane needs to warn about giving you space."

"Jamison heard the story and about booted me out too," Iverson grumbles, but his shrewd gaze is taking in my bruised knuckles, my disheveled, fur-covered shirt, and the kitten giving me moral support.

"I'm just nosy," Haven says, and my chuckle sputters out of me.

"At least one of you's honest." I rest my hand on Sage, letting her slow breathing soothe me. I meet Lane's gaze. He's guarded, like he didn't have a choice but to lead the Hennessys to my doorstep. I give a shake of my head to let him know I don't mind, but I try to convey that I'm not talking about Elodie's business. I'd shone a spotlight on it once already. "I can't tell you guys everything that happened. Elodie's a private person."

"Some jackass harassed her, and you took care of him." Durban shrugs. "That's all anyone has to know."

Appreciation wells for their understanding when it comes to her.

Haven rests his elbows on his knees and presses his fingertips together. "Is he going to be a concern again?"

Lane nods before I can decide how to answer. "Between the five of us, we can keep an eye out for him. I'm sure her cousin will keep an eye out too."

I nod and scrub my face. Good. If she doesn't want me around her, there are still others looking out for her. "Thanks."

"We're worried about you," Lane says. A smile teases his lips. "All of us, apparently."

Haven taps his fingertips. "You left the bakery looking like we all took turns kicking Rufus, and just thinking about that breaks my damn heart."

"I'd kill any guy who hit him. Just like I'd gut a bastard for threatening Elodie." I swallow hard. "But she asked me not to and I did it anyway."

"Give her time," Lane says quietly. "It's a shock to see someone get hit when it hasn't been a part of your life."

Everyone nods. Well, aren't we a group? "What if she's done with me?"

"You won her over once," Iverson says. "You can do it again. She lights up around you."

Fuck, that makes me feel worse. "She asked me not to interfere. I've worked hard to build her trust and then I broke it at the first opportunity."

"But you'd do it all over again," Durban says softly, "because it'd make her life better."

"Feels selfish." I'm only putting part of Elodie first.

I'm using information she didn't want me to know. I could make her situation worse too.

"In some cases, it's not." Durban flicks some of Rufus's fur off his jeans. It's not a long walk between his truck and the house, but enough to get corgi glitter on him. "Sometimes they can't do it themselves. Elodie probably would've kept tolerating that guy's shit out of fear. She only sees how he can hurt her or the bakery. It's not selfish to step in. I did it for Campbell. I didn't know if it'd work, but I had her family's support."

But Elodie's family doesn't know and she wants to keep it that way. Durban might have a point, but I could open a big can of worms and dump them right in her bakery. "I'd do it again, but I think it cost me her."

I trail my fingers over the darker tabby lines on Basil. Tonight's ending differently than I thought it would. I'd be inside Elodie by now. We'd at least be in the dark, talking about the fair and who we saw and our plans for next year.

Instead, I'm here, surrounded by a bunch of well-meaning nosy fuckers. "Thanks for stopping by, guys. I'm fine. Really. I just need to think things through and decide how to talk to her."

I pretend not to notice them all exchanging looks.

"I'll stay behind for a few minutes," Lane says, and that seems to appease the Hennessys.

They all get up, and when I wrap my hands around the cats to rise, Iverson waves me off. "I'm not one to interrupt a guy covered in pussy."

Haven groans. "That's as good as a dad joke."

"He's going to be too far gone before we know it," Durban says. The interaction lifts my mood for two whole seconds.

Lane walks them out, leaving me alone for a few moments. I return to where I was before they arrived.

How do I make Elodie's problems go away? Blackmailing is fucking illegal, so why is Elodie suffering? How much has she paid that asshole ex of hers? I start to ball my hands into fists, but flatten them on the kittens instead. If the guys see my reaction, they might think I'll do something brash.

I'm tempted to drive around town and make sure Damon's gone. If I found him . . .

I'd be back to betraying Elodie.

Lane comes inside. "I tried to tell them."

"Don't worry about it." I slump on the couch. "If we were in Bourbon Canyon, I wouldn't have gotten left alone. I don't intend to complain about people caring about me."

He chuckles and returns to his seat. "True. Still hits odd though, doesn't it?"

"Always." The second I mentally returned to the old, dirty house I grew up in, a Bailey would magically show up to chat, and it didn't matter where I was on the ranch. "I just want to help her. Even if I lose her, I have to know she's safe."

"You don't think that guy will leave her alone?"

"Not him and not her ex."

"Her ex in jail?"

I lift my head. He's frowning, and my gaze strays to the office I barely use. I pay any bills that aren't automatic and keep important documents in it. Junk mail gets tossed there. Along with the letters I don't read from our dad.

I stare a little longer. Her ex needs to be stopped.

"You should talk to Mae," Lane says carefully, "before you do anything impulsive. Maybe even Myles."

"I'm not going to do anything impulsive."

He gives me a hard look.

I did deck a guy today. I would've stomped on him, hooked him to my hitch, and dragged him out of town.

Talking to Myles or Mae is a good idea. They set me on the right path a long time ago and kept me there. "I'd like to go over this in person, but I don't know when I can get to Bourbon Canyon."

"Tomorrow. I can cover the distillery with Haven. The guys won't mind. You know that. Go do what you gotta do." His attention touches on the office. "Take as long as you need."

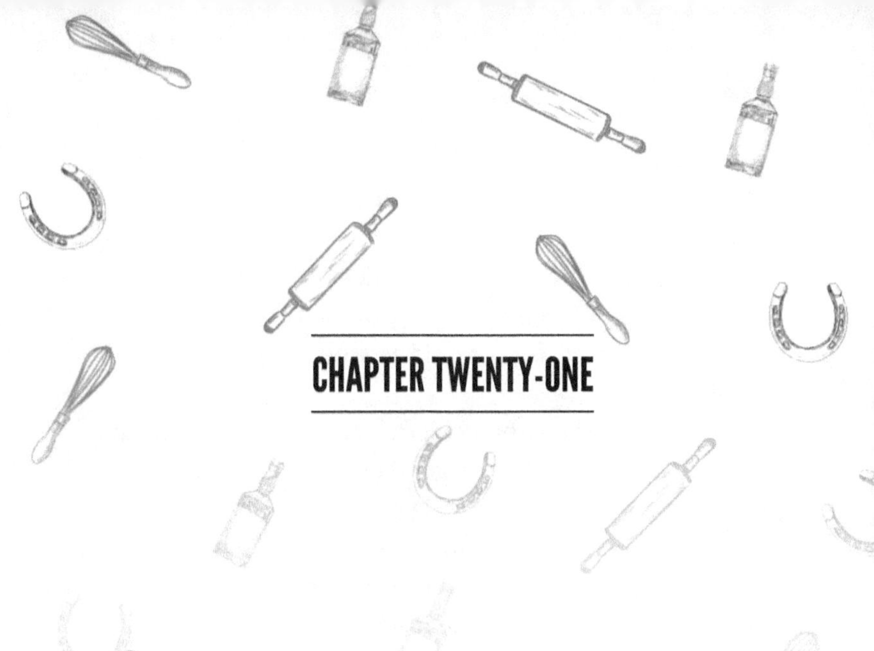

CHAPTER TWENTY-ONE

Cruz

Shortly after lunch on Sunday, I walk into the back door of Mae's house and wipe my boots off like I used to do. Voices and laughter fill the air of the sprawling log cabin. The kitchen opens to my right and the rest of the house sprawls beyond it. To my left is the laundry room. So damn familiar and more homey feeling than my own place.

Tate Bailey, Mae's oldest kid, rounds the corner from the dining room and slaps me on the shoulder. His beard is still neatly trimmed, but there's gray in it when there was none when I first met him. "Nice to see you back, but you missed the meal."

I spent the morning helping with chores to clear my head before the drive and to wake me up after a restless night of sleep. Torn between whether I should reach out to Elodie or wait for her to do so first, I looked at my phone a million times.

It's her choice to reach out to me. I'll leave her alone like she asked. Doesn't mean I won't take care of her.

"Did I make it in time for dessert?" My appetite hasn't made an appearance, but I forced myself to have toast for breakfast. Eggs would've stolen the urge to eat a single morsel.

"It's always time for dessert." Tate grins. "Madison keeps Mama stocked with goodies, but Mama made a pie with the cherries from this year."

I'll stay away from Madison's baked goods. I don't know if I'll get to take Elodie to Scooter's Confections one day. If I have a single cupcake from there, Mae will find me wallowing in a corner.

I leave the kitchen and its many good memories to enter the dining room, where I'm greeted by Tate's family. Myles and Wynter are there with their kids, who push away from the table to give me hugs.

My niece, Elsa, leads me to a seat, and a plate of cherry pie is slid in front of me. Chatter resumes like I never interrupted, and I appreciate that no pointed questions are aimed my way.

I cut a giant piece off and shove it into my mouth. Questions fill my head. Does Elodie like to make pie? Are they too time-consuming when she's the only baker? She mentioned rhubarb and— My throat grows so thick I have a hard time swallowing. Goddammit.

Elodie and her damn independent streak is going to be her undoing.

But it won't be her fucking ex.

I somehow finish the rest of my pie, barely tasting it, and that's a shame. Each bite makes me think of Elodie and one of her baked goods. Does she ever use cherries?

What if Mae gave her some? Would she like some even if she's done with me?

Soon, everyone's done with their dessert and the pie dish only contains crumbs. Tate gathers his wife, Scarlett, and their teens. They all give me another hug before he ushers them out of the house. He must've guessed that I'm here to talk to my brother or Mae.

Myles claps me on the shoulder. "Got a minute?"

My stomach sinks. I punched a guy at a street fair I was at for Foster House, and he's already heard about it? Fuck me. I didn't think of that until now. I let my temper take over and justified it as defending Elodie. She warned me about what could happen.

He leads me to the porch. It's a warm afternoon, but the shade of the overhang keeps it cool. He sits in one of the rocking chairs flanking a small round table, then gestures to the other seat.

When I first met my brother, he was wearing a suit, hair rigidly styled, and his expression set in granite. Now he's relaxed. He's the CEO of Foster House, a philanthropist, and a dad. That hardness is still there, but the refinement was all a put-on, just like me. Myles went from awful foster home to okay foster home until he landed at the Baileys', and then he took off. We can never be easygoing country guys because of the way we grew up. Because of that, we have to be quick to admit when we're wrong.

I plop myself down, kick my boots out, and readjust my Foster House ball cap. The Bailey ranch sprawls across the countryside. I soak it all in and settle on the barn. Every part of this property holds memories, but there's a powerful one by that barn. "I fucked up."

"Sure did."

"Are we going to get sued?"

He rolls a shoulder, his expression unconcerned. "Did the guy have it coming?"

"He called Elodie a whore."

"Good enough for me."

"I shoved him for that. I punched him when he threatened to—" Shit. Everything is her business. What do I say? "She knows him, and he and his brother have a grudge against her through little fault of her own. She heaps all the blame on herself though."

"Sounds like it was self-defense, then."

"He posed no threat to me." Reality sinks in harder than before. "I don't think he'll leave her alone, and I can't promise I won't do it again."

He squints into the distance beyond the hill and the barn and pastures at the bottom. Horses graze, their tails swishing around them. Chickens dart across the yard by a little shed. "If anyone came for Wynter or the kids, I would dismantle them piece by piece and bury them in the hills. I wouldn't give a fuck about Foster House."

That's the Myles Foster not many people get to see.

He rocks slowly. Faint wings of gray at his temples wink in the light. "Our lawyers can handle any trouble that comes our way. I'm not worried."

"Damn, I forget that you're richer than shit sometimes."

He grins and stretches his jean-clad legs out. "Money helps a lot. I have a feeling that something's bothering you that money won't solve."

"I overstepped with Elodie."

He lets out a low whistle. "I don't know her that well, but she seems like she doesn't put up with bullshit."

"She didn't put up with mine for years. She's an island. Family and friends will do anything for her, but she doesn't let them."

"You here to talk to Mae?"

"The last advice she gave me worked."

He snorts. "The first advice she gave me after I reconnected with Wynter got me laid."

I bark out a laugh. "Actually, that's what happened for me too. Eventually." I fall quiet. "I need to do more this time, or those guys won't back off. They need a strong damn message that I will ruin them, and I know Elodie might not ever talk to me again, but at least she'll be safe." Those bastards won't get one more cent from her. "I have an idea, and I think it's a bad one."

"Sometimes, those are the most effective."

"It involves my dad."

"I feel like we need some bourbon for this." He disappears inside and returns with two glasses of amber liquid. I don't bother to ask him what line he poured. It doesn't matter. The flavor will taste like ash, just like the pie.

I take a drink, letting it burn across my tongue and down my throat. "I don't even know if my idea will help."

"Will it hurt?"

"Not her."

"Ah. I see. You're gambling a part of yourself you've never played with before."

"Of all the things Mama passed down, gambling wasn't one of them."

"Yeah, it was." He takes a drink and swirls the glass, staring at the amber liquid. "You bet with your time and your freedom. You got into fights you didn't know you'd win. You put whatever job you had at the time at risk."

The next gulp of bourbon warms the cold his words filled me with.

"The day you showed up here is the day you quit gambling," he continues. "You changed as soon as Mae offered you a job. You weren't going to risk the opportunity. Now you've found something worth risking again. I guess the question you have to ask yourself is . . . are the odds worth it?"

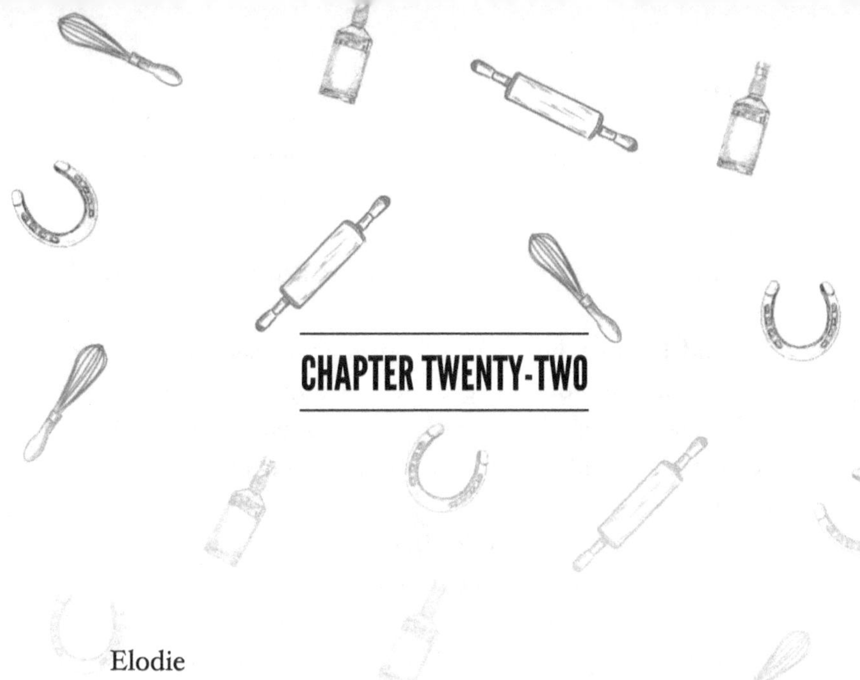

CHAPTER TWENTY-TWO

Elodie

My finger hovers over the transfer button in my bank account. I waited until zero hour, and I'm still stalling. Worry should be clawing at the back of my neck.

It's been almost two weeks since the street fair. I haven't heard from Cruz, and each day that goes by without him coming through the back door breaks my heart a little. Soon, it'll be cracked all the way through in a million different directions.

He left because I told him to. And he hasn't come back.

Grief tears through my chest wall and I glare at the computer screen.

I've been doing nothing but work since the Taste of Springs. The day after, my cousin asked me about the altercation between Damon and Cruz. Apparently, "no one saw a thing," but everyone was talking about it. He also said he ran into a guy with a bloody nose, but that guy skedaddled when he saw Callum's name tag. Deputy Palmer. I would've laughed if my heart weren't cracked in two.

Cruz risked everything to help me, and I told him to leave me alone.

And because he's a stand-up guy, he has. He must think I'm the worst. I've done nothing but push him away, and I don't know what to do about it. I'm still getting blackmailed, and I still don't want him to suffer the drama.

No. It's better that we're apart.

A stabbing pain hits me dead center in my chest.

Since the fair, I've had a flood of inquiries and have been scheduling custom cakes and other desserts. I'm hardly in the front ringing up orders anymore. The drama has been good for the bottom line, which in turn has kept me busy. Nothing will take my mind off Cruz though. If anything, I think about him more.

Like the fundraiser that was his idea. Thanks to Campbell, I'm also planning a low-key kickoff for the cookie dough fundraiser. I'm going to be busy for the foreseeable future and I will have no issues covering the payments to Dwayne and his brother.

My stomach twists on itself, and I close out of the window. I might be late with the payment. It might be never.

Tears fill my eyes. I could destroy everything I've worked for, but the last two weeks have *sucked*. I get up late every day. I slog around in the back, taking way too long to do anything, which makes me work later, get to bed well after normal, and the misery starts all over again.

Is it worth it? Is paying the blackmail worth the emptiness in my life?

Ironically, there's nothing but a vast chasm inside of me that highlights how lonely and isolated I was before.

Enough. I have to get my work done.

I get up and grab my apron off the island. Tying it around my waist, I wander around the counter to look at the next recipe I have to make. Several minutes tick by, and I continue to stare at the paper. The words blur together.

A hot tear rolls down my cheek and there's no tall man with a crooked smile to wipe it away. There's no rough-around-the-edges country boy to reassure me that everything will be fine. Cruz isn't here to tell me I'm not alone.

Because I'm very much alone.

I don't want to be. Swallowing a swell of remorse, I find my phone and pull up the family text thread that's full of supper plans and arrangements for me and Clem to go to their place to clean.

Me: Can you guys all come here? ASAP?

I let out a long exhale. The tension is already untangling at the base of my spine, relaxing all the way up to my shoulders and I haven't said anything yet.

Next, I pull up a number I haven't used for years. Damon Miller.

"What?" he answers and hostility oozes through the phone.

I roll my eyes. How did I *ever* put up with him? "I'm not even officially late yet."

"Late? The payments are over, and I'll return what you've paid before Labor Day, like I said."

I give my head a shake. Did I hear him wrong? I was

calling to tell him that it's over. He can tell whoever he wants anything about me, but the blackmail is over. "What?"

"I have time yet. You don't need to fucking harass me." Is there a thread of fear in his voice?

"Harass you?" Did I call a different Damon, one who's also blackmailing someone and grew a conscience?

"Yeah, those fucking guys you sent made it loud and clear, but it's not Labor Day yet. I need time."

"What guys?"

He huffs into the phone. "You know what fucking guys." When I don't answer, he lets out a frustrated grunt. "Didn't your boyfriend tell you?"

I can't confess that I haven't talked to Cruz since the sidewalk argument. I can't believe I ever risked what I had with him because of this asshole.

"His fucking dad made sure Dwayne and I understand loud and clear to leave you alone."

Shock punches me in the chest and I cough out a breath, but it sounds like a laugh. Cruz's dad? He doesn't talk to his dad.

"It's not fucking funny, Elodie. They broke into my house. Dwayne got his ass kicked in his cell."

My mouth hangs all the way open. "They did what?"

"Sy Lawson and his fucking son."

"Cruz beat Dwayne up?"

"His guys did. The man is in a different goddamn prison, Elodie, and he still got to Dwayne. And me!" Now the terror is unmistakable. "So I get it, okay? I'll leave you alone. Your secrets are safe. We'll pay you back, and we won't tell a soul, but dammit. You have to leave us alone too."

I snap my mouth shut. I don't know what Cruz did

or what he put into motion, but I'm also not going to mess with it. Damon and my ex were prudent in their cons. They got impatient and greedy, but they were otherwise careful about the kind of people they conned. No one violent, and no one with connections.

Who knew I'm the one with connections?

"That's up to Cruz," I say, trying to keep my voice strong when I don't know whether to keep crying or to let out a guffaw and laugh the night away. "Goodbye, Damon. I'd better not hear from you or your brother again."

I hang up, and this time I do chortle. I'm downright giggling when Clem walks into the kitchen. I'm relieved. I'm distraught. I'm hopeful while still feeling hopeless.

"Is everything okay?" she asks cautiously.

Everything might be ruined. Maybe I have no chance with Cruz after I kicked him out. But he went behind my back and tampered with a situation that should've been none of his business, and he didn't tell me. He didn't swagger in here waiting for his accolades. He hasn't even called to nonchalantly see if I drop the fact that he solved my blackmail problem.

Not only did he make it go away, but he obliterated the whole ordeal. Damon's petrified. Dwayne has got to be sleeping with one eye open, and after I think about the way they kept me as their personal chef, housekeeper, and meal ticket, I like the thought of that.

"I don't know what's okay." I toss my glasses on the table as more laughter spills out of me, but so do tears. I'm crying and sputtering when Clem rushes to my side.

"Elodie! Are you okay?"

"No. I don't know." I'm okay because Cruz made sure

of it. Dabbing at my eyes is like trying to block a river with my finger. "I've been so stupid."

"You are not stupid." She darts to the bathroom and returns with a bunch of tissues. "Here. Mom's going to fret."

"I know." Now it's less laughing and more crying. "I don't want to worry her, but I'm going to have to give her at least one sleepless night."

"She'll be fine. She always is—as long as you're okay."

I sniffle and blow my nose. My parents have been through a lot and just because they're older than the parents of most people my age doesn't mean they're feeble. I've suspected for a long time that Mom asks us to weed and clean so we'll actually come over regularly. She grew two independent girls who like to throw themselves into work.

"I've been willfully ignorant."

"I'll accept that." She sits across from me. "You're just like Mom, taking the blame for everything."

I sink my head into my hands. "Oh my god, that's it. I'm not smothering anyone, but I'm keeping you all from stressing."

"Then you need to be more like Dad and talk my ear off."

"Yeah. I will. It's time." I get up to toss my used tissues and take my apron off. After throwing it into the dirty laundry, I grab two more chairs from the front and drag them to the back.

There's a knock at the door. Now it really is the moment where I spill everything. I should've talked to them months ago. I should've talked to them *years* ago. Today, that changes. Cruz crossed a line he never intended to get near, and he did it for me. So I'm going to bound over all the limits I set for myself and hope that at the end, he's there.

My parents greet me. Dad holds on to Mom's hand and concern lines each of their faces. They must be fraught after my text. I never invite them to the bakery. I bring them goodies, but geez, why haven't I asked them to come hang out with me on those long nights?

Because I'm scared I'll be the reason something bad happens. Just like when I crashed with me and Mom.

"Hey, have a seat." I sniffle, and crap, I must look like a rabid mess, just short of foaming at the mouth.

Dad wraps me in a big hug, no questions asked, as if he assumes I wouldn't answer him anyway.

I don't have to. I don't need to do any of this. Cruz took care of the blackmail. Damon and Dwayne are too scared to talk. If they wait longer, until Cruz's dad loses power and influence, then too much time will have passed. I'll have established too solid of a reputation to be affected by whatever the Miller brothers would say.

But keeping what happened to myself hasn't helped me at all. I've been isolated for years—from friends and family. Cruz knows the whole sordid story, and he still did something he swore he wouldn't do. He did it for me, knowing everything. If I hadn't been so jaded and secretive, could I have spent some of those years with him? All of the blackmail would've stopped before it started, I know that. Cruz would've made sure of it.

How's he doing?

The more I think about him, the more anxiety will eat me from the inside out. He talked to his dad. He's been adamantly avoiding everything about his dad, but he must've done it. For me.

I love that man.

I swipe at my drying cheeks, straighten my shoulders, and take a seat. "I have to tell you guys about what happened after culinary school."

Cruz

My place is a mess. I didn't think I'd ever say that again, but it took a little over a week to get cluttered and full of crumbs. At least I haven't crept into disgusting territory, although I haven't cleaned up all the cat treats that Basil spilled yesterday, or the toilet paper from the roll the kittens dragged to the hallway and demolished.

I'm off today, but I've been worthless at work since I returned from my trip to Bourbon Canyon and then Colorado. I've been working every waking moment, and I've needed to in order to fix all the fuckups I caused. A batch of gin was mislabeled as vodka. I got the bottle sizes incorrect, and Haven had to refigure the distribution so we didn't have to dump and rebottle it all. Then I messed up an entire batch of whiskey yesterday, and Lane finally sent me home.

My sleep has been shit. Elodie still hasn't reached out, and she had to have heard something by now. If I expected her to fly across town and into my arms, that's not happening. My appetite is crap, but Lane puts packaged leftovers of his food in my fridge, and the Hennessys must have some food rotation set up. One of them is always casually bringing in something for lunch that's enough for everyone.

I scratch at the stubble at my jaw. Shaving went out

the window several days ago. Without the guys, I wouldn't have eaten. I owe them, and I owe them not to muck it all up at work. So I'll take today to get my head and my heart patched up. Maybe someday I'll feel normal again.

It'd help if I knew what was going on. Have I made everything worse? The worst-case scenario is that I've undone everything I've achieved in the last fourteen years, but even sitting in my quiet house with a kitten chasing a scrap of toilet paper and wondering if Elodie will ever smile at me again, I know I'm not that kid anymore. It'll take more than decking a guy or talking to my dad to turn me back into the old Cruz.

Trusting myself is a mild consolation prize for the mess I've made.

An engine sounds in the distance. Not Lane's pickup. Maybe the mail?

A minute later, there's a knock at the door. Shit. I'm not presentable. My basketball shorts got a hole in them two days ago when I wore them out with my muck boots to do chores, my hair is going in a few different directions, and there's a drop of mustard on my shirt from the brat Lane made and dropped off that I ate for breakfast. Regardless, I push off the couch.

When I open the door to a wide-eyed Elodie in a sundress and sandals, I nearly shut it again. I've gone off the deep end and I'm seeing things. It's been weeks since she kicked me out of the bakery and out of her life.

I blink. "Elodie?"

"I know what you did." She clutches her hands in front of her, and a crease forms between her brows. "Did you really go to see your dad?"

I'm not too far gone to notice the flare of her hips in

the loose material or how the sunflower on the top hugs her tits. Damn, she looks good. Still edible, like her sweet treats. I scratch the back of my neck. A lock of hair falls in front of my eyes. Did I comb it this morning? What was her question?

Right, my dad. Anxiety courses through my veins. Time to face the reckoning. "Yeah. I'm sorry, I couldn't let your ex blackmail you."

The furrow deepens and her gaze intensifies. Damn. As I suspected, my interference is the nail in the coffin. My stomach twists. Now I have to live with it.

"Oh, Cruz." She throws her arms around me, nearly barreling me over.

Her sugar-cookie scent washes over me, along with shock and sweet, cool relief. I catch and embrace her, a smile tugging at my lips for the first time in weeks. The door swings shut behind her as I move us farther into the house. "Are you telling me I'm forgiven, sugar?"

"There's nothing to forgive." Her reply is muffled by my shoulder. "I'm so sorry I pushed you away."

I bury my face in her hair and inhale everything Elodie. "As long as you want me, you're never going to be able to push me that far."

She pulls back, searching my face. She brushes my hair off my forehead. Her lips curve into a small smile that rights my crooked world. "Kind of nice to see you a rumpled mess." She holds me at arm's length. "Not even jeans. Oh my god, is that a hole in your shorts?"

The urge to run and change is fleeting, thanks to her smile rooting me in place. "There are no holes in my underwear."

She laughs. "It's going to take more than ratty undies

to keep me away." Her grin fades. "If you'll give me another chance."

"You never lost your chance. I thought you'd hate me."

She strokes her warm fingers over my face and scratches over my whiskers. "I can never hate you. In fact, I was about to pay Damon last night when I realized that paying him wasn't worth losing you."

I grind my teeth together. That fucker didn't do what he was told to. "He didn't tell you that you no longer owed him?"

Her lips curve up and she puts her hands on my chest. "I think he was afraid of bothering me at all. Terrified even. Your dad has guys?"

The lump is back in my gut. That whole visit was a revelation, a mindfuck, and also oddly settling. "I guess so."

She slips her hand into mine. "Do you want to talk about it?"

I told Lane the gist of my conversation with our father, and my brother eyed me like he knew there was more, but I didn't elaborate. I was trying to figure everything out, but my despair over losing Elodie took over.

I lead her in. The kittens skitter across her feet, batting around the treats I spilled earlier.

"Sorry, I, uh, haven't swept in a while."

"I think Sage has you covered." She turns into the living room and stops. A piece of toilet paper flutters and gets caught on a rug by the coffee table. "Oh my. They got to something."

"Toilet paper isn't safe. But don't worry, it's not used."

Her soft laughter is everything I need to hear when my house is the least tidy it's ever been.

I sit in the corner of the couch, pull her down next to me, and wrap my arms around her again. "I just need to hold you for a while."

She turns into me and I end up with her cradled on my lap. I rest my head against hers and enjoy the pleasure of her weight on me and her fingers dancing across my chest. She doesn't prod me with more questions, and we sit in comfortable, relieved silence.

"He wasn't what I remembered," I say after a few minutes. A tightness in my chest that I've carried all my life loosens. Lane and I don't talk about Dad much, and maybe I should change that. "He's hard. Grizzled. And gray. God, he looked so much older than I remembered. And smaller." I swallow past the lump in my throat. "He's still a tall guy, and he has muscles I've never seen. So excited to see me," I finish quietly. "I don't even remember when he last tried to visit me. I was in high school, I know that. He bailed so often, and then one day, he was there with some burgers. Lane and I ate with him, and he was gone. Then Mom said he'd been arrested after a bad accident and was going to prison for a long time."

Elodie puts her hand over my heart, and it grounds me.

"It was weird, honestly," I continue. "Here's this guy I thought I knew, but he's nothing like the dad I remember. I didn't get long to talk to him, but he's clean and sober, and apparently popular." My laugh is dry. "He's got connections everywhere, and when I told him I needed a guy to leave a girl I love alone, he didn't flinch."

She pushes up, her eyes glowing. "Cruz? A girl you love?"

I play with the ends of her hair hanging over her shoulder. "A girl I'm madly in love with. So in love that I'll burn my relationship with her to make her life better."

She grabs my face and smashes her mouth against mine. I'm hard and aching in an instant. Two weeks have been more like two years when it comes to my dick.

Her lips are still touching mine when she whispers, "I love you too."

A groan rips from me. I lift her across me to straddle my lap. "Sugar, it's been too long since I've had you, and now that I've heard those words on your lips, there's only one thing I want to do right now."

"Fuck now, talk later?" She reaches between us and tugs at the waistband of my shorts.

"My condoms are in my wallet."

"And that's where?" She looks around, but resumes moving fabric out of her way until she wraps her hand around my dick.

My balls tighten, and I moan. It's not going to take much before I lose my control. What the hell did I do with my wallet? "It's, uh . . . it's . . ." Fuck, the way she's pumping me feels too damn good to think straight. I slide my hand up her thighs and under the skirt of her dress. Just a little touch to ground me while I unscramble my brains.

"Do we . . ." She grips me so nice and tight. "Do we need them?"

I stop my trek up her legs. "No condoms?"

She keeps stroking my dick. "I stayed on birth control, just in case, even if I didn't plan to date."

"You've been it for me for a long damn time. I promise I don't have anything. Shit—" I'm going to fuck this up just inches from that dripping-wet pussy of hers. "I can find my results or—"

"I believe you." She lowers herself and rocks her hips. The tip of my erection grazes damp fabric, and I clamp my hands to her thighs. She rocks across the crown again. Blood hammers in my cock. Almost there. "Push my underwear aside, Cruz, so we don't have to wait any longer."

"Yes, ma'am." I yank her panties to the side.

I don't have to slick my fingers through her wet heat and ready her. We have each been waiting for weeks. She sinks farther, taking me inside her.

"You feel so good," she whispers.

"You're fucking velvet." I grip her ass cheeks to hold myself still and not lift and lower her at a frenzied pace. "Do you have to be anywhere today? I want to keep you on your back and under me until the sun rises."

"Nowhere." She rises and slides back down, nearly crossing my damn eyes when she takes me all the way in. "I've got all night. Thanks to you." She pants, her mouth falling open. "I'm going to do more than work now, and a lot more of this."

I'm going to be inside her every minute possible. Without a barrier, every twitch and clamp of her muscles is more acute. The onslaught of pleasure is like trying to stop a tornado with an umbrella.

"It's not going to be long," I say through gritted teeth. I lick my thumb and slide it between us. Her clit is soaked and begging for attention.

"Yes, Cruz." She rides me faster.

"Come for me. Nice and hard." I can barely hold

myself away from my peak. My muscles are straining, but I won't come until she does.

"Yeah," she whimpers and her rhythm is erratic. "Oh god, yes!"

She drops her head back and rolls her hips once, twice, then she shudders and collapses over me. I can finally release. The energy inside me unleashes. I buck up into her willing heat and explode into the most intense orgasm I've ever had.

Elodie

Cruz covers us with blankets and lies down beside me on his bed. My hair is wet, spread out behind me on a towel. His warm citrus scent surrounds us, and I'm boneless. Utterly melted. We enjoyed his massive shower, giving his water heater a workout until me screaming Cruz's name bounced off the walls.

I'm fully in love with the man, and I'm developing an obsession with his house. The bed is comfortable, the kitchen is a dream, and his living area is homey when he's not obsessive about cleaning.

"This bed is so soft." I snuggle deeper into it.

"You look damn good naked in it."

I smile. "What a coincidence, so do you."

It's quiet here. Huckleberry Springs is a mellow town at night, but there are still cars and trucks. After Bootleg closes, it gets loud again with customers going home. The bakery is in an older building. Cruz's house is new and secure. Cozy. We're in a little cocoon just for us, and I can finally talk to him about anything or everything.

"I called Damon." Even in the silence between us, my voice isn't loud. "I was going to inform him that he's not getting a dime from me and to go ahead and tell the world. He thought I was hounding him for the money he's going to pay back." A small giggle slips out. "Should I feel bad?"

The blankets rustle as he moves closer. "You didn't know when you called him?"

"No, but I missed you, and I was sick of how I was living. I called him after I invited Clem and my parents to the bakery. I told them. *Everything*. Including the blackmail. Though I didn't tell them about your dad, and I didn't share your history."

He tenses only briefly. "How'd they take it?"

"Worried. Mom blamed herself and I asked her not to. I blamed myself enough for everyone. I know you're going to be shocked, but they didn't crumble from the stress."

His grin is big enough to see in the dark.

"Clem tried to play it cool," I continue, "and she was concerned and righteously angry, but I think she was taking notes and getting plot bunnies, or whatever she calls them, for her stories."

He laughs and tangles his fingers through mine. Ever since I arrived, he hasn't quit touching me. "What if word spreads?"

"I don't care. I'll open another business, or get a job at the café, and actually get weekends off once in a while. But I think it's time I hire another baker."

"No shit?"

"A full-time one at that. Like I said, it's because of

you I have the funds and the time. That cookie dough fundraiser idea has legs. And if Damon and Dwayne really pay me back? That'll go a long way."

"Good." He lifts my hand to kiss my fingers.

Everything he did made my life better. I'm closer to my parents and Clem, I won't be working every waking minute, and I might get an influx of funds. But what did it cost him? "Is everything done with your dad? Are you really okay after seeing him?"

His soft exhale tickles the skin of my hand. "Yeah, I'm okay. It was like taking a pressure bandage off. I don't have this . . . restlessness . . . when I think of him, like he's waiting in the shadows to ditch me for a lunch date again. Or that he only wanted to tell me what a loser I am."

"Did he do that when you were younger?" I'll never forgive myself for driving Cruz to speaking to his dad again if that's the case. I don't know how I'll make it up to him.

"No, but he was always pushing me and Lane to do more and be more. If I lost a fight, he'd coach me on how to win it. When I said I'd be late for work, he said it was a shit job anyway. That kind of stuff. If we were gonna be bad, we'd better be good at it."

"If he's not proud of you now, then he's not worth another second of your time." I've got enough for everyone.

"I owe him some of my time. It's part of the deal."

Fear strikes through me, and I prop myself up. "What? No, not for me."

He gives me a kiss. "Relax, sugar. I just have to answer the phone when he calls—if I'm able. He gave me freedom for that."

Anxiety curls through my stomach. "Cruz, if he's trying to control you—"

"No, Elodie. He won't. He can't. He knows it, but he's used to bargaining. It's his life, and it'll be ours dealing with him. He's always going to test our limits. It's fun for him, especially when his boys prove stronger."

That's a warped father-son relationship, but it could be worse. I wiggle closer to Cruz. "I can't believe you did that for me."

"I have to name my first kid after him," he says abruptly.

I shoot up to a sitting position. "What?"

He's not laughing. Is he even smiling? Oh god. He's not kidding.

"It's okay." He tugs me back down and gives me a quick kiss. "I said it'd be a middle name."

"You really are serious."

"Mom never gave us Dad's name, and that's always bugged him. This is the only way he feels like he can live on."

I root around my brain for a quick fact. "Sy Lawson? That's what Damon called him."

"Sylvester Lawson."

"A strong name." An image of a dark-haired little boy or girl pops into my mind. "Lawson's a cool name."

"Yeah?"

"Yeah. Assuming, you know, you want kids." I do not sound casual.

"I'd like kids. If the right woman wanted to have them with me."

I suck in a breath through my teeth. "Ooh, she might be hard to find."

"Or . . . she might be right here."

My heart stops. Is he proposing?

"When I ask you to marry me," he says like he's reading my mind, "it'll be with a ring and more romance than lying in bed after a sex-fest. But it's going to be you that I ask."

Giddiness fills me. He wants to be with me. The man who's seen me at my worst and at my frumpiest wants to spend his life with me. "Okay. Until then, I'll figure out the answer."

"Do you want kids?" His question is hesitant.

"Do I want a Lawson Foster?" Using our connected hands, I pull him on top of me. The towel for my hair falls to the floor, and he nestles between my legs, keeping his weight off me. "You gotta admit—has a nice ring to it."

"It does. Sylvester Foster?"

I laugh. "Sylvie Foster?"

"Damn, sugar. That's a good one." His erection nudges against my leg. If I shifted, he could slide inside, but I don't. Our conversation sounds lighthearted, but it's serious. We're working out our future.

"Both are very good names," I say softly. "How do we decide?"

"I don't know." He lines kisses along my jaw and down my neck. "Maybe we have to have more than one."

"Assuming I say yes."

"And that's after I propose." He drags his mouth back up to nibble at my ear.

Shivers race across my body. How can I be ready to go again? "Of course."

"I think you should move in with me."

Pure happiness fills me full enough to float away.

Yesterday, my world was spinning out of control and I was at the end of my rope. "Are you going to ask me that someday too?"

He touches his lips to mine. "I'm asking now. Want to move in? I have a big closet." He scoots down and takes my nipple into his mouth.

I arch into him. "How do you know I won't use you for your big . . . closet?"

He flicks his tongue across my sensitive skin and smiles against me when I grind into him. "I have a lot of big things you can use me for."

"I'm going to have to think hard about it."

He switches to the other side and slides his hand between us. I hiss when his fingertip hits my clit. Just as I think my pussy can't take more, pleasure carries me away.

"Okay," I gasp as he notches the broad tip of his cock at my entrance. "I'll move in."

He thrusts in and out, his hips pumping underneath the blankets. "Go ahead and think about that longer. I'm going to take my time convincing you."

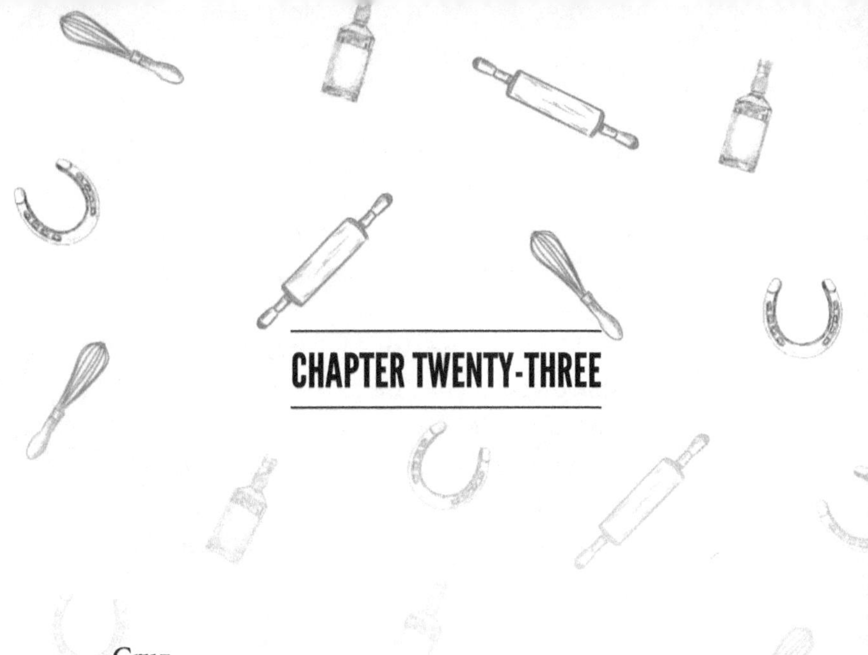

CHAPTER TWENTY-THREE

Cruz

A month after reconnecting, I'm flanked by Bob and Karl at the grill again. Elodie's sitting in a camp chair by her mom and sister. These family grill-outs are becoming a thing, and I don't foresee a change when the weather turns cold. Bob's already sketching plans for a four-season addition to the house.

"I always had it in mind," he says about his idea and hitches up his jean shorts, which are secured with a plain brown leather belt. "But then it got delayed with the accident. Elodie moved away and Clem went to school for even longer than me." Despite what might sound like complaining, the man radiates pride for his girls.

Karl nods. He's dressed like he should be Bob's twin instead of a former brother-in-law. I'm the standout in jeans, boots, and a T-shirt.

"Both girls are back," Karl says, "and if looks don't

deceive me, Elodie might be staying awhile because of this guy."

Bob's grin stretches wider. "The bakery was going to keep her here, but thanks to Cruz here, it's not her prison."

"I wish I could've seen that punch," Karl mutters and does a quick shadowbox. Then he looks around like he's afraid the townsfolk might've seen him.

"Thank you for that." Bob's solemn as he glances at the girls to make sure they don't hear. "I hate that she felt like she had to keep it from us, but I'm glad someone helped her."

My lungs freeze. I'm not prepared to talk about this, but I don't hear censure. Elodie didn't tell them any of my personal details. She glossed over my past, and I'm forever appreciative that she tried to protect me. But if this whole situation has taught me anything, it's that being ashamed of our past has no good purpose. It leaves our history open to be used against us.

I'm not going to let something that Elodie accepts about me be a weakness like that. "I can't take full credit for helping her. I called in a favor from my dad. He's got connections I'd rather not know about and he made sure Dwayne left Elodie alone. He's, uh . . . he's in prison."

Bob's bushy brows rise. Karl makes a *how 'bout that* expression. Both guys study me. Karl's probably heard worse confessions in his time, but Bob's mouth doesn't turn into a frown.

"I didn't have the best childhood," I continue. Might as well get it all out. "Got in my share of trouble. Mom was an addict. Left us alone a lot. Dad was in and out of my life before he was out for a long time." I swallow, determined to tell it all. "Elodie was afraid for me when

I hit that bastard, Damon. Worried that I'd hate myself for regressing into someone I worked hard on not being anymore. What she doesn't understand is that I'd do worse for her, and the last thing I would do is regret it."

Silence falls between us. The chatter of the women is a low murmur. The burgers smell good on the grill, but my appetite starts retreating. If I get kicked out, so be it. Elodie and I will figure a way to win her family over. I just don't want her to stress, and dammit, I really like her dad and uncle. I drop my gaze and study the tips of my boots. I wiped them off before I came over. Good habits are just good habits.

Karl claps a big hand on my shoulder. "Sorry to hear about what you went through. You've obviously taken charge of your own life and chosen a different path than your parents, but I'm glad to hear someone has Elodie's back no matter what."

"Me too." Bob leans in closer. "Between you, me, and the fence posts, I'll take the fall if she ever needs a problem dealt with again. I'm old and won't be in jail for long."

My laugh is as unexpected as his words. Bob and Karl snicker with me.

Karl nudges Bob. "He's got her back, and we've got theirs, ain't that right?"

They dissolve into delighted chortling that tells me they might even have fun saving me and Elodie from a hypothetical future scenario like the one we just got out of. My humor rises, but I'm humbled to my core. Not since Mae Bailey offered to give me a decent future have I realized how goddamn lucky I am. I told these guys who I am and where I come from—dirty house, felon dad, and all—and Bob's offering to take the blame for anything I do to benefit his daughter. Instead of chasing me away, a guy who used his father's prison network to threaten and intimidate, he's bringing me into the Palmer fold. And he didn't ask me to name any kids after him for the privilege.

Elodie appears at my side, wrapping an arm around my waist. "You all sound like trouble."

Bob's smile is secretive. "Just telling your guy that it's nice to see more of you."

Elodie hugs me harder. "Angie's been great."

Her new employee is originally from a small town in eastern Montana and went to pastry school. She's thrilled to be working in her home state again, and that her kids can be so close to their grandparents.

With Angie, Elodie can expand her menu and her hours and take more time off. She even has temporary workers arranged to help with the cookie dough fundraiser and the holiday orders, working with the high school for both volunteer hours and extra fundraising opportunities to help pack and deliver orders.

She's going to take her first week off right before she has to work on holiday orders, and I'm taking her to Bourbon Canyon and Bozeman. She wants to see where I grew up, literally and figuratively.

I have a ring in a drawer at my house, waiting patiently for that trip. I know just where to pop the question.

Elodie

. . .

I press my hands against my stomach to keep it from churning and smooth them down the rest of my dress. Over it I have on a robin's-egg-blue cardigan, and boots beneath it. I've never thought so hard about what to wear when meeting someone.

Cruz leads me up a path to the back door. The view from here is stunning. The Bailey Beef ranch encompasses rolling hills and tree-covered inclines. Down another path is a cute shed with chickens darting around it. There's also a huge barn, a shop that Cruz said Lane used to do a lot of work in, and fenced-off pastures with horses and cattle. A couple of goats even amble by the barn.

Cruz puts a hand at the small of my back. "You should see it when it's green."

The air is cool and the grasses are more brown than green today, but it doesn't diminish the vista. "It's stunning now. The trees on the foothills and the shadows from the clouds? Gorgeous."

"I never would've been able to move far away. Myles would've had no issues bringing the Hennessys into the Foster House Gold deal, but he also wanted to watch out for me and Lane. We wanted to be close to this and the Baileys."

The door opens and I spin around. A woman a little older than my mom appears in the doorway. She's got a ruffled apron on and her salt-and-pepper hair pulled back.

"I thought I heard you pull up." Her warm gaze lands on me. "So nice to finally meet you, Elodie."

"I've heard so much about you." I hold out the box of poppy seed cruisers, the muffins I made with the whiskey Cruz served me for a tasting at the distillery.

Why did I bring these? She has a daughter-in-law who's also a baker. Mae probably gets yummy goodies all the time.

Her smile brightens even more. "Now I want dessert first. Come on in."

She waves us inside and we pile in after her. The house is as inviting as everything else. I'm lucky I got to know Cruz. He probably wouldn't have left if the Foster House opportunity hadn't opened up.

For a large log home, it's warm and inviting inside. Cruz leads me around a corner to a long dining room table. He pulls a seat out for me at the far end.

I don't sit. "Can I help with anything?"

"You can help by sitting your sweet ass down and letting me and Mae spoil you." He grins. "She'll let us do the cleanup."

My relief allows me to sit. As long as I'm not getting waited on. I take my seat. "Okay. I should've offered to cook."

"You'll have plenty of time for that. For today, she pulled a roast from the freezer, and the potatoes are fresh from the garden. And the onions, the carrots, the berries."

I would push back and jump up, but he's blocking the way. I crane my head back to stare up at him. Home-grown ingredients and meat so local it used to moo in the backyard sound divine to work with. "Everything she's using is from the ranch?"

"Mae's industrious, but she doesn't churn her own butter." He drops a kiss into my hair. "Now relax. We'll be doing the dishes."

Several minutes later, the three of us are at the end of the table, eating the best pot roast I've ever tasted.

After a few minutes of chatter, I feel like I've known Mae all my life. She has a disarming way about her, unassuming and accepting. All remaining tension drains from me. I get the whole week in town, and Cruz is going to treat me to a private Copper Summit Bourbon tour.

We have the cupcakes for dessert, and then Cruz and I clean up while Mae pours us each a glass of bourbon on the porch. Cruz leans against the railing, while Mae and I rock in some well-used wooden rocking chairs.

This is a lot like the times Cruz and I sat on his back deck, enjoying a drink after a meal. I messed up the first time he tried, but I've made up for it. Mostly with a blow job the next time we tried it.

My face warms, and I catch Cruz's intense gaze. Is he thinking the same thing?

Mae rocks slowly. "Are you going down to the barn?"

He sets his glass on the end table between us. "Yes, ma'am. Gotta show her where it all started." He holds out a hand. I take it and rise. He doesn't let go of me as he leads me along the path to the barn.

The chickens streak across the yard and moos ring out in the distance. A horse whinnies and another nickers. We continue past the barn to the fence of the closest pasture.

The slight breeze. The frogs and the bugs. We could've gone anywhere for my vacation, but I can't think of a better place. "It's so peaceful out here. I bet there's amazing fly-fishing."

He laughs. "Tate and Teller already offered to take your dad out whenever he can get here next year."

"That's so sweet. Your family is welcoming."

"They are my family," he murmurs. "You know, when Myles first brought me out here, I remember this longing deep inside me that I was afraid to admit to. I wanted the welcoming home and the good food and to be surrounded by people who wanted me."

"You have all that."

"I didn't feel like it at the time."

"Oh, Cruz." I turn to him and cup his cheek. My heart hurts for that young man.

He kisses my palm. "But this spot, where I was shown the horses and told about what I would be doing for work? This is exactly where I made a decision. That I would be someone who could have it all. Now I do. I have more. And there's a woman who loves me that I want to spend the rest of my life with."

He slips his hand into a pocket and withdraws a twinkling ring. He drops to his knee, and even though he told me this day would come, tears spring into my eyes and I put a hand over my mouth.

"Elodie Palmer?" A sexy grin curves his lips. "Sugar? Will you marry me?"

"Oh my god, of course. Yes!" I wave my left hand in front of him. "Put it on, put it on."

His grin is bigger than I've ever seen. The ring slides into place, a perfect fit. Cruz Foster is a prepared man.

He rises and sweeps me into his arms, letting out a big whoop. I cling to him, laughing as he spins me around.

"I'm going to make you a happy woman, Elodie. You and little future Lawson and Sylvie."

"You already do." Cruz keeps his word. I slide down his hard body when he sets me back on my feet. "Should we call or text everyone?"

The suggestive grin is back. "The rest of our bourbon is waiting for us, but the barn is right here, and you have a dress on, and we need to celebrate." He takes my hand again and tows me toward the opening of the barn. "I've been planning for a long time to bring the love of my life here—and get inside of her."

"I'm happy to make your dreams come true."

"Aw, Elodie." He spins me around. "You already do. Now grab the post and hang on. I'm about to make you mine again."

———

Thank you for reading Whiskey Flirt!

Is Haven going to find love like his brothers, or will he keep avoiding relationships? Or will he find a former pet influencer rescuing strays in the ditch right when the wind blows her skirt up? Find out in Whiskey Charm!

Cruz and Elodie invite you to their wedding in a special bonus epilogue when you sign up to my newsletter at walkerrosebooks.com/newsletter.

ABOUT THE AUTHOR

I live the dream in my own slice of paradise where I get to enjoy colorful sunsets from my rocking chair while I'm working. I have my very own romance hero with Mr. Rose and there's more than a few little rose buds running around. A couple aren't so little anymore! We keep things interesting with cats and a dog and the critters that roam though the yard (fingers crossed the mountain lions stay away).

walkerrosebooks.com

ALSO BY WALKER ROSE

Foster House Series

Whiskey Cowboy

Whiskey Bargain

Whiskey Flirt

Whiskey Charm

Bourbon Canyon Series

Bourbon Bachelor

Bourbon Lullaby

Bourbon Runaway

Bourbon Promises

Bourbon Harmony

Bourbon Summer

Bourbon Sunset

www.ingramcontent.com/pod-product-compliance
Lightning Source LLC
Chambersburg PA
CBHW051210190726
48288CB00006B/1889